Hell to Pay

The Harry Russo Diaries, volume 4

By Lisa Emme

Hell to Pay – The Harry Russo Diaries, volume 4

By Lisa Emme

Print Edition
ISBN 978-1-988117-07-2

Cover design by
The Scarlett Rugers Design Agency
www.scarlettrugers.com

Contact Lisa:
www.lisaemme.com

To my home team:

My family and friends,
my alpha, beta and advanced readers,
and all my hometown cheerleaders.
I never thought I'd be publishing
book one, let alone book four.
I'm where I am today because
of your support and encouragement.

Thank you!

OTHER NOVELS BY LISA EMME

The Harry Russo Diaries

Dead and Kicking

Tooth and Claw

Deadlocked

Home Again

The Yacht Club

(available Spring 2017)

Chapter One

"You're leaving me too?" I flopped back against the leather bucket seat, crossing my arms, and pouted at Tess, my BFF. We may not be biologically related, but we had been raised as sisters, and I couldn't help it if her news left me feeling a little abandoned.

Tess looked back over her shoulder at me and rolled her eyes. "Don't be such a baby. It's not like I'm going that far. It's just across the street for crying out loud."

I sat forward to lean over the front seat. Tess had won the game of rock-paper-scissors-lizard-Spock and called shotgun. I should have known better than to accept the challenge. Tess is a real *Big Bang Theory* geek, so she had the whole lizard-Spock thing down pat.

I glanced at Isaac, who was behind the wheel of his big Escalade as usual. He was studiously avoiding making eye contact.

"This is your fault," I griped at him in the rearview mirror.

Isaac shrugged. "I can withdraw the—"

"Don't you dare!" Tess interrupted with a growl. She narrowed her eyes, giving Isaac a dirty look before turning back to me. "Listen, Harry. Quit being such a drama queen. It's not like we were going to live together forever. We both need our space now, and this is too good an opportunity to pass up."

I sighed and settled back in my seat. Tess was right. It was a great opportunity. I mean, how often do you get offered a high-end condo for a dollar? She'd have to be crazy not to take it.

I scowled at the back of Isaac's head. It really was his fault. If he hadn't a) bought the building across the street; and b) decided to renovate it; and c) decided that he didn't need the entire penthouse floor for himself but instead had it subdivided into two units, both looking over the converted fire station I called my home and place of business; then he wouldn't have d) made such a sweet deal to Tess.

"I just thought we'd be roomies for a bit longer, is all." Ugh, even I thought I sounded whiny. "There's plenty of room at our place, especially now that Isaac has moved out." It had been over two weeks and I hadn't gotten used to how much quieter the apartment felt without Isaac.

"And Nash has all but moved in," Tess replied, referring to the sexy yet sometimes infuriating werewolf police detective who had growled his way into my life. "And believe me, your place isn't big enough for two werewolves."

I scowled at Tess. "He hasn't moved in. All his stuff is back at his place." Well, except for a couple changes of clothes and his toothbrush. We were still pretending to be moving slow even though he had already marked me as his mate. Between the hours he put in chasing bad guys and cleaning up supernatural messes as liaison for the Riverton Police Department and the Magister of the Cimmerian (the supernatural underworld) and the time I spent trying to run two businesses, we didn't get as many opportunities to be together as we would have liked. Often it meant he arrived in the middle of the night, sliding in next to me in my bed. Not that I'm going to complain about that. He had this amazing way of waking me up...but I won't get into that right now. "Half the time he's over we're holed up in my room. You barely even know he's there."

Isaac sputtered out a laugh. It was so uncharacteristic of his usually staid demeanor that I gaped at him in surprise, but his mask of neutrality had already slipped back into place.

"Are you fucking kidding me?" Tess's voice rose an octave. She turned back to look at me with a smirk. "Don't fool yourself, Harry. Just because you're in your room, doesn't mean we don't know he's there." She rolled her eyes and then faced the road in front of her.

"But we soundproofed all the rooms!" I frowned as I thought about what Tess was insinuating with her little outburst. When we had renovated the old firehall we called home, we had splurged, taking supernatural hearing into consideration, and paid for extra soundproofing. I thought that it had been enough. My mind churned through the implications.

Oh. My. God.

I face-palmed, shaking my head, thoroughly embarrassed. Nash and I weren't particularly shy in the sex department, and while we may be going through the motions of taking things slow, that didn't mean we didn't have sex. Lots of sex.

My eyes met Isaac's in the rearview mirror and he gave me a Gallic shrug. My face burned two shades brighter. How embarrassing. No wonder Isaac, with his vampire super-hearing, had been eager to move out.

I was spared further discomfort when the Escalade came to a halt in front of a tiny bungalow on a quiet residential street. I tumbled out of the backseat, eager to leave the conversation behind.

"Are you sure this is the right address?" Tess asked as she stepped down from the vehicle. "It doesn't look like a haunted house."

They usually didn't, but still, I reached for the slip of paper I had stuffed in my pocket to double-check just as the front door burst open and a woman, close in age to Tess and me, ran down the steps towards us.

"Harry!" she called out, and then stopped short, her relieved smile giving way to a wary frown as Isaac stepped around the side of the SUV.

"Hi, Susan," I replied quickly, moving between her and Isaac, blocking her view. Tall and lanky, his dark hair and beard trimmed neatly, Isaac didn't particularly appear menacing especially when you considered he was a vampire, although Susan wouldn't know that last part. In fact, he was, quite frankly, drop-dead gorgeous, if male metrosexual was your type. It didn't matter to Susan. She was wary of all men, the cause of her wariness being the reason we were here today. "These are my friends, Tess and Isaac." I waved my hand out to them and took a step closer to Susan. She looked like a deer caught in the headlights, unsure whether to flee or not. I gently grasped her elbow, hoping to keep her from choosing the flee option. She turned to face me, the haunted look that had first drawn my attention to her settling over her features. Is it ironic that someone who was being haunted actually looked haunted? Ever since I heard that song by Alanis Morissette, I'm a little confused about what really is ironic.

"Yes, right. You told me you would be bringing friends to help." She bit her lip and shook her head slowly. "I'm so stupid sometimes, I—"

"Don't worry about it," I said, interrupting her. "It slipped your mind. You have a lot going on. Completely understandable." I smiled at her encouragingly. "Did you get everything ready like I asked?"

"Yes! I did everything you said. It wasn't hard. Most of my stuff is already broken." Wringing her hands nervously, she bit her lip again. "Can you...? I-I mean are you...?"

"Yes, I really can help you. It's a gift that runs in my family." Of course I didn't bother to tell her how screwed up my family was, or that while I was a witch I was also half vampire—otherwise known as a dhamphir—or that my ability to see and control ghosts was just one of my many freaky talents, necromancy among them. There was only so much a norm, or non-supernatural human like Susan, could process. "Give us a minute to gather some equipment, and then you can show us around." I gave her arm a reassuring squeeze before walking over to the back of the Escalade, Tess following on my heels.

"Crap, Harry," she whispered, casting a furtive look over to where Susan stood still clutching her hands. "You weren't kidding about her. She's as jumpy as a cat in a room full of rocking chairs."

"Can you blame her? She escapes her ex-boyfriend, who used her as a punching bag on a regular basis, only to have him die in a car crash and come back to haunt her?" I scowled at the thought. The first time I had bumped into Susan was at one of those survivor support groups, which was being held in the basement of the church I was busy decorating for a wedding later in the day. Nature had called, and I found myself in the ladies' room with a hyperventilating Susan, who was in the middle of a panic attack. I knew right away she was in need of my help. It was kind of hard to ignore the two-hundred-and-eighty-pound bully standing over her shoulder spewing vitriol, even if he was a ghost and I was the only one there who could see and hear him.

I had haltingly coaxed the story out of Susan over a cup of very bad, support-group coffee and made her promise to come by the coffee shop for the real thing. At first she was reluctant to believe she was being haunted, but then Darryl, her dead ex, had upped the ante, going into full poltergeist mode, charging through her life like a bull in a china shop. By the time Susan had decided to take me up on my offer and visit me at the coffee shop, she had found herself trying to live and work in what amounted to a war zone, with personal items regularly flying off shelves and smashing against the walls.

Bryce, my personal computer hacker and literal ghost-in-the-machine, had done a bit of poking around through police records and discovered there had been over a dozen domestic dispute calls to Susan's house in the last eighteen months. Susan had even filed a restraining order, but it hadn't stopped the abuse. The last incident, about six months ago, had left her with a dislocated shoulder and a cracked cheekbone. Charges had been laid, but before Darryl could appear in court he died in a drunk-driving accident. Luckily, it had been a single vehicle crash, and the only one who had been hurt was Darryl. If the asshole wasn't already dead, I'd seriously consider killing him myself. Banishing his spirit was going to be extremely satisfying.

I grabbed the black duffle bag I had placed in Isaac's trunk and threw it over my shoulder before heading back towards the house. Susan fell into step beside me hesitantly. As I passed Isaac, I leaned towards him. "Maybe you should just wait outside for now. Tess and I have it covered. You'll hear if we get into trouble."

"As you wish," he replied, moving to rest nonchalantly against the Escalade. He was the most accommodating vampire I had ever met. Of course, that might have had something to do with the fact I was his Master (yes, with a capital M) after inadvertently binding him to me in a moment of self-preservation. At least his association with me and Tess seemed to be rubbing off on him. He never would have replied so cheekily three months ago. "I feel I must remind you, however, that we are on a bit of a tight schedule." He raised an eyebrow at me expectantly.

"I know, I know," I replied with a frown. "This shouldn't take long. We have plenty of time." Which was true, but part of me was hoping this little excursion would take longer than expected, giving me an excuse to skip out on the next event on our agenda this evening. Although on the other hand, skipping out probably wasn't a great idea. I was sure there would be hell to pay if I missed Salvador's big show.

It had been a month to the day since my deadly encounter with the Mariposa, the evil vampire empress, and the apprehension of the three rogue vampires who had been terrorizing the city. As had been decreed by Salvador, the rogues were to be punished by spiking. I wasn't too sure what exactly spiking entailed, but I had found out it started off by starving the lucky spikees for two fortnights. As the prescribed time was now up, my presence and that of many others from the supernatural community was required to witness the meting out of the Magister's justice. Needless to say, I wasn't particularly eager to attend the show. Having recently learned that Salvador was my father, I was sorely tempted to see how much leeway that relationship might buy me and skip what was sure to be a macabre spectacle altogether, but since both Nash and Tess had to be there, not to mention Isaac, I sort of felt obligated to go too.

But first things first. We had a ghost to get rid of.

***

I dropped the duffle bag on the floor in what appeared to be Susan's living room. It held a well-worn sofa and an equally ratty-looking La-Z-Boy chair. The walls were pockmarked, the paint chipped away in several places exposing the plaster beneath.

Susan glanced around the room and then back to Tess and me, running her hands self-consciously over her T-shirt and jeans. "I feel a bit underdressed," she said with a halfhearted smile. "You didn't say this would be a formal affair."

I gave her a smile and then glanced at what I was wearing with a little shrug. I was dressed in a short, canary-yellow Roberto Cavalli feather-print dress. It had a formfitting flare silhouette with a black-banded crossover waist. I had matched it with a pair of kick-ass, peep-toed, micromesh ankle boots with a stiletto heel that could best be described as vertiginous. Tess was similarly attired in a rocking bandeau-style dress in lipstick red. It hugged her curves like a second skin, leaving very little to the imagination. "No worries. We just have a thing to go to afterwards, and we were afraid we might not have time to go home and change in between."

I crouched in front of the duffle, pulling items out and putting them on the floor beside me. "So have there been any incidents today?"

I paused to look at Susan, who swallowed, her gaze darting around the room nervously. "No, nothing, uh, physical, but I can feel him all the time." She cast a furtive look over her shoulder and then leaned towards me to whisper, "Can you see him now?"

I made a show of examining the room, although to me it was obvious he wasn't there at the moment, before replying, "No, but I'm sure he'll show up." I pulled my Taser from the bag and checked the charge. "Let me just get a couple more things ready, and then we'll begin."

Susan nodded vigorously, clasping her hands nervously. She started to speak several times, but stopped each time before finally blurting out, "I can't believe that you believe me. I thought I was going crazy."

Tess stepped towards Susan and wrapped her arm around her. "It will be over soon. Harry's the best. Before you know it that asshole will be nothing but a distant memory." She gave Susan another reassuring squeeze and then bent down to grab one of the boxes of table salt I had pulled from the bag. "Why don't I take a look around and then get started in the dining room?"

"Okay, that sounds like a good idea. Susan, you stay here with me." Since Susan had previously given me the layout of her house, I had decided that the dining room was the best room to use for our plan to exorcise Darryl's spirit.

In most cases, the ghosts I had banished were tied to a particular place or item, so making sure they stuck around for the actual banishment wasn't an issue. Darryl proved to be a bit trickier. He seemed to be able to go wherever he pleased, sometimes wreaking havoc in places he personally had never been to but were associated to Susan. I wanted to make sure he stayed put once he arrived, so we were going to make it impossible for him to leave by setting a circle of protection. The dining room was the best choice because it was in the centre of the house and had no windows that could be easily broken. Susan had prepped the room by removing all the breakables and pulling any furniture away from the walls. Tess would start by pouring out an almost continuous circle of salt around the perimeter of the room leaving openings at each of the three doorways leading into the room. Once we lured Darryl in, we would close the circle, making it impossible for him to leave. Or so I hoped.

***

"Say his name," I said, coaxing Susan into the middle of the room. Tess stood off to the side, her eyes fixed on her mini-tablet. She was mesmerised by the new toy, courtesy of Bryce. Being the computer genius he was, he had taken the functionality of a K2 meter commonly used to measure electromagnetic radiance and somehow morphed it into an app that worked on the tablet, turning the camera into an EMF meter. With it, Tess would be able to see Darryl when he arrived. Or at least that was the theory. So far the only things showing up on the display were the electrical lines behind the walls. They appeared as fuzzy yellow lines running the perimeter of the room.

"D-Darryl," Susan said, her hands clutched at her chest. "Darryl Leroy Sutcliffe."

"Leroy? Seriously?" Tess looked up from her tablet. "Sounds like a real hick. No wonder he was such a loser."

I shot Tess a grin and turned back to the centre of the room. "Darryl Sutcliffe! Come on, Darryl. We're waiting for you."

A few minutes passed, and nothing happened. Susan was a nervous wreck. The waiting was getting to her. I led her over to the table and sat her down in front of a stack of paper Dixie cups. "Here, why don't you stack those up like I told you? It'll give you something to do." I watched as she began to build a pyramid of cups and then nodded encouragingly at her before moving back to the centre of the room. "Darryl Leroy Sutcliffe!"

"Oh Darrrrryl," Tess chimed in a sing-song voice. "Darryl, you big piece of shit, come out, or are you too big of a coward to face us?"

A whiff of cold air rushed past, lowering the temperature enough to raise goose bumps on my arms. Tess gasped and held up her tablet, scanning in front of her. Suddenly, one of the books we had left on the edge of the table slammed to the floor, causing us all to jump.

"D-Darryl? Is that you?" Susan looked around anxiously.

"I don't see anything," Tess complained, frowning at her tablet. She held it up, checking the area around Susan.

"That's because he's not all here yet. He can't manifest. He's too weak."

SLAM! Another book hit the floor. There were several books left, scattered over the table. Poltergeists love to smash things, so we had made sure to leave a few items for Darryl to play with.

Plunk! Plunk! Plunk! The Dixie cup tower Susan had been building toppled to the table, cups rolling across its surface and falling to the floor. Susan let out a scared little shriek.

"Is that all you've got, Darryl?" I put as much contempt as I could in my voice. "What a big man you are, having a tantrum, knocking things down like a toddler."

"Yeah, he's not a real man," Tess replied. "I bet he didn't have any staying power in bed either." She laughed and held up her index finger, letting it curve slightly.

An empty chair beside the table toppled over just as Tess started in surprise. She pointed to the screen of her tablet. "Holy shit, Harry. Look!" An amorphous blob of yellow and red appeared on the screen. The edges of the object seemed to flow and change, the colours shifting and darkening from yellow to red at the centre.

I didn't need the tablet to see the six foot, two hundred and eighty pounds of angry man.

"You fucking little bitch! Who the hell do you think you are? I'll fucking show you who's got staying power." Darryl swept out with his beefy arm, his less-than-corporeal hand passing through Tess.

Tess sucked in a breath and jumped back as the screen of her tablet turned red. "Whoa! What the fuck?"

"He's here and he's pissed."

"Darryl?" Susan looked around, fear etched on her face.

"It's okay, Susan. He can't hurt you."

"Like hell I can't! I'm going to fuck her up like she fucked with me. The worthless whore." The remaining cups on the table rattled, and several rolled off the edge.

"It's time, Tess," I said quietly. Tess nodded and casually walked over to the nearest doorway. Using the box of salt, she quickly finished the circle, moving from one door to the next, connecting the continuous line until the room was completely enclosed. I turned to Susan. "Talk to him, Susan. Tell him how you feel."

"I don't fucking care how she feels. She's nothing but a worthless slut."

"Talk to him, Susan," I coaxed again, ignoring Darryl's outburst.

"D-Darryl? Darryl, you have to leave me alone." Susan slowly rose from her chair, her hands clenched in fists at her sides. "You...you're nothing but a bully. You were a bully in life and now you think you can bully me in death and...and I won't have it."

"Whoa, good for you, Susan. You tell him." Tess smiled encouragingly at her.

While Tess and Susan continued to distract Darryl, I circled the room, chanting under my breath, setting the protective circle. When I reached the final doorway, I beckoned to Susan, taking her by the hand. "It's time for you to leave," I said, indicating she should step carefully over the salt. Once she was out of the room and into the living room, I finished my chant, sealing up the circle. Darryl was trapped.

"You should probably go outside now, Susan. Isaac is there. He'll keep you safe."

Susan stood for a moment, looking through the door at me. She bit her lip, obviously struggling with her fears.

"Go on. You can trust me. You can trust Isaac. Not every man is an asshole like Darryl."

"You fucking bitch! You stay right there! Don't you leave!" Darryl rushed towards the door, intending to follow Susan, but when he reached the doorway, he was repelled back towards the centre of the room.

"Cool!" Tess said, sounding slightly awed. She had her tablet open again, pointed at the doorway. "He bounced off it like a ping-pong ball."

Darryl roared in frustration, throwing himself at the barrier again and again. Each time, he was pushed back, unable to leave the protective circle.

"What have you done to me, you bitch?" He came to stand in front of me, fists clenched.

"That's witch to you, asshole. And now it's time for you to leave. You're not wanted here. Your time on this plane is over. You must cross to the other side."

Of course he didn't listen to me and wasn't going to make things easy. I listened to him bellow and spew his hatred for a few more minutes, sorely tempted to pull out my Taser and give him a few thousand volts, but that would only mean we had to start all over, so I managed to contain the urge.

Finally, I'd had enough. It was clear Darryl wasn't going to leave voluntarily, which would have been easier and less costly for me, energy-wise. I'd have to make him. Quietly I started to chant my banishing spell. It wasn't really a spell. Like a lot of the incantations I use, it was more of a means to focus my will. The words weren't important, only the intent mattered. Just as well, since I banished my first ghost at the age of five at a time when I was on a bit of Dr. Seuss jag, the spell itself was kind of embarrassing.

"You're not wanted here or there,
You're not wanted anywhere,
On this plane you cannot stay,
You should really fly away.
I do not want you in my house,
I do not want you in my car,
I do not want you in my space,
You really need to leave this place!"

It wasn't until the third time through that I felt my power kick in. Up until then, Darryl had continued to rant and roar, sending the occasional Dixie cup flying across the room. As my will rippled over him, however, he became more desperate, which seemed to focus his efforts, and in a burst of power, the cups and the books that had been lying on the floor suddenly rose in the air and began to swirl around us.

"What the fuck, Harry?" Tess threw her arms up as a cup came close to whacking her in the head.

"Tess!" I pulled her in close beside me as I tried to extend my shields to deflect the flying objects. "He's going out with a bang," I yelled at her, forgetting that she wouldn't be able to hear most of the ruckus he was making. I gave her an apologetic shrug and turned my attention back to Darryl.

"You can't stay here, Darryl. It's time to leave!"

I began my chant again, focussing my will. Darryl's spectral form had disappeared when he directed his energy at the vortex of flying objects. He wasn't strong enough to do both. The books and cups swirled around us like a mini tornado, spinning faster and faster. The sound was almost deafening as Darryl's shouts became more like the wail of a banshee.

Finally, with a last push of my magic, I felt the shift in the power balance and I knew it was time. Darryl's exit had arrived. There was no bright light or doorway, at least not that I could see, just a sense of a rift opening in the fabric of our plane of existence. Frankly, I don't understand the mechanics of it, and I've never had the urge to explore what might be on the other side so that's the best I can do to describe it.

The whirling tornado stopped, the books and cups coming to a halt, hovering momentarily before crashing to the floor. Tess yelped in surprise. Darryl flicked in and out of view like the picture on an old TV set, his spectral state much more translucent and fuzzy than it had been before.

"What's happening?" he said, his voice trembling. "What is that?"

"You need to leave now, Darryl," I replied quietly. "You don't belong here."

"I-I…yes, I need to go." He began to fade and I relaxed as I felt his power slowly dissipate.

Suddenly a chill came over the room and I was overwhelmed by a sense of what I can only describe as evil. There was a pull on my aura, like something was sampling my power, and I staggered, almost falling to my knees as I struggled to clamp down my shields.

Tess grabbed my arm. "What the fuck's happening, Harry?"

"No!" Darryl shouted. "Who are you? Wait! Stop!"

"Darryl? Darryl, what's happening?" I stared at the ghost in confusion.

Darryl's spectral form fizzled and popped as he winked out of sight, but not before I saw his look of pure terror. There was a rush of air and then everything went still.

"What the fuck, Harry?" Tess peered around cautiously. "Is he gone?"

"He's gone," I said, stumbling over to a chair. I was drained. Never in all the dozens of banishments I'd performed had I ever felt like I did now. Something really weird had happened. Or at least something weirder than usual had happened.

"Harry!" Isaac's worried voice echoed through the house.

"We're in here, Isaac. We're fine," I called back, rising to my feet.

Isaac came to the doorway and stopped, his brow wrinkled in concern. "I felt..." He paused as if trying to find the right words to describe it. "There was a presence."

"You sensed something?" I gaped at him in surprise. With a wave of my hand, I mumbled the words to release the protection of the circle, and Isaac crossed the threshold, Susan close on his heels.

"Is he gone?" Susan looked around suspiciously.

"Yes, he's gone. Darryl won't bother you anymore."

With a cry of relief, Susan's knees buckled, and Isaac grabbed her elbow to keep her from falling. He carefully eased her over to a chair. "Have a seat, Ms. Cooper. You have endured much."

Susan gazed up in surprise at Isaac with a tentative smile. "T-thank you, Mr....uh..."

"Isaac. My name is simply Isaac."

"Yeah, he's like Cher that way." Tess grinned.

"Yes, well…thank you, Isaac." Susan bent and absently picked a book up off the floor. Flattening her hand across the cover, she set it gently on the table in front of her. "I can't believe it's finally over. It is over, isn't it, Harry?"

"Trust me. He's never coming back." I shared a look with Isaac and Tess. We needed to figure out what exactly happened, but now wasn't the time nor place.

Isaac glanced at his watch. "Harry, we really must be going, or we will be late."

I rolled my eyes, but gathered my things. Despite how the evening had gone so far, I couldn't help feeling like I was moving from the frying pan and into the fire.

Chapter Two

"Ugh, it burns." I grimaced and made a disgusted face.

"We simply must work on refining your palate, my dear Harry." Salvador raised an eyebrow patiently. I found it disconcerting that he seemed to be taking on more and more characteristics of a long-suffering parent the more time we spent together.

We were sitting in the spacious, open lounge area of Salvador's private penthouse. Despite Isaac's worries, we had arrived in plenty of time. Enough time, in fact, for me to give Tess a tour of my closet here in the penthouse.

A month ago, when the whole Mariposa deal started, I had learned that Salvador was keeping a suite reserved for me in his penthouse. Like the rest of the place, it was over-the-top luxurious, right down to its massive dressing room—the place was too big and too decked out to be called a closet. Of course, since Salvador seemed to have a penchant for treating me (and subsequently Nash) as his own personal dress-up dolls, the closet was loaded with high-end designer-label clothes. As expected, Tess was suitably impressed.

"Ahhh, that's nice stuff," Tess purred. She took another sip of the twenty-one-year-old single malt scotch and grinned at me.

"I'm glad you agree, Miss Fuentes, or may I call you Therese?" Salvador gave Tess an appraising glance.

"Please, call me Tess."

"Tessss." Salvador rolled the name off his tongue like he was trying it on for size. "Yes, I think that will do." He nodded his approval.

Tess turned her head and made a face at me, but thankfully held her tongue.

"So, tell me, young Tess, what is it that you do?"

I frowned at Salvador. What was he up to? I was sure he knew full well what Tess did. He probably had a dossier on everyone in my life over the last twenty-three years.

Tess glared at me and I threw her a little shrug. "Well, mostly I work for my Uncle Rodrigo at his gym, teaching martial arts and self-defence classes."

"Yes, yes, but what is it you really want to do?" Salvador smiled slyly at her, leaning forward to give Tess his attention.

"Shouldn't we be going or something?" I said quickly, hoping to divert Salvador's gaze. I knew it was a mistake to bring Tess up to the penthouse. The last thing she needed was to be on Salvador's radar. It was bad enough he had taken an interest in me. Although now that I knew I was his daughter, it made more sense and was a little less creepy.

"We have time if I say we have time, Angharad." Salvador waved a dismissive hand at me, his eyes never leaving Tess. Damn, I hated when he used my full name, not that I hated my name or anything—although I did prefer Harry—it was just so *parental* when he did it.

Tess shifted uncomfortably under Salvador's stare. "Well, I..."

"If you would allow me?" Salvador extended his hand to Tess. I shook my head at her, but she was already instinctively reaching out to place her hand in his. When their fingers touched, Tess froze, her eyes going blank as Salvador dipped his head to graze his lips across the inside of her wrist.

I shared a concerned look across the room with Isaac, but there was nothing we could do but wait for Salvador to finish. Salvador was a Reader, a very rare talent that allowed him to read the potential for power in someone's blood. He was, in fact, the most powerful vampire I had ever met. So powerful, he didn't even need to take blood. He could sip your life force right off your skin. With the small sip of Tess's essence he had taken, he would be able to know her abilities and see the possibilities for her future. It wasn't really fortune-telling or scrying the future, but more a glimpse at the possible future.

After a moment, Salvador nodded and released Tess's hand. "Yes, that will do. That will do nicely," he said more to himself than anyone else.

Tess pulled her hand back slowly, confused.

Salvador jumped to his feet with the grace of a cat. "You are absolutely right, my dear Harry, we should most certainly go." He paused, giving me a once-over as I scrambled to stand. His eyes narrowed, and I could tell when the katana I had strapped across my back and hidden with a no-see-me spell snapped into view, the enchantment broken. I was really going to have to upgrade that spell. "And might I add that you are particularly lovely this evening."

"I'm glad you think so. Maybe you'll be less inclined to need me to do anything that would require my new dress to get bloodstained?"

Salvador laughed and held out his arm for me. "We shall see, we shall see. And what of your wolf this evening? Will he be joining us?"

"Nash is caught up dealing with a multiple homicide. Sounds like nasty business, an entire family murdered. He wasn't sure if he would be able to get away." The lucky bastard.

"Ah, well then, I shall have you all to myself." He threw a glance over his shoulder as he led me out to wait for his private elevator. "And, young Tess, you will join us front and centre as well." It wasn't a request.

***

Luckily for Tess (and me) front and centre was really front and to the side. The audience chamber below Dante's was packed to capacity, including the raised platform where Salvador customarily sat on a chair that was suspiciously throne-like in appearance. He quite often made me sit to his left as he listened to the petty gripes and complaints of his vampire vassals. Tomas, a fellow dhamphir and Salvador's second, usually sat to his right, although come to think of it, recently Tomas had been MIA. Not that I was complaining. Tomas could be a real tool sometimes.

Tonight the dais was full, as there were several matters affecting both the witch and werewolf communities that would be discussed. As a result, Tess and I were relocated to the floor to the left of the stage. A large semi-circular space had been cleared directly in front, with Salvador's guards hemming the perimeter. The crowd was restless, eager even.

Tess, who seemed to have recovered from her encounter with Salvador, practically vibrated with nervous energy. She looked around the large room excitedly until her eyes cast over the stage, and she suddenly froze.

"You didn't tell me that *he'd* be here," she muttered angrily, grabbing my arm.

I followed her gaze, spotting the object of her dismay. Maxwell Hart, the newly elected leader of the Coven's governing body, the Conclave, was seated on the dais along with Eleanor, Nash's mother and pack alpha. Eleanor was a member of the Triad, one of the leaders of the werewolf pack. I searched the stage, but neither Charles Harris nor James Martin, the other two alphas of the Triad, were there. No surprise really as neither was quick to hide their dislike of vampires, and they both tended to avoid these sorts of gatherings unless absolutely required.

"What is your problem with Max?" I was truly baffled by Tess's reaction to the man. He was a nice guy and an extremely powerful practitioner. He was also easy on the eyes in a ruggedly handsome kind of way, his black, wavy hair with its signature white lock at his temple giving him an air of distinction.

"So tell me what goes on at one of these things?" Blatantly ignoring my question, Tess turned to Isaac, who stood a discreet distance behind us. I frowned at her. There was something going on with her. It wasn't like Tess not to share.

Before I could push the issue, a commotion across the room drew our attention. The large double doors had swung open, and someone stood at the entrance. The crowd, now focussed on the new arrival, buzzed, their conversations getting louder and more excited.

"Is that?" Tess stood on her tip-toes, grabbing my arm to keep her balance.

"Whoa. It's Tomas, but..." I stared across the room, at a loss for words, watching as Tomas walked towards the dais.

"Tomas, two-point-oh, more like," Tess replied, sounding awed.

I had to admit, it did look like Tomas had had some sort of upgrade. It wasn't just the navy pinstripe suit tailored to fit perfectly, or even his neatly coifed hair, there was something else. He had always been handsome, like he stepped off the pages of *GQ*, but now he was almost god-like in his beauty. He appeared bigger, healthier, more robust. He was...well-fed. And then it dawned on me.

"Omigod! He's a vampire." I looked at Isaac, who merely nodded in agreement.

"Well, duh," Tess scoffed. "He's always been a vampire."

"No, I mean he's really a vampire, a full vampire." I turned back to Isaac. "Is that where he's been all this time?

He died his first death?" Tomas was a dhamphir, a born vampire like me, and as such had already lived well beyond a normal mortal life-span, but as a living man. To become a full vampire meant that he had given up his mortal life or had it taken from him. "What happened? Do you know?"

Isaac frowned and shook his head. "I do not. I am no longer, as you say, in the loop with such things."

"I can't believe that Salvador never told me." You would think that the transformation of his right-hand man from living to undead might have come up in one of our weekly conversations over the last four weeks.

Tomas stopped in the centre of the empty semicircle in front of Salvador. "Magister, *Patrón*," he said, invoking the title reserved for when a vampire addresses his sire. He dipped gracefully into a low, respectful bow as the crowd exploded in a fury of excited chatter.

"He'll be insufferable now," Tess said with a roll of her eyes. She was probably right. Tomas had always been a bit of a vampire snob, and now he could claim Salvador as his maker.

"Welcome back, my son," Salvador said as he rose from his seat, his arms held up in benediction. "Welcome." He cast his gaze over the mass of spectators. "Friends, allies, join me in congratulating Tomas on his ascension."

As one, the vampires in the crowd snapped to attention. "We are one! We are legion! Together in blood!" The words, spoken by every vampire in the room, echoed through the chamber as the crowd burst into applause.

"Wow, it's like the Stepford Vampires." Tess eyed the room nervously.

I turned to look at Isaac, raising an eyebrow in question. "Is that like your team cheer or something?"

"Some traditions need to be observed. They are the very glue of our civilized society."

Admonished, I tried to appear contrite. "Yes, you're right. I'm sorry, Isaac. I shouldn't have made light of the occasion." I shrugged and then grinned as Tomas approached. "But that doesn't mean I can't have some fun." I nudged Tess with my elbow. "Do you see that, Tess?" I put my hand up as if fending off a bright light.

"Omigod, Harry! What is it? It's blinding." Tess held up her hands, pretending to shade her eyes. "Where are my sunglasses when I need them?"

"It's positively glowing," I replied, struggling to keep from laughing. "You might even say it..."

"Sparkles!" Tess and I shouted out together. We gave Tomas our best shit-eating grins.

"Yeah, ha-ha, Russo. So funny." He lifted his chin haughtily. "Your time will come."

He came to stand beside me. I guess even with his new status, he wasn't invited up on the stage either. I couldn't help but stare at him. The transformation was remarkable. He was still Tomas, but...more. I narrowed my eyes and examined him with my nifty supernatural power meter ability—an ability that seemed to come from my necromantic gift. He had received a power boost as well as a makeover with his transition into full vampire mode.

"What's the matter, Russo? Like what you see?" Tomas leered at me, opening his mouth slightly to seductively run his tongue over his teeth. "It's true what they say, you know. Even the sex is better as a vampire."

"That's funny." Tess leaned across me to address her comments directly to Tomas. "I heard they suck."

Tomas bristled, his smile becoming a scowl.

"Ewww, put your fangs away, Tomas." I pushed myself between the two of them before they decided to come to blows. "No one here is interested in hearing about your sex life, fangboy." I turned away and focussed on the dais, where Salvador had begun to address the crowd, not really listening but glad to have the distraction. I couldn't help but be curious about Tomas's transformation. One day the same thing was very likely going to happen to me. I tried not to think about it too much, but when I did, I just assumed I would still be me, that nothing, other than I could kiss watching the sunrise goodbye, would change. I glanced at Tomas again out of the corner of my eye. He at least seemed happy with the change. I bit my lip in thought.

Tomas snorted and leaned towards me. "Spit it out, Russo. You know you want to ask." He kept his voice low as Salvador and the other leaders began to address some matter of joint importance.

"Did it...I mean, how...?" I bit my lip again, unsure what I wanted to know.

"Yet another betrayal by your mother." Tomas all but spat out the words.

"My mother!" I slapped my hand over my mouth at my outburst and glanced around to see if anyone noticed. "My mother?" I repeated, quietly.

"She and I were friends once. Or so I thought." For a moment, Tomas had a faraway look in his eye, like he was remembering something, but then he scowled, giving his head a shake. "Deirdre used our friendship to lure me out. The Mariposa's guards were waiting."

I stared at Tomas, wide-eyed, unsure what to say. My mother, who I had thought dead my entire life, had proven to be a real piece of work. She had plotted against Salvador with the Mariposa, going so far as to conceive a child to be used against him in a grab for power. That she had turned out to be less than maternally inclined and a back-stabbing bitch to boot came as no surprise.

"I hear you killed the bitch," Tomas continued.

I stared at him in confusion. I hadn't killed my mother. She had done what she did best, run off and abandoned me yet again. Not that I was going to complain about that. Good riddance, as far as I was concerned.

"The Mariposa," he said, seeing my bewilderment. "Impressive, Russo. I didn't know you had it in you."

"She tried to kill me first," I blurted out.

Tomas smirked and then turned his attention back to the dais. It appeared that the minor petitions had been dealt with and the main event was about to begin.

***

There was no trial. It was, for all intents and purposes, an execution. Very few vampires survived spiking, or so I was told. The three vampires had been caught after rampaging across the city, feeding viciously on humans, discarding their torn and mutilated bodies like so much trash. The killing spree had created a citywide panic in the norm population who believed a sadistic serial killer was on the loose. Of course, that wasn't why the vampires were being punished. No, this whole dog and pony show was for the sole offense of disobeying Salvador, the loss of human life taking a backseat to ignoring the Magister's edict.

As Magister, Salvador was the law within the supernatural community. While the leaders of the other two main supernatural groups in town, the Werewolf Triad and the Witch Conclave, ruled within their own communities and were often consulted on matters affecting the Cimmerian as a whole, they had ceded their rights to govern when they had agreed to support Salvador as Magister. It was a move that prevented a lot of bloodshed over the years and was fairly unique compared to other territories around the globe where the various supernatural communities jostled for position, often gaining power through bloody show of force, the various species constantly at war with one another.

In preparation for the Mariposa's arrival a month ago, Salvador had restricted vampires to only feeding within the confines of designated clubs, like Dante's. The Mariposa's people had been apprised of the edict, and assurances had been made on the Mariposa's part. We quickly learned how worthless her word was, when the first body turned up.

The volume of the crowd suddenly rose, pulling my thoughts back to the present as the spectators on the far side of the chamber parted, and several vampire guards marched in, escorting the prisoners across the room to stand in front of the dais. The first of the rogue vampires was barely able to remain upright and had to be supported between two of the guards. He was gaunt, his eyes sunken and his cheeks hollow. Silver shackles had been fastened to his wrists for the transport, and I could see them burning the surrounding skin, turning it angry red. The prisoner appeared to be mumbling incoherently and didn't look up as he was brought to a halt to stand before the stage.

The second prisoner walked on his own accord between his vampire guards. He was the worse for wear, his hair unkempt, his clothes in tatters as if he had been in a fight, and he had the desperate, hungry look of a predator. Starving, he was probably even more dangerous now than he had been four weeks ago. He was also shackled, the silver burning on his wrists, but he showed no visible discomfort. As he came to a stop beside his fellow prisoner, he raised his head and I glared at him. It was Juan Carlo, the creepy, little vampire who had the ability to tamper with people's minds. He had used his ability to render his victims helpless, terrorizing them and silencing them at the same time. He had also tried to use it on me, but my shields had withstood his invasion. As if my thoughts drew his attention, he turned to stare at me, lifting his shackled hands to tap his temple in salute. Even facing final death, he was still a cheeky bastard.

"I thought there were supposed to be three of them," Tess said, interrupting my thoughts.

"The third was so weak he couldn't even survive the month-long purge," Tomas answered with a sneer.

"So what happens next?" I asked, taking advantage of Tomas's talkative mood.

"Watch and see," he replied, turning back to the stage. So much for being talkative.

A tall, severe-looking vampire, dressed in black tails and carrying a long, ebony staff, stepped to centre stage and bowed to Salvador. Salvador nodded and with a wave of his hand indicated the man should get on with it.

"Who's that?" I had never seen him before despite all of my weekly trips to Dante's.

Isaac leaned forward to answer. "He's Grimes, the Magister's Orator."

Before I could ask Isaac to elucidate, Grimes began to speak.

"Hear ye, hear ye, all those gathered do act as witness. Prisoners, you stand before the Magister charged with the crime of willful disobedience to his word. Know that his justice is swift and without mercy."

Grimes brought his staff down to pound on the stage three times, and the crowd once again parted as what appeared to be two large, wooden coffins were wheeled to stand upright behind the prisoners.

Juan Carlo merely lifted his chin haughtily, but his fellow rogue moaned and begged for his life, falling to his knees between his two guards. They hoisted him to his feet, just as the coffin lid was lifted open.

Beside me, Tess gasped in surprise. "Damn! He's going to be a vampire pin cushion."

I nodded in agreement. The inside of the coffin was lined with some type of smooth stone—granite or marble maybe. The lid had been fitted with row after row of shining, silver spikes concentrated in the torso area of the box. Each spike was at least ten inches long. When the lid was replaced on the coffin, they would pierce its occupant's body, leaving the head and heart free from harm. Because each spike was made of, or at least covered in, silver, the piercing would not only be painful, but the vampire would not be able to heal his injuries as the silver poisoned his body. If he didn't bleed to death or die from organ failure, he would eventually die of silver poisoning.

As the first prisoner was dragged to the coffin, Tomas turned to me, a grin on his face. "Do you think you can stomach it, Russo? You might want to step back out of the splash zone."

"The what?" I glanced around. It did appear, in fact, like some spectators were backing away through the crowd, while others pushed forward, eager to be closer to the action.

"Tomas has a point, Harry. You may wish to move a little farther away." Isaac stepped to the side, clearing a path for us to move if we chose.

"No, wait!" Tess grabbed my arm and then pulled something from her purse. "Every time you go to one of these vampire things you end up wrecking your clothes. I came prepared." A clear plastic rain poncho materialized, followed by a second.

"Rain ponchos?" I stared at her in surprise. "Great idea!"

We quickly pulled them on, ignoring Tomas's mocking laughter.

"Laugh all you want, fangboy," I said to him. "I refuse to ruin another dress because of vampire shenanigans."

I turned my attention back to the stage where Salvador sat with a bored expression. His eyes met mine, and he frowned as he took in Tess's and my new fashion accessories. The frown gave way to a look of amusement and he barked out a laugh. The crowd hushed momentarily, the guards eyeing Salvador in confusion. He simply nodded and waved at them to continue.

The guards hauled the vampire to the coffin, pulling his shackled hands above his head and attaching them to a hook at the top of the coffin. Next they shackled each leg at the bottom of the coffin, stretching the vampire out, immobilizing him. Without pause or fanfare, the lid of the coffin lowered shut. The vampire screamed as the tips of the spikes drove into his body. The crowd roared their approval. It was almost deafening, yet you could still hear the agonized cries of the prisoner. I clenched my teeth, refusing to appear weak and look away.

The lid continued to close, slowing as it met resistance. The crowd hushed, straining to hear the prisoner's screams, which had become wheezy cries as the spikes pierced his lungs. As the lid lowered the last few inches, there was a hiss followed by a loud pop. The coffin blew open, bits of gore and blood spraying outward as its occupant exploded violently, a common occurrence with vampire true death. The crowd went wild.

I looked down at my poncho, which was now covered in blood spatter. Tess was a genius.

Chapter Three

"And the second one went about the same as the first, except for the whole exploding-into-gooey-bits part." I shook my head as I thought of Juan Carlo. He had stepped up to the coffin with no prodding from the guards whatsoever. There had been a brief moment when I thought I saw fear in his eyes, but then the lid was lowered. He never made a sound, much to the crowd's disappointment. The coffin lid had closed tightly and had been secured in place. Juan Carlo would be locked up until Salvador decided to let him out, if he decided to let him out.

"Omigod! It's so barbaric." Barbie, a werewolf and one of my daytime staff in the coffee shop, shivered and made a face. "Don't get me wrong, the evil little bugger deserved it, but still...I'm glad I didn't have to be there." She shuddered again then turned away to wipe down the already pristine counter-top.

Tiffy, another of the daytime staff who was also Fae, a brownie to be precise, licked her lips. "What did they do with the remains of the first vampire?" She ran her tongue across her perfect human teeth, deep in thought, and I tried not to think of the shark-like double row of razor-sharp choppers hiding behind her glamour, or what she might have wanted with a bucket of liquefied vampire guts.

"I don't know. Probably left them out in the sun to be turned to ash."

Tiffy shook her head at the apparent waste and then returned to the task of restocking the coffee supplies. It was midmorning, and the commuter rush of coffee drinkers had passed. We were in the lull before the lunch-rush crowd. The coffee shop was my latest business venture. I already owned Contain Yourself, the flower shop next door—although Mrs. Potts, Tiffy's aunt, really took care of the day-to-day business—and since I now owned the entire building thanks to a deal with Salvador, it made sense to fill the remaining vacant shop space on the main level. A coffee shop seemed like the logical choice, not only for the neighbourhood but because it turned out Isaac was a foodie and liked to bake. Even with our overactive metabolisms, there was only so much baking that Tess and I could eat by ourselves. I called the shop the Full Fat Coffee Company due to Isaac's refusal to serve anything low calorie or low fat. It had been open for about a month and had succeeded beyond my expectations. Not only had we built up a steady base of norm customers—they loved our coffee and our bakery items—our later-than-usual nighttime hours allowed us to cater to a whole other clientele of the supernatural variety. We were so busy, in fact, I'd hired two more staff besides Barbie.

First there had been Willow, a vampire friend of Isaac's who was an extremely talented artist—a talent she put to use as our chief cake decorator. She was one of a half-dozen vampires who wanted a change and had taken up residence across the street in Isaac's new vampire condos. Next came Hector, a werewolf and outrageous flirt who styled himself as a Latin-lover type. He charmed all the ladies, norm and supernatural alike, working a split shift to cover the lunch crowd and then returning to work the evening shift. Between the hired staff and Hilde, Isaac and me, we managed to always have at least two people on shift at any given time.

The bell above the door rang, and I glanced up, expecting to see Hector arriving for his lunch shift. Instead it was a rather stuffy-looking norm in a dark, tailored suit.

He paused inside the door, letting his eyes adjust from the bright sunlight outside, and then zeroed in on me.

"Miss Russo?"

"Yes, that's me. How can I help you?"

He bobbed his head and reached into the breast pocket of his suit. Both Tiffy and Barbie tensed, as if ready to spring to my defense, but he merely pulled out a business card and held it out to me. "Reginald DeGrasse. Martins, Newburg and DeGrasse."

I took the card and glanced at it. He was a lawyer, a partner obviously, in one of the city's larger, well-known law firms.

"How can I help you, Mr. DeGrasse?"

DeGrasse scanned the shop and then leaned towards me. "It's of a sensitive nature. Is there perhaps...?"

"Of course. Why don't we step into my office?" I swept my hand out indicating the first booth closest to the counter. Tess and I had decided it would be our personal table, and unless the shop got really busy, we kept a small sign on it that read *Reserved for the Owner*.

DeGrasse paused, momentarily disconcerted by my less than private office, but then stepped over, unbuttoning his suit jacket before sliding into a seat at the booth.

"Can I offer you a cup of coffee?"

"Yes, thank you. That would be quite welcome."

I signalled to Barbie, who nodded, and then I joined DeGrasse at the booth. A moment later, Barbie arrived with two steaming cups of coffee and a plate of Isaac's to-die-for chocolate chip cookies.

"Am I being sued or something?" I asked, half-joking but genuinely worried, as I took a cautious sip of coffee.

"No, gracious, no. Nothing like that. I have a rather delicate situation, and I was referred to you by a well-known member of the business community, Mr. Salvador Arroyo."

At Salvador's name, I almost snorted my coffee out my nose. "I see. And what exactly is this sensitive matter?"

"You will have heard of William Koenig?"

I nodded and replied, "The founder of K-Company Distribution. Yes, I know who he is, I mean, was." Koenig, a Riverton titan of industry and well-known philanthropist, had just recently passed away. The flower shop had been busy for three days straight handling all the orders that came in for sympathy floral arrangements. "I'm not sure what Mr. Koenig would have to do with me, though."

DeGrasse cleared his throat and shifted uncomfortably in his seat. "Yes, well…I've represented Mr. Koenig for going on forty years, and I continue to represent his daughter, Elise. In two weeks' time, there will be a reading of the will." He paused and took a long sip of coffee. "For years, it was known that Mr. Koenig was grooming his son, William Jr, to take over the business."

I couldn't help myself and I let out a disgruntled "Hmph". Of course it was the son who was expected to take over the family business. I raised an eyebrow at DeGrasse, communicating my impatience. I still didn't see what any of this had to do with me.

DeGrasse cleared his throat again before continuing. "Recently, William Jr. has, to put it mildly, fallen in with a bad crowd. He has no interest in the day-to-day running of the company and has voiced his opinion that it would be worth more if they split it up and sold it off."

"*What?*" K-Company Distribution was a huge employer in Riverton. If the company was sold off, there could potentially be a lot of people put out of work.

"Mr. Koenig made provisions to prevent this. I personally drew up a new will for him, leaving the company to his daughter with the stipulation that it remain intact and in Riverton."

"I sense there's a *but* coming."

DeGrasse grimaced. "Unfortunately, yes. The will is missing. It had been signed and witnessed, but before it could be entered into the record, it disappeared. No one knows what happened to it. It was last seen with Mr. Koenig at his bedside."

I let out a long, slow breath. I had a bad feeling about where this conversation might be headed. "And what do you expect me to do about it?"

DeGrasse leaned over the table towards me and lowered his voice. "Well, we, that is, I was led to believe you could assist in this matter. That you have a particular..." DeGrasse glanced around the room furtively, "...talent that could be of use."

I frowned at him, inwardly cursing Salvador and wondering what exactly he had told DeGrasse I could do. How much did he know? Did he merely think I was some sort of psychic? Norms readily believed in their existence. Or was DeGrasse all on board, so to speak, and one of the minority of norms who knew about the existence of the Cimmerian and all its denizens?

As if sensing my hesitation, DeGrasse coughed nervously and then, holding his right arm above the table, pulled back his sleeve to reveal a small black tattoo on the underside of his wrist. Holy shit! To the unenlightened, it simply looked like two commas stacked one on top of the other, but within the Cimmerian, it signified that DeGrasse was a trusted blood donor. DeGrasse was a fang-banger!

"I still don't know if I can help," I said, shaking my head. "There's no guarantee that his spirit will remember—"

"No, Miss Russo, his spirit will not suffice. For it to be binding, all parties have agreed that we require visible proof. We must be able to see and question Mr. Koenig directly ourselves." DeGrasse paused and arched a brow at me. "We require you to raise his zombie."

Chapter Four

I was still steaming over DeGrasse's visit to the coffee shop later that afternoon, as I pulled my truck into the loading zone at Riverton Memorial Hospital and began to unload my deliveries. I couldn't believe Salvador had basically pimped me out to one of his cronies in the business community. To a norm, no less! Although with DeGrasse being a blood donor, he was probably already aware of my particular talents. You don't execute a pedophile vampire, bind a couple of vampire servants, and bring the undead life of a big, scary, ancient vampire like the Mariposa to an end in a rain of blood and gore without getting a bit of a reputation. But still, raise a zombie that could not only talk, but remember its past life? Salvador obviously had more confidence in my abilities than I did.

I didn't know what to say to DeGrasse. That he offered me an obscene amount of money to do it didn't help either. I'd finally told him I needed to do some research and would get back to him in a couple days. I wasn't worried about him blabbing to anyone about my bizarre talent, because who would believe him? Besides, the tattoo he had marking him as a blood donor also meant he was under a geis that prevented him from speaking to the uninitiated. Basically what happened in the blood den, stayed in the blood den. As if to offer me incentive to call sooner rather than later, on his way out the door DeGrasse placed a rather large envelope full of cash on the table in front of me as a retainer.

"Hey, Harry!"

"Shit!" Startled, I almost dropped the basket of flowers I was placing on my delivery cart. I looked around, groaning when I saw who was approaching.

"Hey, Harry! Pull my finger." The finger in question was attached to a scrawny arm wrapped in a red-and-white-striped shirt. Green, polka-dotted overalls that had seen better days and a purple bow tie completed the ensemble.

"Not now," I replied, turning my back on the clown. Yes, he was literally a clown. Yellow frizzy hair under a bowler hat, whiteface paint and red rubber nose included.

"Ahhh, c'mon, Harry. Be a sport." He waggled his index finger at me. "Pull my finger."

With a sigh, I looked heavenward in defeat and reached out to pull the appendage. At the point where our fingers should have made contact, mine simply passed through the air as if nothing was there, which in fact, was true. That didn't stop the resulting sound effect, however.

BRRR-ATT!

The farting sound echoed around the loading dock, but only my ears could hear it. I couldn't help but be impressed that he had enough spectral juice to recreate the sound of a whoopee cushion that didn't exist.

As you probably guessed, Mofo the clown was a ghost. And yes, that really is his name. Of course Mofo was named in a simpler time, back in the fifties when novelty gags like squirting flowers and whoopee cushions were all the rage. It was just as well that hardly anyone could see or hear him. His name took on a whole new meaning these days.

"Ha-ha," I deadpanned. "You're so hilarious, Mofo."

"Of course. That's always been one of my most popular gags." Mofo preened, my sarcasm lost on him. "Haven't seen you around here much lately, Harry."

I shrugged. I had been trying to give more of the hospital deliveries to Jimmy, my part-time delivery guy, but he was at his other job this afternoon, teaching a class at

Uncle Rigo's gym. I didn't particularly enjoy the hospital deliveries, for obvious reasons. For a place that was supposed to heal you, there were sure a lot of dead people.

"It's been kind of busy the last couple of months."

"You should come up to the children's ward, Harry. With you there, I'd knock it out of the park."

Ha! No kidding. With all the little psychic believers up there—many young kids can see ghosts—plus my recently super-charged powers, I wouldn't be surprised if I could pull his finger.

"Sorry, maybe another time."

"Okay, Harry. Smell ya later!" With a guffaw, Mofo winked out of sight. I smiled to myself as I pushed my loaded cart towards the double receiving entrance doors. I really should try and stop by the ward soon. It was always fun to watch the kids interact with Mofo. They loved him, which is why he probably stuck around. The baffled looks on the faces of the nursing staff and parents were also kind of priceless.

***

I was making my last delivery when it happened. I was just placing the *Thank-you* succulent arrangement on the corner of the ICU nurses' station when I heard a plea for help.

"Oh my God, oh my God! No! This can't be happening. I'm not ready. Someone help me. Help me!"

I looked around, but of course no one else could hear the cries. The source of the sound appeared to be the room across the hall where a small group of people stood vigil at a woman's bedside. From what I could tell, they had unplugged her, and the inevitable had occurred.

"No! Why isn't anyone doing anything? Why aren't they helping me?"

The ghost, a blonde woman in her mid-forties, flitted from one person to the next, attempting to get their attention. I watched, hoping she would quickly accept her death and move on.

"John! John! I'm right here. Why can't you see me? I'm right here." The woman stood beside a man who was holding her body's hand, visibly crying. "Can't anybody help me? Anyone? Please, I'm beg—"

I blinked in surprise as the ghost disappeared mid-sentence. I'd never seen it happen that way before. Usually they sort of just faded, their pleas for help turning to acceptance and assertions of love, before they crossed over.

I shrugged to myself and started to turn away, only to stop in shock when the room erupted into happy shouts, the woman's family now laughing and hugging one another. The medical staff looked equally surprised and baffled as they fussed with monitors and tended to their patient who'd apparently returned from the dead.

Huh. Well, that was weird.

***

Returning to the loading dock, I wheeled my now-empty cart into the back of my truck and closed the tailgate, only to find myself pinned against it. Instinct and years of self-defence training kicked in, and I pushed myself off the truck, surprising my attacker, who fell back a step, allowing me to spin around to face him as I brought my knee up to deliver a crippling blow to the 'nads.

"Careful now, minx," a familiar voice growled at me. "You don't want to damage the goods." Nash grinned, swiftly moving his hands to protect the family jewels.

"Nash!" I slowed my knee, stopping as it made contact.

Nash caught my raised leg, wrapping it around his thigh as he leaned into me, flattening me against the truck. He dipped his face to my neck and inhaled with a groan. "Mmmm, you smell good, Harry."

Before I could respond, his free hand raked through my hair pulling my head back as his mouth descended on mine. Nash kissed me like we hadn't seen each other in weeks rather than just twenty-four hours and when his hand brushed against the mate mark at the base of my neck, it was a good thing I was pinned to the truck or I would have slid to the ground in a boneless heap.

When we finally came up for air, I gave him a once-over and frowned. "You look like shit."

Nash barked out a laugh and ran a hand through his hair. "Thanks. I feel like it, too." For a moment his eyes looked haunted and then he covered them, rubbing his hand down his face.

"It was a tough one," I said, making it more a statement than a question. I had expected him to arrive in my bed sometime in the night, but he had never showed. From the state of him, he probably hadn't even gone to bed yet.

"Yeah, you could say that. We chased the bastard halfway across the city." He let out a sigh. "I caught an hour or two of sleep at the station."

"I heard about it on the news." I shuddered, thinking about it. A local man, a norm, had gone berserk, murdering his wife and two of his children before rampaging across the city, leaving a trail of bodies in his wake. He had finally been cornered down at the docks, going down in a hail of bullets after opening fire on the police officers surrounding him. His body had fallen off the pier and into the river below. When all was said and done, five people were dead and several million dollars of property damage had occurred. The only bright note in the whole affair was that his fifteen-year-old daughter had survived the attack.

"Is the girl here at the hospital?"

Nash nodded. "Yeah, I was on my way up to see her when I spotted your truck."

I pulled him into a fierce hug, resting my head against his chest. "I'm glad you found me."

Nash's arms tightened around me, returning the gesture. "Me too." He kissed the top of my head. "Listen, I should have this wrapped up in a couple of hours."

"Why don't you swing by my place after? I'll cook you dinner."

"You'll cook?" He pushed himself back so he could look down at me in surprise.

"What? I can cook," I replied defensively.

Nash gave me a skeptical look and then glanced at his watch. "Make it three hours, and I'll slip home first to shower and change."

"Deal."

Grinning, Nash swooped me up by my forearms, pulling me up on my toes to lay another big kiss on me before turning to head back into the hospital.

Holy crap! Cook dinner? What had I done?

Chapter Five

"You told him you'd do what?" Tess laughed and gaped at me in amazement.

"I told him I would cook dinner. What's the big deal? How hard can it be?"

"Harry, you've never cooked anything in your life."

"Sure I have."

"Macaroni and cheese from a box doesn't count."

I frowned at her. She had a point. "Well, I guess it's about time I tried then, isn't it? Now are you going to help me find a recipe or not? I still have to run to the grocery store."

"*Perhaps I can be of some assistance*?"

The computerized voice came from the speakers on the desk in the corner just as the screen blinked on, its now familiar animated robot waving at us from across the room.

"Bryce! Where have you been? No, scratch that. I don't want to know." Now that Bryce had unlimited, nearly instantaneous access to anywhere in the world the Internet could take him, he tended to disappear for long periods of time, more often than not surfing porn sites. I didn't need to hear a play-by-play of his latest stop.

"*I'm eager to hear how the GhostCam 3000 worked,*" Bryce replied.

"The what? Oh, the tablet app. It worked great, didn't it, Tess?"

"Yeah, it did."

"*Cool. I'm accessing the tablet now via the network so I can analyze the recording.*"

"It recorded everything?" Tess looked surprised. "So we can watch it again?"

"Can we skip the technical conversation right now and find me a recipe instead?"

The printer suddenly beeped and spit out a page. I walked over and grabbed it.

"*Easy Chicken and Rice,*" Bryce intoned, his computer voice taking on an accent that suspiciously sounded like Julia Child. "*It only has five ingredients and a difficulty rating of one spoon. Even you should be able to handle it, Harry.*"

"Gee, thanks." I bit my lip, peering over the instructions. "Actually, this is great. Thanks!" I sat down beside Tess at the kitchen island and made a list. The chicken was supposed to take an hour and I still had to go to the store. I needed to get cracking.

"So now that Bryce has solved your cooking crisis, can we talk about something else?" Tess turned to face me.

"Sure, as long as it doesn't have anything to do with you moving out," I replied, only half-joking.

Tess snorted and then pulled a green sheet of paper from the stack of mail that had been sitting on the counter. "Did you see this?" She shoved it towards me.

I looked at it with a puzzled frown. It was a flyer advertising a new nightclub called Wishes. "No. I've never heard of it." I pushed the flyer back to Tess.

"I think we should go check it out. There's a two-for-one drink special every night this month," she replied, tapping at the flyer.

"Sure, why not? What's the big deal? Why are you acting weird about asking me to go to a club?" It wasn't like we had never been out dancing together before, and my dating Nash hadn't changed anything.

"It's...well..."

Tess bit her lip and tapped the flyer again, this time pointing to the address listed at the bottom of the page. I stared at it a moment, trying to figure out why it sounded familiar.

"Omigod! Is that where I think it is?"

"If you're thinking that it's the same address as the warehouse where DiCastro tried to sacrifice you to the Egyptian god Osiris, then yes, it is."

"They made it into a nightclub? Who? Who owns it?"

"I don't know, but I heard from some of the guys at the gym that it's been completely renovated and totally tricked out. You won't even recognize it." She clasped her hands under her chin and batted her best puppy-dog eyes at me. "Puh-lease, Harry? Can we go?"

I wrinkled my nose at the idea. I didn't particularly have fond memories of the place. I still had the occasional nightmare about it. "I don't know. I'll think about it, okay?"

Satisfied with my answer, Tess nodded and hopped down off her stool. "Great. I've gotta go. I promised Uncle Rigo I would inventory the new crossbow supplies tonight." She turned and waved on her way to the door. "Good luck with your dinner, Harry." She gave me an impish grin. "Don't forget the fire extinguisher is under the sink."

"Oh, ha-ha," I replied, flipping her the bird. "Just for that, I won't save you any leftovers."

"Promises, promises." Tess grinned at me again and then hurried out the door.

"I'll show them," I muttered to myself. I was going to cook Nash dinner, and he was going to eat it whether he liked it or not.

Chapter Six

"I don't like it," Nash complained, leaning forward to grab his beer off the coffee table. He took a swig and then reached for another slice of pizza.

We were eating pizza and not the easy chicken and rice due to a small technical difficulty I had with the oven. It turns out that if you're running late, doubling the oven temperature does not actually cut the cooking time in half. Who knew?

On the plus side, my kitchen catastrophe meant we ordered a pepperoni and sausage pie from Minetti's, and since Mama Minetti thought I looked "to-ah skeeny", she had sent a double order of tiramisu as well. It was no chocolate cassata, but nothing to sneeze at either.

The apartment still smelled like burnt rice and chicken, despite having every window open. I shivered, and only partly because of the cold, night air. "I don't either, but what can I do? The guy just showed up at the coffee shop. Salvador *referred* him."

Nash grumbled again at Salvador's name. "What was he thinking?"

"Who knows? It's probably just another one of his tests."

"Can you do it?"

I thought about the wolf zombies I had raised six weeks earlier when the psychotic Elf prince, Elian Navarre, had hunted Nash and me through the forest, and then nodded. "Yeah, I think so. The only thing I'm worried about is making sure I can control it and keep everyone safe."

"I should be there when you do it. Isaac too."

I nodded absently and snuggled up to Nash. It gave me a warm, fuzzy feeling knowing he was looking out for me but still willing to let me be myself. I snuck my hand under his shirt, enjoying the heat coming off his body as I trailed my fingers up and down his torso. "So, are you ready for dessert, or…" I waggled my eyebrows at him, "*…dessert*?"

Nash grabbed my hand, and I squeaked in surprise as I found myself lifted up to straddle him. His hands tugged at my shirt, yanking it out from where it was tucked into my jeans. "Mmmm, let's have *dessert* first." He pulled me down with a growl and our mouths connected just as his cellphone trilled.

"Crap! I suppose you have to get that." I made a pouty face as I slid off his lap.

Nash grabbed his phone, punching his finger at it. "Yeah, Nash. Speak." As he listened to the voice on the other end—I was guessing it was his partner, Dev—he slowly rose to his feet and raked a hand through his hair. Oh no. That wasn't a good sign. It appeared our date had come to an end.

***

The next few days passed by uneventfully, at least for me. Nash and Dev, however, were practically run off their feet as one norm after another seemed to go psycho, apparently hell-bent on wreaking as much havoc as possible.

First there was the seventy-five-year-old woman who went ballistic when she didn't win at seniors' bingo night. She had attacked the man calling the game, beating him senseless with the bingo ball cage. She had then proceeded to chase all her fellow bingo players around the hall (not as hard as it sounds since most either used a walker or a cane), tackling them and then dabbing them all over with the multicoloured bingo dabbers while laughing hysterically. When the police finally arrived, she was sitting under a table humming to herself and tearing the lids off the dabbers so she could drink the liquid ink. The responding officers had understandably been less than worried about the near catatonic woman. That is until she wrestled one of them to the ground, pulling his side arm from the holster and wildly opening fire on the room. She had managed to shoot both officers and three of the cane-and-walker crowd—luckily all superficial wounds—before putting the gun to her chest and blowing a hole through her heart.

The second incident was just as bizarre. A salesman at a local car dealership inexplicably went nuts, stripping off his clothes and running around the dealership. It all seemed rather harmless until he dumped several gallons of motor oil on himself, jumped into one of the showroom cars and fired it up, driving it through the large plate-glass window. He then careened through the lot, crashing into one new car after another like he was playing bumper cars or smash-up derby. When the police arrived, they managed to hem his car in, but before they could apprehend him, he slid out of the car and across the hood (the motor oil making him particularly slippery), and made a dash for the busy street. The driver of the bus that flattened him like a pancake, didn't even have time to slam on the brakes when the salesman threw himself in front of the hurtling vehicle.

With three bizarre incidents involving norms going homicidally, or at least suicidally, loopy, it was hard not to jump to the conclusion that we had some sort of epidemic on our hands. It was also hard not to assume, at least for those in the know, that a supernatural influence could be at play. I was discussing just that possibility with Isaac while he puttered around my kitchen. After my easy chicken and rice incident, I had been banned from cooking until Isaac could give me a few basic lessons, so he was making dinner.

"Do you think it could be some sort of mind control?" I asked, helping myself to another scoop of his homemade guacamole. It was unbelievably good with chunks of avocado, onion and tomato, and plenty of garlic to give it some kick—that whole vampires-hate-garlic thing is hogwash. He had even made his own crispy tortilla chips to go with it. What can I say? There are benefits to knowing a foodie who loves to cook.

Isaac placed a long salmon fillet on a cedar plank skin-side down and then brushed it with sauce. We were having one of my favourites, grilled salmon with chili glaze and lime crème fraîche.

"That is a possibility, I suppose, although the only known supernatural in the area with the ability to do such a thing on that kind of scale is currently incapacitated." Isaac arched an eyebrow at me, and I shuddered, thinking about Juan Carlo.

"It just seems like too much of a coincidence for there not to be a supe involved. They've already ruled out hallucinogenic drugs. The tests all came back clean. Nash and Dev are really getting pressure from higher up to put a stop to it all." I grabbed the pitcher of margaritas and topped mine up. Isaac had a real theme going tonight. Tess was going to be sorry she had to work late and miss out. "Nash must be getting desperate for answers because he even asked me to go to the funeral for the bingo lady to see if I might be able to find something out." And you know Nash *must* be desperate if he was asking *me* to poke my nose into things.

"Yes, well..." Isaac cleared his throat. "Speaking of the detective, there is a topic that I wish to discuss to further your vampiric education."

Isaac was my guru when it came to all things vampire. Seeing as how I had been kept in the dark about my parentage for most of my life, I was embarrassingly lacking when it came to knowledge about my own kind. "Sure," I replied. "Shoot."

Isaac finished garnishing the salmon with lime slices and then set the plank aside, ready to go on the grill.

"As you know from our conversation the other day, I am aware that you and Cian enjoy a sexual relationship—"

"Omigod! Stop right there." I held up my hands as if warding him off. "We are not going to talk about my sex life." I frowned at him. "Besides, you're a little late for the birds-and-the-bees talk, don't you think?"

Isaac gave me a long suffering look. "I'm sure you are more than capable of handling the mechanics of your relationship or any contraceptive issues you might have. But, as I was saying, I am aware that you enjoy a sexual relationship that involves the sharing of blood."

Heat rushed to my face. While it was true there had been several times where, in the moment, I had taken Nash's blood, it wasn't something I wanted to think too closely about. The experience was beyond anything either of us had ever felt. Nash got off on it as much as I did, his blood strengthening our mate connection to the point where we were in each other's mind, sharing each other's sensations. It had led to some mind-blowing orgasms. Not that I had any intention of telling Isaac that.

"There is nothing for you to be embarrassed about," Isaac continued, ignoring my discomfort. "It is a perfectly natural instinct due to your heritage. In fact, the vampire's ability to feed during sex and provide his or her donor with an extraordinary sexual experience is key to our species' survival."

"Great. So I'm not a freak. Can we change the subject now?" I gulped the last half of my margarita and then poured another.

"No." Isaac folded his arms over his *Oh Crêpe* apron. "I would be remiss in your education if we didn't go over a few...safety precautions." He crossed the kitchen to pull something out of the breast pocket of the suit jacket he had left hanging over the back of a chair and handed it to me.

I took it hesitantly. It was a glossy, trifold pamphlet with *The Human Circulatory System* written on the front. "You have a brochure?" I gaped at him.

Isaac shrugged, gesturing for me to take a look. Inside, a full-length colour depiction of the human body with all its arteries (in red) and veins (in blue) was laid out and labelled. I flipped the page over to glance at the back. There was a small white rectangle at the bottom where *Riverton Blood Services* and an address had been stamped. The rest of the page was taken up by what appeared to be a menu of sorts, listing blood type and price per litre. The strangest part was the words *We Deliver!* written in—what else?—blood-red letters across the top.

"Is this the equivalent of a vampire takeout menu?" I snorted, feeling a little less embarrassed.

"While it is preferable to use a live donor, in a pinch, a blood bank can be a feasible alternative. As you are probably aware, the life essence found in a being's blood slowly dissipates once that blood has been spilled. As a result, you require a larger quantity of bagged blood than you would from a fresh meal."

Ewww, he'd just referred to Nash as a meal.

"Of course, as a dhamphir, the taking of blood is not yet a necessity for you. However, over time, as your powers continue to grow, you will find the lure much harder to resist." Isaac paused as I squirmed in my chair. "It is nothing you should feel uncomfortable about." He gave me a pointed look, took the pamphlet from my hand and opened it fully, laying it flat on the counter. "What we need to discuss are the safe places on a human from which to feed."

I did a face-palm, shaking my head. My life had become nothing if not entertaining. If you had told me six months ago that I would be sitting in my kitchen getting an anatomy lesson from a vampire, I would have said you were crazy.

"Now, the first thing you need to remember is to always select a vein rather than an artery. I'm sure you can ascertain why."

"I'm going to go out on a limb here and say it's so I don't use Nash to recreate a Jackson Pollock on the nearest wall."

"Correct. The velocity of blood flow through a punctured artery would result in probable death for your meal." He looked pensive for a moment. "Although, with your penchant for werewolves, there is a greater chance that they could survive a puncture to a major artery."

"My *penchant* for werewolves? There's just one werewolf." And I was pretty sure I was in love with him, although I wasn't ready to admit that aloud to anyone.

"As I was saying, avoid the arteries and instead choose the veins. There are several excellent locations on the body that lend themselves to both the practical as well as the sensual considerations." He pointed to the diagram in front of us and ticked locations off. "In the neck you will find the external jugular. At the collarbone, the subclavian is also a safe choice. Then there are the extremities. The femoral vein in particular can be quite erotic due to its proximity to certain regions of the body. And, of course, you have already discovered the radial vein at the wrist."

I felt my face flush again. He was referring to where I had first bitten Nash. It was a totally in-the-moment thing, although Nash had known what I had intended and encouraged me. His blood had called out to me, and I had responded. The result had been two small scars on his wrist.

"So how come the bite I gave Nash didn't heal completely?" Usually, when a vampire licks the wound made during a blood exchange, the magic that is vampire spit instantly heals it. For some reason the bite I had given

Nash had left a permanent mark. That it had become an erogenous zone for Nash like his mate mark at the base of my neck was for me, was just a lucky turn of events. The spot was so sensitive, Nash had taken to wearing a leather bracer on his wrist to protect it.

Isaac gave another of his annoying Gallic shrugs. "This I do not know. It could be as your powers are so newly acquired combined with your half-vampire status, your saliva does not contain enough of the component that gives it the ability to heal. Or, it could be something related to your mating with Cian. He did, after all, mark you as well."

Nash had said pretty much the same thing. "So are we finished then?" I couldn't keep my voice from sounding grouchy. *Aunt Flo* had arrived for her monthly visit, and talking about my sex life with Isaac was making me cranky.

Isaac grabbed the salmon plank and moved towards the stairs. He'd have to go up to the roof to use the grill. "Yes. You are, as they say, off the hook." He looked back at me and then pointed to a bag of basmati rice sitting on the counter top. "Your first cooking lesson is in reading and following the instructions exactly. If you begin now, the rice should be ready when the salmon is done." He started to walk away, but then turned back again, taking a deep breath, his eyes narrowing as he looked at me thoughtfully. "Oh, and, Harry, you should probably suggest to the Magister that you take this week's meeting somewhere other than Dante's."

"Not necessary. I've already been informed that we will be dining at Cirque." With Tomas—another reason I was cranky.

With a nod, Isaac turned and left the kitchen. It wasn't until a full minute later when it dawned on me. Did he just sniff me and imply that he knew it was that time of the month? Eww!

***

After dinner (which was delicious and I didn't even screw up the rice) Isaac disappeared to spend some quality time with Christina, Nash's sister. Christina was also a foodie, and although they never came right out and said it, it was pretty clear they were doing more than just trading recipes.

Nash was working on yet another case involving an HRN—a homicidally rampaging norm—so I didn't expect he'd show up until the middle of the night, if at all. From what I gathered on the news, this time the incident had gone down at a Gas & Shop. A man had apparently stopped to get gas. While his car was filling, he entered the store and started stuffing his face with junk food he hadn't paid for yet. When the clerk confronted him, the man ran wild up and down the aisles, tearing things off the shelves before bolting from the store, grabbing the gas pump from his car and dousing himself with gasoline. Witnesses said he laughed gleefully and then pulled a lighter from his pocket and set himself on fire. Because he had been standing right next to his car with the gas tank open, the flames had jumped, causing his car to explode as well. This set off a chain reaction, taking several more cars with it. By the time the fire department arrived the entire gas station was in flames, and the whole block had to be evacuated.

With Isaac out and both Nash and Tess working, I was feeling at loose ends, so I went downstairs to hang out at the coffee shop. Both Hector and Barbie were working out front, while Hilde was busy baking up a storm in the kitchen. I really liked Hilde. She was a character. She appeared to be a typical sixteen- or seventeen-year-old Goth chick—dressed in black with an ear full of hoops from lobe to helix and a spiky mop of hair dyed a fiery red—but then you looked into her eyes and saw the old soul starring back. I wasn't sure how old Hilde was, younger than Isaac for sure, but not by much.

At first our relationship had been kind of strained and awkward. I admit it was mostly my fault. I just didn't know how to deal with the idea that she was bound to me like Isaac was. Isaac had been an accident, but Hilde had been on purpose at her request, and she looked at me like I was some sort of saviour, her gratitude and devotion making me extremely uncomfortable. I think Isaac must have finally taken her aside and spoken to her because eventually she toned down her hero-worship towards me, and we settled into a much easier friendship. She was a real asset to the bakery side of the coffee shop. Boy, could she bake. And if she went out of her way to make sure there were always plenty of my favourites, I wasn't going to complain.

A few hours later, Barbie was gone, leaving Hector to take the late shift. It was quiet in the shop, so when Isaac arrived, flushed and fed and already rolling up his sleeves preparing to bake up a storm, I decided to head back upstairs and call it an early night.

I was just climbing into bed when Gran popped in, taking me by surprise. Gran is a ghost. She passed away about seven years ago, but because my gift lets me see the spirits of the dead, I guess she didn't see much point in moving on when she could continue to boss me around from the grave. Lately, her visits had become more and more sporadic, and while we had come to an understanding of sorts regarding her attitude towards vampires, our relationship was strained.

"Harry!" She sputtered into view, her spectral body glimmering faintly. "Harry, can you feel it? There's been a shift."

"What? Gran?" I had no clue what she was talking about. "What's wrong?" I looked at her in concern. Usually she was able to manifest much more clearly. Something was definitely wrong. She could barely hold form. It was like watching an old TV trying to tune in, the snowy picture fading in and out, full of static.

"The balance has…can't stay…every…gone…"

"Gran!" I leapt from the bed, reaching out to her, thinking I could lend her some power to help stabilize her apparition, but she popped out of sight. "Gran?"

Shaken, I sat on the edge of the bed and pushed my senses outwards, trying to find her, but she was nowhere to be found and I was alone.

Chapter Seven

The next day I was still feeling unsettled by Gran's brief visit. The weird nightmare I'd had didn't help either. Neither did being shaken awake in the safety of Nash's arms.

"Harry! Wake up, minx. You're dreaming." His lips brushed across the back of my neck as he spoke quietly in my ear. "Wake up."

Thrashing in his arms, I suddenly sat up, banging Nash's face with my shoulder in the process, and gulping for air like a swimmer coming to the surface after a long dive.

With a groan, Nash fell back against the pillows, gingerly touching his lip where it had mashed against his teeth. "Shit, Harry. Are you okay?" He reached out to me, his hand on my elbow.

"Nash!" I turned and fell back into his arms, snuggling up to him. His skin felt warm against mine. As usual, I had gone to bed wearing an oversized T-shirt. And, as was always the case when Nash appeared in my bed, the shirt had mysteriously disappeared. It was Nash's super power or something. "I'm sorry. It was a bad dream. Are you okay?"

"I'll survive," he replied, rubbing at his now-swollen lip. "Was it the same dream as before?"

I let out a long breath, trying to calm my racing heart. "Yeah, or at least a variation on the same theme." I had been having recurring nightmares for the past few weeks. While I could only remember fragments, they were always the same: I was helpless, naked and chained up like I had been when DiCastro had kidnapped me and tried to sacrifice me to Osiris. Sometimes DiCastro was there, other times it was Holly, my former friend who had betrayed us. We were always surrounded by an amorphous mass of beings, wailing and crying, pressing in towards us, the circle surrounding us getting smaller and smaller until it felt like we would be smothered under a wave of bodies. Sometimes, Nash lay dying at my feet, his body riddled with stab wounds. Other times it was Tess. "But there was more this time. I had a strange visit from Gran last night and…I don't know. Something's wrong. I can't shake the feeling."

"You're safe now." Nash's arm tightened around me, pulling me closer. He tucked me under his chin, turning on his side to hold me against his chest so I could hear his heartbeat. "Go to sleep, Harry. Sounds like we've both had tough nights. We can talk about it in the morning." He sounded drowsy, so I stayed quiet, letting the steady rhythm of his breathing lull me back to sleep.

When I woke again later, I didn't have the heart to disturb Nash, who still looked exhausted—and that's saying something when you consider Nash has the recuperative powers of a werewolf. The HRN case was running him ragged.

Instead, I slithered out from under his arm and out the bottom of the bed. That I made my escape without waking him was another testament to just how worn out Nash must be. I showered and changed into workout clothes and then mixed myself a quick protein shake before heading out for a run to the gym.

I try to get to the gym to train every other day, but truthfully it can be hit or miss. Today I had an appointment though, so I had to go. A while back Max had asked me to spar with him so he could improve his bladework. In return he offered to help me set a better no-see-me spell on my own blade. The spell I currently use relies on a person's expectations. You don't expect to see a sword strapped to someone's back, so the spell just makes it easier for you to ignore what you are seeing. Now that it had become commonly known that I was often armed with my katana, too many people expected to see it, making the no-see-me spell practically useless. I wanted a stronger enchantment so that I could keep the element of surprise when needed, and so I had readily agreed to Max's deal. Today was our first session.

The gym is only a few blocks away from the firehall, but I usually run a roundabout route of three miles or so in order to warm up first before I get there. Today I tacked on an extra mile to make sure I didn't get there too early. I hadn't told Tess about my little arrangement with Max or that he would be joining me at the gym today because of the weird way she had been acting around him. If I got there too early, I'd have to spill the beans. It was better to just surprise her instead.

As I ran along the quiet, tree-covered streets of my neighbourhood, I mulled over Gran's cryptic message from the night before. What could she have meant? What had shifted? And who was gone? I couldn't remember hearing about any missing-persons cases. Of course due to its attention-grabbing, tabloid-headline nature, the HRN case was hogging all of the spotlight these days. Not that Gran would have been overly concerned about missing norms. I'd have to ask Max if he knew anything.

With my mind on Gran's visit, I hadn't paid much attention to my run, and I arrived at the gym with five minutes to spare. Normally, I can run a mile in about five minutes if I don't try too hard (three minutes if I put some effort into it). But since that's kind of fast for an average person, I try to keep my pace down to about an eight-minute mile. It's one of the reasons you don't see werewolves jogging, because they just don't jog. It's too slow. Tess could easily run a mile in about two minutes—a minute and a half if she really tried.

I was met by the familiar sounds of the gym as I walked through the door—the grunts and groans, the clanking weights, the incessant pounding beat of whatever playlist happened to be on the go. During the day, from six in the morning until ten at night, the gym catered to norms. They were the bread-and-butter of the gym. After hours, it was werewolves only, but since werewolves don't need to work out, it was more a time to hone skills than to exercise.

"Harry!"

I had a second to register Tess's scowling face and then my arm was wrenched as she dragged me across the lobby.

"What is *he* doing here?" Tess hissed at me, giving my arm another yank to pull me in beside her behind the half-wall of glass bricks that screened the entrance to the change rooms. From where we were standing we had a clear view of the front half of the gym. It was an open area filled with the usual equipment and machinery you'd find at a fitness centre. I glanced across the room to where she was pointing. The treadmills and elliptical machines were all in use. On the second treadmill on the right, running at a fair clip I might add, was Max. Oops! Busted.

I took a moment to watch Max in appreciation. He looked pretty fine in his skimpy running shorts. They came to about mid-thigh, and from this direction, did a great job of showing off his *ass*ets. He had taken off his shirt, and it was hanging over the front of the machine. His dark-tanned, well-muscled torso glistened with sweat.

"Damn! Max is hot!" I couldn't contain my surprise. The suits he always wore had obviously hidden how buff he really was.

Tess scowled at me again. "What the hell is he doing here?"

"He's here to meet me. We're going to spar together." I put on my most innocent face. "Didn't I mention that?"

"No, you did not. And don't give me that little-miss-innocent face either." She glared at me through narrowed eyes. "You purposely neglected to mention he was going to be here today."

I let out an exasperated sound. "Only because I knew this is how you'd react. What is it with you? Why don't you like Max?"

"I never said I didn't like him," Tess replied sharply. She crossed her arms and looked away, refusing to make eye contact.

"Omigod! That's it, isn't it? You *do* like him. You like him a lot." My eyes widened in surprise.

"Shut your piehole, Harry." Tess turned to glare at me.

"Naa-na-na-naa-naa, you like Ma-ax," I teased in a singsong voice.

"Shut it, Harry. I mean it."

She said it with such vehemence that I gaped at her in shock. "Tess? Are you okay?"

"I…I don't know." Tess turned away, but not before I caught the sad, confused expression on her face.

"What's wrong? Did Max do something to you? Did he hurt you?" I grasped her by the shoulders, spinning her around to face me again.

"No! No, it's not that. It's nothing like that." She shook her head.

I let out the breath I'd been holding in a long sigh of relief. I liked Max. It would be a shame if I had to kick him in the balls for hurting Tess. I paused, waiting for Tess to elaborate, but she gave me a tight-lipped stare. "Listen, Tess. I don't know what the hell is going on with you, but I don't want you to be upset. I'll ask Max to leave. We can set up another day to spar when you aren't here."

I brushed past her, intending to go speak with Max, but she grabbed my arm. "Harry, wait. It's okay. I'm just overreacting."

"Are you sure?"

Tess nodded.

"Well, okay. I wish you'd tell me what's going on."

"I can't right now, Harry. I need to work something out first."

"All right, I'm here when you're ready to talk."

Tess gave me a weak smile, and I squeezed her arm and then went to get Max. I had booked us the Kendo room at the back of the gym, so at least we would be out of sight.

***

Kendo, which means "the way of the sword", is the art of Japanese fencing, its techniques and traditions hailing from the time of the samurai. Over the years it has evolved into a fine art of strikes and blocks using a bamboo sword or *shinai* while wearing protective armour, *bōgu*. Max and I had pretty much thrown tradition out the window, however. Well, except for the bamboo-sword part.

After a few warm-up exercises, where I ran Max through a series of movements called *kata* that he could practice at home by himself, we basically just decided to have at it. The only concession we had made was that we both donned the *men*, a stylized helmet with a metal grill to protect the face and a series of hard leather and fabric flaps to protect the throat and neck. Other than that, it was no holds barred.

"Shit!" Max laughed and rubbed his wrist where I caught him with a quick blow past his guard. "That's going to leave a mark."

"Are you sure you don't want to suit up?" I asked, pulling off my *men*. While I would heal supernaturally fast from any bruises I might receive, I didn't think Max had the same recuperative powers. I had offered him the full gear in order to protect his arms and torso, but he had declined. "You're going to be black and blue by the time I'm done with you." I smiled at him.

"You're awfully cocky there, *Miss* Russo," Max replied.

I shrugged and replaced my helmet. "Your funeral," I said with a laugh, cutting it short to bring my *shinai* up in time (barely) to block Max's advance. We sparred back and forth across the floor, Max's shouts echoing through the room. Max was a traditionalist when it came to his Kendo, employing a *kiai* or shout to express the fighting spirit when striking. I had abandoned that practice early on in my training, preferring to think of myself as being quiet as a ninja.

I lost track of the time as Max and I battled around the dojo. He was rusty, but not as bad as he had led me to believe, even getting in a couple of good shots that hopefully would fade before Nash saw me naked tonight, or I'd have some 'splaining to do.

"What the hell do you think you're doing?"

I stopped short, quicker than Max, who scored a hit across my unprotected wrist. "Ow! Damn." It stung like a...well you know the expression.

"Sorry, Harry!" Max pulled off his *men* and gave me a contrite look. We both turned to stare at the source of our interruption.

Tess stood in the doorway of the room, hands on her hips, her entire five-foot-nothing frame bristling with anger. "Are you trying to damage yourselves? Where is your gear? Why aren't you wearing the *bōgu*?" She scowled at me. "I thought you were just going to run through the *kata*?"

"We did. Now we're sparring." I smiled conspiratorially at Max. "It's more fun than just running through some exercises.

Tess scowled at me again. "Don't you have some place you need to be?" She waved her hand at the clock. It was ten minutes to one. I was supposed to be going to the bingo lady's funeral with Nash at two. "And you." She pointed at Max. "If you want to improve your skills, there are no shortcuts. You start with mastering the *kata*, or you can go somewhere else."

Max gave Tess a cheeky look, his eyebrows rising in question. “Are you offering to teach me?”

“I….” Tess swallowed, momentarily uncomfortable, but then cleared her throat and straightened her spine. “Damn straight. But don’t expect it to be all fun and games.” She paused as if waiting to see if he would protest. When he didn’t, she nodded. “Call me tomorrow, and we’ll get started.”

“This doesn’t get you off the hook for your side of the bargain,” I said to Max as Tess stormed out of the room.

“The thought never crossed my mind,” Max replied absently. His eyes fixed on Tess’s retreating form. Now that was interesting.

Chapter Eight

It felt weird being at a funeral and not having to worry about the flowers. The bingo lady's service was being held at a church located on the far side of town, so I had only been there a couple of times in the past for work. It was a nondenominational deal, set up in a nontraditional manner. The building was made up of several overlapping, circular rooms with a large worship area at the centre. The sanctuary sat in the middle of the space, surrounded by seating for the congregation on all sides. Because Nash had been at work, we had arrived separately, but we were sitting together off to one side of the main aisle. I had made it home in plenty of time to shower, get ready and drive across town. I had even dug through my closet to find a suitable LBD that Nash had yet to have seen. It was a soft wool pencil dress with a sheer silk chiffon panel at the shoulders and a black pearl ribbon across the chest where chiffon met wool. It was obviously a good choice because I had noticed several women taking note and pointing me out to their friends when I arrived, not that I cared about that sort of thing. As usual, Nash was turning heads himself in a charcoal-grey suit.

"Yuck," I whispered to Nash, making a face. "That is the ugliest funeral spray I have ever seen. I can't believe they used orange carnations and yellow roses together like that. And what is it shaped like? It looks like a mutant porcupine." I shuddered at how hideous it was.

Nash frowned at me. "You're here to check for ghosts, not critique the competition."

"I'm not critiquing the competition, I'm just saying it's a shame that someone's hard-earned money went to pay for that awful thing."

"Focus, Harry. Do you see a ghost?" He reached for my hand. We had discovered that our mate bond enabled me to share my gift with him, allowing him to see and hear ghosts provided he was touching me. As his hand brushed over a particularly nasty welt leftover from the morning's workout with Max, I flinched and he frowned. "What's this?"

"It's nothing. Max and I—"

"Max?" Nash interrupted, his voice low and rough. "What were you doing with him?"

"I told you. I promised to spar with him in return for some technical help on a spell."

"I don't like it," he growled again in reply.

"Why? You're not going to act all jealous, are you?" I huffed out an exasperated breath.

"No. I'm not jealous." Nash leaned close to brush his lips across my nape and his mark. A shiver rippled down my spine, and I gasped, heat instantly rushing to my core. Nash took a deep breath and smiled a toothy smile. "You're mine."

The Neanderthal-like statement should not have turned me on, but it did and Nash, the bastard, knew it. He grinned at me again, and I rolled my eyes.

"So what's your problem with Max then? He's a nice guy and he's been doing a great job as the Coven's new leader."

Nash shrugged. "I've got nothing against the guy. It's just...there's something about him. He rubs me the wrong way."

"It's weird. Tess was acting all strange about him too."

"You should trust our instincts and be cautious around him."

"Actually, I think Tess has a crush on him," I said with a snort.

Nash grunted noncommittally and, grabbing my hand again, scanned the church.

The conversation was obviously closed, so I huffed out a breath and gazed around, searching the room for any sign of a ghost. I looked around the nave and then towards the sanctuary in the middle where the casket had been placed.

"It's an open casket?" I blurted out, drawing a few stares from the other funeral-goers. I lowered my voice and turned to Nash. "I thought she shot herself. Why would they be having an open casket?"

"She shot herself in the chest. Not a mark on her face." He slid out of his seat to stand beside me. "I'm going to go pay my respects. Are you coming?"

"Ugh. No, thanks." I hate open-casket funerals. I just don't understand why anyone would want to stare at a dead person if they didn't have to.

Nash sauntered up the aisle, turning heads along the way. Not even the blue-haired set was immune to his steamy good looks. Several of them actually staggered to their feet and toddled on after Nash, joining him in the queue in front of the coffin. I watched for a few minutes as two little old biddies jostled for position to see who got to stand next to him, their walkers crashing into one another. Nash, oblivious to the commotion his presence was causing, nodded and smiled at the fawning women.

"Hey! It's the flower lady!"

I looked over in surprise to see Tosh, the spirit of a young, teenage girl I could only describe as a skater chick. She could have been an extra from an Avril Lavigne music video, wearing baggy jeans that ended six inches above her converse shoes, and a black T-shirt that read *Shred It* worn over another white, long-sleeved shirt. Her hair was straight and black with a neon-pink streak, and she wore a random collection of studded, black leather bracelets on each wrist. Both her nose and her left eyebrow were pierced.

Tosh smirked at me and said, "Nice dress."

I glanced around to see if anyone was watching before answering quietly, "Uh, thanks?" There was a tone in her voice that made me think I wasn't getting a compliment.

Tosh's face broke out into a wide smile. "You definitely 'wore it better'." She held her hands up, finger quoting in the air.

"What?" I gaped at her.

"Dude, you're wearing the same dress as the corpse."

Oh. My. God! No wonder I was getting so many funny looks. The bingo lady and I were twinsies! I scanned the church. Nash was headed back down the aisle towards me. Reading something on my face, he frowned and quickened his pace.

"What are you doing here?" I whispered at Tosh, giving Nash a hand sign to wait. "Don't you usually hang out near St. Anthony's?"

"Yeah, it's too crowded there now." She shrugged. "They all think they need Father Mike's juju to keep them safe, but hallowed ground is hallowed ground, I'm thinking."

"Keep them safe? Keep who safe? From whom?"

The congregation suddenly rose to its feet, and I had to follow suit. Nash slipped in to stand beside me, a question in his eyes, but the service was starting so we couldn't talk. I searched for Tosh, but she was nowhere to be seen.

During the service, I stewed over what Tosh had said. Was she talking about other ghosts? If so, why were they afraid and in need of protection? When I added Tosh's information to Gran's cryptic message, the mystery only deepened.

After the service ended, I jumped to my feet, eager to leave. I needed to get some answers from Gran. Not to mention the fact that I was pretty sure it was some sort of fashion faux pas to be wearing the same thing as the dead body at a funeral, and I didn't need to give anyone else the opportunity to notice.

"I'm heading off," I said to Nash.

"Aren't you sticking around for tea and cookies?" Nash asked with a grin. The last time we attended a funeral together I had insisted we were owed cookies for sitting through the long, boring service.

"Are you kidding? I can't be seen at coffee time."

"Why the hell not?"

Stunned by his response, I gestured with my hand at what I was wearing. "Because of my dress, of course."

"What's wrong with your dress?" Nash appeared thoroughly perplexed and a wee bit impatient.

"Omigod! I can't believe you didn't notice that I'm wearing the same dress as the bingo lady."

"The bingo lady?"

"The dead woman," I muttered, lowering my voice. "Mrs. Whatever-the-hell-her-name-is."

"You are?"

I levelled an incredulous look at Nash and then turned with a growl. I strode up the aisle, shaking my head. Men! They can be so clueless. Why do women even bother? I might as well wear a burlap sack.

"Harry! Harry." Nash hurried after me, catching up in the vestibule where I had hung my coat. "Wait up. Is it really that bad?" He valiantly tried to keep the smirk off his face, but failed. He grabbed my coat from my hands and held it out to help me into it.

I rolled my eyes and huffed out a breath before turning to shove my arms in the sleeves. "Of course not. I could care less about what the bingo lady is wearing. But a girl does like to know that her efforts don't go unnoticed."

Nash, standing at my back, settled the coat on my shoulders and wrapped his arms around me. "Trust me, Harry. I noticed," he replied quietly, his breath tickling the back of my neck. "I noticed how this long zipper starts right here..." he paused and placed a kiss right above the zipper, sending a shiver down my spine, "...and how it runs down to the small of your back. I spent the whole service thinking about slowly pulling that zipper down and kissing your bare skin, until your dress slips from your shoulders and falls to the floor."

Um...yowza! Good answer.

I turned in his arms, wrapping mine around his neck and pulling him in for a kiss. "Mmmm, I almost forgive you," I replied with a grin.

Chapter Nine

"This doesn't mean I forgive you." I put my spoon down on my now-empty plate. "Even if you did just bribe me with chocolate soufflé."

I was at Cirque, the swankiest restaurant in town, with Salvador and Tomas. As was the case the last time I ate there, the food was divine, prepared specifically for us by the chef. Then, we had the restaurant to ourselves—Salvador had arranged a private meal on an evening when the restaurant was usually closed. This time, however, the place was packed. Salvador wasn't just the kingpin of the supernatural underworld, he was a mover and shaker in the norm world as well, so we had been given the best table in the house. The wait staff practically fell over themselves to serve us, and the entire restaurant eagerly watched our every move while pretending total indifference to our presence.

Salvador sat back, elbows resting on the arms of his chair, his hands wrapped around the bowl of a large wine glass—although I doubted it was only red wine in the glass.

"Why, whatever do you mean, my dear Harry?"

I gave my hand a little wave to indicate the restaurant. "This! This whole, forgive the pun, circus." I narrowed my eyes at him. "What are you up to? I don't appreciate being paraded out on display." And paraded was an accurate term for it.

We had arrived at Cirque in Salvador's stretch limo, only to be met by a barrage of paparazzi—okay, so barrage might be a bit of an exaggeration. This is Riverton, after all. But there were at least two of them. Somebody had obviously tipped them off that we were coming. I should have known Salvador had some sort of spectacle planned when a familiar box with the blood-red ribbon arrived at my door. Inside was a gorgeous silk chiffon dress in a shade of red that almost matched the bow on the box. The dress was scandalously short, but with filmy cape sleeves that floated down to skim the ground at my feet. Speaking of feet, never one to skimp, Salvador had also sent a to-die-for pair of Valentino's So Noir 100 pointed pumps in ultra-soft, black leather with gunmetal stud accents.

"Can a man not enjoy a quiet dinner with his protégé and his beloved, long-lost daughter?"

I stared at Salvador for a moment and then shook my head. "I really have no idea how to respond to that." I paused, trying to regroup, and then I remembered the other reason I was pissed at Salvador. "And then there's Mr. DeGrasse. The lawyer?" I arched an eyebrow at him. "You pimped me out to him."

Tomas, sitting across the table from me, smirked, but Salvador merely shrugged, unconcerned at my accusation.

"I merely acted the part of emissary, the go-between if you will." He took a long sip from his glass. "Am I to assume that you won't be assisting *Señor* DeGrasse with his request?"

"I don't know. I'm thinking about it."

"Don't think too long, Harry. Jobs lie in the balance."

"Sure, no pressure."

"But of course, of course," Salvador replied, choosing to ignore my sarcastic tone. "Whether you accept *Señor* DeGrasse's proposal or not is totally up to you. It does not fall under the purview of our agreement."

The agreement he was referring to was our deal for the title to the firehall. Salvador had given it to me in exchange for having dinner with him, but then he had managed to renege, forcing me to renegotiate the deal so it ended up being nine months of weekly dinners instead of just one. Damn those vampire loopholes.

The deal also included a proviso that I would occasionally use my particular talents to assist Salvador when requested. I had assumed DeGrasse was one of those times. I guess I had assumed wrong.

"There is a matter, however, that does require your cooperation and possibly your particular talents," Salvador continued.

Ah, here we go. The other shoe just dropped.

"I'm all ears." I leaned back in my chair and signalled to the waiter with my empty glass. I had a feeling I was going to need another drink.

The waiter came, quickly replacing my glass with one that held a generous inch of tequila. Salvador waved him off impatiently.

"You have heard of this new club, Wishes?" Salvador paused, continuing at my nod. "You will visit this establishment, observe, and report back to me."

"That's it?"

"I think you will find that is enough. I feel this establishment is much more than it seems. Take your wolf if you would like, and Maxwell Hart has agreed to accompany you."

Surprised, I looked at Tomas. The last time I had to go somewhere sketchy, he had been sent to babysit me.

Seeing my glance at Tomas, Salvador shook his head. "Alas, young Tomas will not be able to assist in this endeavour. Neither, might I add, will our friend Isaac."

"Why not?"

Tomas scowled. "The place is crawling with norms and mutts," he said, using the derogatory vampire term for werewolves, "but no vampire has been able to enter. There's dirty magic involved, a barrier of some sort."

"Magic!" No wonder Max was going to join me on my little field trip. If there was a rogue involved, it was the

Coven's responsibility to handle it. They had a lot of face to save after the whole DiCastro incident. "Max is better suited to the job. I don't see what you need me for."

"There is something in the air, my dear Harry. A shift."

I started forward in my seat at Salvador's words. It couldn't be coincidence that I had heard that word again. "I'll do it," I replied with a sigh.

I guess Tess was going to get her wish.

Chapter Ten

"Whoa, Harry! Maybe you had better slow down there." Barbie eyed the mammoth double shot mocha latte I had in front of me. It was my second this morning. Added to the four, yes four, *pain au chocolat* I had scarfed down, I had a real caffeine and sugar buzz going.

"Yeah, I guess you're right. I'll cut myself off...after this one." With my hyper metabolism, the buzz wouldn't last long, and neither would the calories, but too much caffeine made for a cranky Harry, and I was already in a bad (okay, admittedly sexually frustrated) mood. Nash had been a no-show last night, much to my disappointment. Another HRN. Things were getting seriously out of hand, and I couldn't shake the feeling that all the weird stuff lately was somehow connected.

It had been a busy morning rush in the shop, busier than usual. I wasn't even on the schedule to work today, but I had woken up early, unable to go back to sleep (more bad dreams) so I had decided to pop in and help out. To top it off, everyone seemed to be acting weird. At least the customers were, I mean. The whole shift I felt like I was being watched, and in fact I had caught several people staring at me. Then, when I was clearing tables, I got close to one of the four tops by the window where three women were engrossed in a hushed conversation. When they noticed me, they suddenly fell silent, going out of their way to avoid making eye contact with me. It was enough to give a girl a complex.

I quickly realized that part of the reason for the rush was because customers who normally grabbed their coffee to go had decided to stay and sit, so the tables and casual seating area were packed all morning. The other reason, from what I could tell, was that *all* our regular customers, even our once-or-twice-a-weekers and Sundays-only customers, had decided to come for coffee today. It was a good thing I had decided to drop by because it was more than Tiffy and Barbie could handle on their own. I ended up spending most of the morning bussing tables and restocking supplies.

The rush was finally done, although the shop was still over half full with sip-n-sits (what Barbie liked to call the customers who paid for one cup of coffee and then dawdled at a table for hours). Hector was due in shortly, so I figured it was safe to sit down with my latte and relax for a few minutes. Besides, I had a call to make.

I punched in the number DeGrasse had given me and was surprised when the line went to him directly, bypassing any sort of switchboard or receptionist.

"Mr. DeGrasse? This is Harry Russo."

"Yes, Miss Russo. I'm glad to hear from you. Have you come to a decision?"

"Yes, I have. And yes, I will attempt to raise your zombie, but there will have to be some hard-and-fast rules about how things will be handled…for safety reasons."

"Yes, of course. I understand."

"I'll put together a list and send it to you later today. You can review it and then decide if you want to move ahead."

"That won't be necessary. I'm sure whatever safety precautions you wish to take will be acceptable. I'll have my client and her brother sign the nondisclosure contract and courier it over to you by end of day."

"The nondisclosure contract?"

"Yes, Mr. Arroyo insisted that there be one in place if you were to agree to help us. It simply states that whatever occurs, you will not be held legally responsible, and that my client, her brother, as well as his attorney, will not discuss you or your particular talents with anyone. A failure by any of the parties in this regard would result in compensation being paid to you in the amount of ten million dollars."

"Ten million dollars!" My voice had risen, and I looked around the shop to see if anyone had noticed. Barbie raised a questioning brow, but I pointed to the phone at my ear and then lowered my voice and continued, "Ten million dollars if they blab to anyone?"

"Well, yes. If it were to get out to, say, the media, or something like that. I assume this is acceptable?"

"What? Oh, yes. More than acceptable."

"Wonderful. I'll get the papers to you as soon as possible. Do you have a date and time in mind?"

"I need a few days to prepare. I'd like to do it as close to the new moon as possible. The new moon is Tuesday, so sometime early next week. I'll have to get back to you. I want to make sure I have everything I need first. Where was Mr. Koenig buried? Depending on which cemetary, getting in there at night without getting arrested for trespassing might be an issue."

"Not to worry. I'll take care of access to the gravesite on my end. Mr. Koenig was interred at Hillside."

I nodded to myself. I shouldn't have been surprised. If there was such a thing as a high-class cemetery, Hillside was it. The oldest cemetery in Riverton, it was the resting place of all of Riverton's rich and influential corpses. Being raised a witch, I didn't buy into the whole burying-your-dead ritual. Witches burned their dead—you can't raise a zombie from a pile of ash.

"Great," I replied. "That will make things easier."

The door dinged as I was signing off with DeGrasse, and Mrs. Flannigan, a neighbourhood local, came in for her daily sweet treat.

"Good morning, Mrs. F," I called out to her, pasting on my customer service smile.

She paused, a frown on her face, and then with a sniff in my direction, turned on her heel, and marched over to Barbie to place her order. That was weird. Mrs. Flannigan may have been an odd bird at the best of times, but today she was acting positively loopy.

Concerned, I started to rise from my seat. "Is everything okay, Mrs. F?"

"I'm fine, thank-you very much," she replied, her words clipped. She waved me off, muttering something about "not abiding a cheater" and "gold-diggers", grabbed her to-go cup of coffee and cinnamon roll, and stomped out the door. Tiffy, who was standing right beside me, gave me a baffled look. She was still learning about human behaviour, and this apparently required an explanation.

"Don't ask me," I said, holding up my hands in defeat. "I think everyone has gone a little nuts this morning." I didn't get a chance to say more because Tess burst in the door waving a newspaper at me.

"Harry! You're famous!"

"What?" I snatched the paper from her hands.

"You made Page Six!"

Page Six was the society gossip page. It was usually reserved for celebrity gossip because there wasn't much to report in Riverton in terms of society news. I flipped through the paper, laying it out flat on the counter.

"Holy crap!" I gaped at the page in front of me. They had gone for a full-colour spread, and I and my attention-grabbing red dress were front and centre. The first picture was rather tame and only showed Salvador giving me a hand out of the limo in front of Cirque (although let's say it was a good thing I was wearing panties). With the second though, they had gone for a more provocative pose, choosing to use a picture of the moment when Tomas stepped out of the limo and put his arm around me, hand on my ass. That they didn't use the photo of the moment immediately after when I removed his hand by grabbing his thumb and threatening to break it if he tried that again, just shows how biased the news can be.

The headline screamed "Who's that Girl?" followed by a second line in smaller print that read "And Whose Girl is She?" The article went on to discuss my dress ("attention-grabbing and daringly short"), my hair ("a pixie cut with attitude"), my shoes ("killer pumps that would be equally at home at the Ritz or at the local MC clubhouse") and lastly posed the question of just who I was there with. Was I the latest arm candy of Salvador Arroyo, the devilishly handsome billionaire (a billionaire? That was news to me, but I guess it shouldn't have been a surprise. You can amass quite a fortune when you live forever), or was I the latest conquest of the well-known lady's man, Tomas Guerra? (Tomas had a last name? Huh...that was news to me as well.)

The only bright spot of the whole thing was the inch and a half of space the article spent debating whether Tomas's mysterious disappearance the month before was due to a drug problem (rehab) or if he had some "work done" which would explain his remarkable transformation from handsome to drop-dead gorgeous (their words, not mine).

"Oh man! I can't believe they did this." I continued to scan the article, but Tess grabbed it out from under my gaze.

"Listen to this! It's a hoot." She dodged my attempt to snag the paper back and started to read directly from the article.

"The mystery woman, obviously comfortable in her own skin—and why wouldn't she be?—ate with a healthy appetite, and sources say she finished off the evening with Cirque's signature chocolate soufflé—a dish that has to be special ordered—and a shot of tequila."

I growled and reached for the paper again. "Will you keep your voice down?" I grumbled at her. We were drawing attention.

"Wait," Tess continued, lowering her voice, "it gets even better."

"If this mystery woman has her sights set on either of Riverton's most sought-after bachelors, one might suggest a change in demeanor is in order. One witness (name withheld on request) attested to hearing the young lady threaten to "snap his thumb off and shove it where the sun don't shine" if Guerra didn't remove his hand from her bottom. While as the picture below attests, if she has a bigger fish in mind, she may want to lose the attitude."

"Omigod, Harry. The picture is priceless."

"Let me see!" I succeeded in stealing the page back.

The last part was written directly above a small picture of Salvador bidding me good night with his customary kiss to the top of my hand. I guess my impatient eye roll was considered bad attitude.

"Crap. I can't believe this is happening." I leaned over the counter, head in hands, slowly giving it a shake. Well, I guess I knew what Mrs. Flannigan was all about earlier. She had a soft-spot for Nash. Oh no, Nash! I straightened, grabbing my cell phone from behind the counter. "I'd better call Nash and warn him," I said, just as the bell above the door rang.

"Yeah," replied Tess, laughter in her voice, "I don't think that's going to be necessary."

Nash stood in the doorway and scanned the room with narrowed eyes. His gaze met mine, and I could hear him growl from across the room. The next thing I knew he was behind the counter, pressing me up against the wall, his hands shoved roughly through my hair, holding my head. "Mine," he rasped, pulling my face to his. His lips captured mine in a demanding kiss as he slid one hand down to grip my ass, melding our bodies together.

When we finally came up for air, minutes later, we had the attention of the entire shop. "Nash, you Neanderthal, quit making a scene in front of the customers."

I clutched his hand and dragged him down the hall and into the kitchen. "I guess this means you saw this morning's paper?"

"Yes," he replied with a scowl. "In fact, my locker at the precinct was papered with it, and several of the guys wondered if I would get your autograph for them."

Oh. Well. I could see why he might be a little worked up. Being a werewolf, he kind of took the whole alpha male thing to the extreme. A trait I found equally sexy and annoying.

"It's not like any of this is my fault." I glared at him. "Salvador obviously set the whole thing up." I crossed my arms in front of me. "Although why, I have no clue."

"I don't like it," Nash groused.

"So what else is new?" I snorted and grabbed the front of his shirt, pulling him towards me. "You never came home last night to help me out of my dress." I tugged him closer so we were face-to-face. "I *really* wanted you to help me out of my dress." I ran my free hand down his torso towards the bulge in his pants. As my fingertips touched the waistband of his jeans, he groaned and I found myself once again pinned against the wall, my hands captured in his. He slid my arms above my head and leaned into me, dipping his face to my neck and taking a deep breath.

"Damn work," he said, speaking into the curve of my neck, his lips tickling my sensitive skin. He nipped at my collarbone, and I sucked in a surprised breath. When his tongue flicked over the same spot, I let out a heated sigh, squirming in his grasp. Our bodies rubbed together, and I could feel him hard against me. "I'll be home for sure tonight." He let my hands drop, sliding his to my hips as he boosted me up. My legs automatically wrapped around him, my arms falling to his neck. His mouth found mine, and he ground his body against me, pushing me up against the wall.

I was a bit lust-dazed, so it took a minute for what he had said to register. When it finally did, I reluctantly pulled my mouth from his. "I have to go out tonight," I said breathlessly.

"What? Where?" He nipped at my neck again, working his way down to my collarbone, moving his hand to cup my breast. "I'm sure I can persuade you to change your plans."

With a grunt of effort, I pushed Nash away, my feet falling to the floor. "I wish, but they're not *my* plans."

Nash paused for a second then scowled. "Damn Salvador. What does he want now?"

***

"Yippee!" Tess squealed and clapped her hands. "Don't worry, Harry. It's going to be fun."

I had just told her about my assignment from Salvador. I shook my head slowly. "I don't know. Weren't you listening? *Salvador* thinks there is something hinky going on there, and vampires can't even get in the door. It doesn't bode well for *fun*."

"Don't be such a downer. I've heard it's totally lit."

"What's totally lit?" Barbie paused on her way past to the kitchen.

"We're going to Wishes, the new club."

"No way! Can I come?"

"Sure!" Tess smiled at her. "The more the merrier."

"Wait, wait." I held out a hand. "I don't think that's such a good idea."

Barbie's smile disappeared. "Oh, okay." She shook her head. "Yeah, you're right. It would be weird with you being my boss and all."

"What? No! That's not what I meant. Of course you can come if you want. Like Tess said, the more the merrier. I just think you should know what you're getting yourself into first. The last thing I need is your entire posse of brothers coming down on me for taking you into danger." Barbie had four older brothers. The oldest, Martin, was a cop in the SRU—the Supernatural Response Unit—the force that Nash headed up. “Maybe you better sit down a minute and I’ll explain.”

Chapter Eleven

When all was said and done, we ended up with quite a group heading to Wishes. Tess and I were riding with Isaac, who insisted on coming even if it meant he would end up only playing chauffeur and waiting outside. After a tense moment when Max arrived (all the tension being on Tess's part and no one else's), it was decided he would follow in his own car, a snazzy Lexus. Tess had breathed a sigh of relief and climbed into the back of Isaac's vehicle, leaving shotgun for me without even a token fight. That left Barbie and her beefy werewolf boyfriend, Tank, who were meeting us there.

As we were leaving, a sapphire-blue Porsche roared into view, spraying gravel in the parking lot behind my building as it came to a stop.

"What the hell are you doing here?" I asked when Tomas climbed out.

"Russo," he replied, his eyes taking a trip down the length of my body. "As charming as ever." He smirked and leaned against his car, arms folded casually across his chest. He was dressed in a dark blue suit with a similarly coloured shirt. The shirt was open at the neck with no tie. He looked sexy as hell. "Where's your little pet?"

"Nash is working. He's joining us later."

Tomas made a face. "Not him, the other...the little *chica*." He waggled his eyebrows. "She's a feisty one, that one. I like them feisty."

There was a movement behind me, and then suddenly Max was in Tomas's face.

"Watch your mouth, buster." Max bristled, his hands in fists at his sides.

"Whoa, there. No need to bring the hammer down, Elder." Tomas grinned at his joke, playing on Max's official title as leader of the Coven.

"Miss Fuentes is a lady, and you will give her the respect she deserves." Max turned his back, dismissing Tomas, and looked at me. "I'll meet you there, Harry."

"Yeah, okay, Max. We'll be right behind you."

Max hopped in his car and drove off, tires squealing. Tomas grinned. "What got him so riled up?"

"Just leave it alone, fangboy." I put my hands on my hips.

Tomas gave me another lazy once-over. "You know, you clean up nice, Russo. You look equal parts ready to kick-ass and party girl."

I shrugged. I'd take that as a compliment. It was, in fact, what I had been going for. I was dressed in a killer, black leather mini dress with a large paisley print detail. The leather was soft and supple, giving me optimum flexibility. I had paired it with my favourite pair of thigh-high, black leather boots. I was wearing my katana strapped across my back, but with the new invisibility enchantment Max had put on the sheath, no one would know it was there until I wanted them to.

"We should get going," Isaac said, lifting an eyebrow at Tomas.

Tess popped her head out of the window. "What's the hold up? Are we going, or what?"

Tomas smirked again and then sauntered back to his car. He hopped in and gunned the engine before roaring off, his taillights winking at us in the distance.

"Definitely must be compensating for something," I muttered to myself as I climbed into the Escalade.

***

I have to admit to being nervous about going back to the warehouse. I didn't particularly have the best memories of my time spent there. I needn't have worried though; it looked nothing like it did before. The entire building had been painted canary yellow. The entrance, originally a single, nondescript steel door, had been widened, and two bright green doors hung there instead. A gaudy neon rainbow with *Wishes* written in flashing orange script stretched across the side of the building, arching over the entrance. There was a small crowd gathered up against one side of the doorway, held back by a purple, velvet rope. They stood just at the edge of the red carpet that lined the front of the doorway.

Isaac parked a ways up the street, and the three of us climbed out of the vehicle and simply stood staring at the monstrosity.

Tess made a disappointed little sound. "That's not at all what I was expecting."

"It's like it was designed by someone colourblind," I added.

"It looks like a clown vomited," Tess replied.

Isaac shrugged. "Appearances can be deceiving."

"Yeah," Tess said, the smile returning to her face. "Maybe it's like The Lodge." She was referring to the werewolf pack's local hangout. On the outside it looked like a tired, old, western-themed dive bar, but that was just a front for one of the hippest nightclubs in town.

We walked towards the entrance, joining up with Max and Tomas, who had each been waiting in their respective cars. We were standing on the sidewalk across the street from the building when Tank and Barbie appeared.

Barbie gave us a skeptical look.

"We're thinking it's better on the inside," Tess said in reply.

"Don't fall for temptation! Evil is among us!"

The voice rang out from the front of the building. A brief commotion erupted and a man dressed in dark clothing stood in front of the gathered crowd holding up a paper. "Step away! This path only leads to damnation." The man handed out leaflets to the people in line. He turned to face the street. There was a flash of white at his neck and I started in surprise.

"Father Mike?" He was the priest from St. Anthony's.

Father Mike looked up at his name and, spotting me, crossed over to join our little group.

"Harry! You shouldn't be here." He shoved a leaflet into my hand. It was an invitation to a special Mass at St. Anthony's. "This is a place of evil."

"Father Mike, since when have you started picketing nightclubs?"

"It's more than that, Harry. Can't you feel it?" He tucked the remaining leaflets into a satchel at his side and placed a hand on my arm. "It's infecting the whole city with its evil. I've felt the shift."

"The shift!" I grabbed his hand. "What do you mean?"

"Evil, Harry. Pure evil. Don't go in there. Nothing good happens in there."

"What are you talking about? Has something happened?" Max's voice seemed to startle Father Mike, as if he had been so focussed on me he hadn't noticed any of the others. His eyes widened as he took in Isaac and Tomas, but then he turned back to me.

"I've had parishioners go in and come out changed. They stop coming to Mass, stop living their lives. They neglect their families, their jobs. It's like some sort of drug." Father Mike turned back to me. "You must feel it, Harry. I know you are...different. That you have a gift."

"I..." I let out a long breath. I didn't see much point in denying it. "That's why I'm here...to check it out."

"You have a pure soul, Harry. You do God's work." Father Mike patted my arm.

"You know I don't follow your religion, Father Mike."

"We all find God in our own way," he replied, pulling something from his pocket. It was a small bottle of clear liquid. Before I could protest, he tipped a bit out on his thumb and then rubbed it on my forehead, making the shape of a cross. "Lord Father, bless this child. She is a warrior of the light. Shield her with your strength and keep her safe from harm." I blinked at him in surprise and he clasped me on the arms. "Be safe in there, Harry."

"Thanks, Father Mike. I will."

"Well, that was weird," Tess said as we watched Father Mike hurry back across the street to continue to preach to the waiting crowd.

"He's right though," Max said, "there is something here. I can feel it." He looked at me. "Can't you, Harry?"

I frowned at him and then turned my senses outwards. As soon as I did, I was hit by it—a wave of, well, of what I wasn't sure. It just felt wrong. "Yes, I can feel it, but I don't know what *it* is." I looked at the rest of the group. "Can anyone else feel anything?"

Tomas, who had been pacing impatiently stalked across the street then stopped less than a quarter of the way across. "I can," he said. "It starts right about here."

Isaac cocked his head as if trying to sense something and then strode towards Tomas. He came to an abrupt stop right beside him. "Yes, I can feel it too."

"What? I don't feel anything," Tess said with a frown. She stepped up to stand beside Isaac. With a shrug she crossed the street to stand on the sidewalk in front of the building. "Come on. We're wasting time. Let's check it out."

I approached Isaac and Tomas, walking across the street to join Tess. I looked back, but neither of them had moved.

"I'm afraid this appears to be as far as I am able to go," Isaac said, his face puzzled.

"Really? Why?"

"I don't know. I am just unable to move forward." He put his hand out, reaching towards me. His arm wasn't fully extended when it suddenly stopped, as if encountering a barrier.

"What do you feel?" asked Max, coming to stand beside Isaac. "Does it feel solid?"

"Yes, it feels as if there is a solid wall right in front of me. I am unable to pass it."

"Interesting." Max nodded absently. He walked across the street to where Tess and I were waiting and then turned and walked back to Isaac. "Most interesting."

Tess rolled her eyes. "Are we going to stand here all night?"

"You go ahead," Max replied. "I want to explore this barrier. I wonder if it goes around the entire perimeter of the building?" He looked at Tomas.

Tomas nodded. "It did when I checked it out the other night. Although it was closer to the building then. It's widened. Last time I was here I was able to make it across the street to the sidewalk."

"You mean it's growing?" I gaped at him in shock.

Tomas shrugged. "It appears so."

"Okay, then. Max, you stay out here and do your thing. Tomas, you go with Max." Tomas gave me a look as if to say he didn't like to be told what to do by me. "Someone has to watch Max's back while his senses are tuned elsewhere. If not you, then Isaac."

"I didn't say I wouldn't do it," Tomas replied.

"I will wait here," Isaac said, moving back to lean against Max's car.

I looked at Tank and Barbie, who still stood on the other side of the street. "What about you two? Are you coming?"

"I've got a bad feeling about this." Tank shook his head.

"Oh, come on. We have to go. What can go wrong if we all stick together?" Barbie grabbed his hand and tugged him across the street towards us.

"Alrighty, then. That's settled." I turned to Tess. "Ready?"

She patted her tiny purse with a grin. "Locked and loaded. Let's go." I rolled my eyes. She had insisted on tucking a small revolver—a Ruger LCR—into it. Since I currently had an invisible sword strapped to my back, I couldn't really complain.

I glanced over at the line to get in. It had only gotten longer in the time we spent discussing everything. "I guess we'll have to get in line," I said with a sigh.

"Tank doesn't wait in lines," Tank replied, striding up to the door, bypassing the crowd. They started to complain, but he turned and glared at them and they quickly fell silent. Have I mentioned that Tank works as a bouncer and is about six foot four and almost as wide? If you think of the most muscled-up bodybuilder you know and added about fifty pounds more of muscle to him, you'd get Tank.

The bouncer at the door didn't even blink at our approach. He merely nodded at Tank and waved us through. Either he recognized Tank as a fellow bouncer, or he decided it was safer just to let us in.

As we passed through the doors, we entered a darkened vestibule, and I tensed for a moment, feeling slightly claustrophobic. As soon as the outside doors closed, a man stepped out of the shadows to greet us. Dressed in a white tuxedo, complete with tails and a top hat, he was flanked on either side by two rather well-endowed, curvy women dressed in white corsets and not a heck of a lot else.

"Welcome! Welcome! I am your host, Mr. Zed." He bowed deeply, tipping his hat.

"If he says 'welcome to *Fahn*tasy Island', I'm bolting," Tess chirped with a smirk.

"Welcome to Wishes," Mr. Zed continued, "where dreams really do come true. We can fulfill your every desire…fame…fortune…love…*lust*." He gave us a cheeky wink. "Your wish is our command here at Wishes." He paused and waved the women forward. "If you would be so kind to check your coats and purchase your admission, Miss F and Miss J would be more than happy to assist you. I must see to our other guests." He turned as if to leave and then stopped, spinning around to add, "And please, don't forget to help yourself to the complimentary champagne."

After one last parting bow, he disappeared as quickly as he had appeared. I walked over to the coat-check girls and peeled off four twenties to pay the cover charge.

"I'm putting it on Salvador's bill," I said to Tank, waving him off when he motioned to pay. Tank grinned and put his money clip back in his pocket.

One of the alphabet girls (I wasn't paying attention to who was who, and come on, it's not like those were their *real* names) approached holding a tablet with the outline of a hand displayed on the screen.

"If you would just place your hand on the device and state your name, we'll get you all checked in." She smiled a completely vacuous smile and held out the tablet.

With a shrug, Tess stepped up and put her hand on the screen. "Therese," she said, giving her actual name. The scanner beeped, and a thin line of light passed over its surface, reminding me of a photocopier. When it beeped the second time, the screen turned green, and Tess removed her hand.

Barbie went next, and it was a near-exact repeat performance (except she said her name was Barbara). When it was Tank's turn, he looked less than enthused as he choked out the name *Thadeus* (OMG, I thought *my* name was bad!). His hand barely fit on the screen, and when the scanner completed its pass, the surface glowed yellow. The alphabet girls' smiles dimmed slightly, but they nodded and held the scanner up to me.

I placed my hand on the screen and felt a slight tingle. There was more to this scan than met the eye, I was sure. "Harry," I said, somewhat defiantly as the scanner beeped and began its pass. When it beeped a second time, the screen flashed red. Surprised, I glanced at the alphabet girls, but their faces were suspiciously blank.

The one holding the tablet pulled it away and gestured to a second set of double doors that swung open. "Enjoy your stay at Wishes."

Impatient to get going, Tess hustled through the doors, followed by Tank and Barbie. I brought up the rear, but as I crossed the threshold of the inner doorway I stumbled, suddenly overwhelmed by a feeling of vertigo. My stomach did a roll, and for a second I thought I was going to be sick.

"Harry!" Barbie turned and caught me by the arm, preventing me from falling on my knees. "Are you okay?"

I stood bent over, my hands resting on my thighs, while I tried to catch my breath and settle my protesting stomach. I could only remember feeling this way once before, right after I had been translocated against my will to this very warehouse. Was I having some sort of flashback? After a moment or two, I got things under control by giving my shields an extra boost. The pressure I had been feeling lessened, and I was able to take a deep breath. I straightened and looked around, awestruck.

"Whoa," I said, at a loss for words.

The space we were standing in was huge—much larger than I remembered. The club itself was hard to describe. The closest I can think of was if you took a casino, a roller-derby arena, a Vegas cabaret and a glow-in-the-dark bowling lane and mashed them together, you would get something that looked like the inside of Wishes. What lighting there was appeared to be either of the black-light variety or neon. Anything and everything that was white was glowing in the dark. And there was a lot of white. Most of the people in white appeared to be serving staff wheeling around on roller skates, trays of drinks and food held high above their heads. Like the alphabet girls, they were dressed mostly in leather variations of fetish wear—corsets and miniskirts, leather pants and vests over bare chests. Directly in front of us at the centre of the building was a huge fountain. It was out of place with the rest of the decor and more like something you would see in Rome, the water flowing from ornately carved figures to splash into the marble basin below. There was a large central figure in the fountain that loomed over the others, but we were too far away to see it clearly.

"What the hell happened, Harry?" Tess was suddenly by my side, full of concern.

"I don't know. I felt...something. Did you feel anything when you walked through the door?" I turned to Barbie and Tank. They were shaking their heads.

"I don't feel any different." Tess gave me an assessing look. "Are you sure you're okay?"

I put a hand to my head. My temples were throbbing with the music. "Ugh. Why do they always have to play Metallica?"

Tess cocked her head, listening for a moment then she wrinkled her nose at me. "That's AC/DC's 'Thunderstruck'. Not Metallica. Geez, Harry, you're always getting it mixed up. Do you want to leave?"

"No, I'll be okay. Let's get this over with." I paused to look around again, not quite believing what I was seeing. "Is it just me, or does this place seem like it's one big, drunken orgy?"

"It's not just you." Barbie's eyes widened at the sight of a man and woman grinding up against one another. Her voice sounded uncertain, and Tank squeezed her hand.

People, mostly norms, were everywhere, and they all looked to be having a *very* good time. Their behaviour was odd though. Everything they did seemed manic and frenzied, like they were trying extra hard to have a good time. I watched as a scantily clad woman dashed by, tearing open her blouse as she ran, giggling hysterically. She was being chased by two obviously drunken, half-naked men. She stopped and pulled off her top, swinging it above her head while shaking her hips seductively. The men caught up to her, and she squealed, grabbing the nearest one and planting a big, sloppy-looking kiss on him. The other man groped her breasts, and her hand slid down to grab his crotch. I averted my eyes, but it wasn't the only such scene. Everywhere you looked people were pawing each other and making out.

As we moved towards the dance floor, the crowd got bigger and even wilder. "We should try and stick together," I said, half yelling to be heard over the music. "But if we get separated, let's meet up at the fountain." After catching everyone's nod, I pushed ahead through the crowd.

We came to our first break from the crush of bodies when we arrived at a lounge-type area off to the side of the dance floor. It featured a bar and low, cushioned seating. Men and women were draped over the seats, drinking and laughing boisterously. The neon and black lights made everything glow, even the drinks. At one table, a very large man sat surrounded by an array of food. He was eating ravenously, stuffing one thing after another into his mouth using both hands. He seemed oblivious to anything else around him. I frowned and squinted at him. Something was off about him, like he was slightly out of focus. I shook my head and blinked, but it didn't help.

"Complimentary champagne?" A woman wearing roller skates and two little scraps of white leather appeared, holding out a tray. She smiled and fluttered her eyelashes at Tank.

"No," I said, reaching out to stop Tank's arm. "I don't think we should drink anything here. Or eat anything for that matter. I have a bad feeling about this place."

Tank shrugged and lowered his arm.

The server's eyes narrowed briefly, and I thought I saw anger in their depths, but then she smiled and replied, "Suit yourself. Your wish is our command at Wishes."

Tess grabbed my arm, pulling me down to shout in my ear. "Let's go check out the casino." She pointed to the other side of the building where there were several banks of slot machines and what appeared to be blackjack tables and a roulette wheel.

The music was blaring out some sort of electro-dance-party mashup and I recognized Fifth Harmony and Rhianna in the mix. We left the bar and the dance floor behind and started across the club. Twice more we were approached with free drinks. Each time we declined we were given the same "Your wish is our command at Wishes" reply, and each time I sensed that our response was not what they wanted to hear.

We were about halfway across the large space when a shout erupted from the surrounding mass of revellers, and I found myself being jostled and pushed back towards the dance floor. Five burly men dressed in worn football jerseys waded through the crowd. They held some sort of cup like trophy over their heads, and they were shouting, "Chug, chug, chug!" They stopped, and a white-clad server appeared as if from nowhere holding two bottles of champagne above her head. The men cheered as she began pouring champagne from both bottles into the cup. When the bottles were empty, one of the men grabbed the trophy and hoisted it to his mouth to take a drink, champagne spilling out the sides to run down his face. His buddies all laughed and pumped their fists, their cries of "Chug, chug, chug!" being picked up by the surrounding crowd.

I turned to say something to Tess and then stopped in surprise.

"Shit!" I looked around frantically. She wasn't there and neither was Barbie or Tank. We had somehow been separated during the distraction.

I scanned the crowd. Surely I should be able to spot Tank. He was kind of hard to miss. The crowd seemed to close in around me as I struggled to see over their heads. I couldn't find Tank, Tess or Barbie anywhere.

I was jostled back and forth by the crowd, making it hard to get a sense of direction. It felt like I had been all turned around. A hand brushed against my back, and I spun around, expecting to see Tess, but it was just a drunken norm.

"Hey, sexy! You look *hawt*!" His breath was warm and boozy and right in my face. "Wanna dance?" He reached out a hand towards my breast. With a scowl, I grabbed his thumb, pulling it back to his wrist. He shrieked in pain and dropped to the floor on one knee.

"Don't fucking touch me," I shouted, giving him a push so he rocked back, falling on his ass. I strode away, my heart pounding with adrenaline. I don't know why I'd over-reacted. I guess the place was getting to me.

I elbowed my way through the crowd, keeping my back to the dance floor. It felt like I was stuck in quicksand, but instead of sand, it was bodies. I'd push past one, only to have another fall in place in front of me. Where were they all coming from? I tried to focus on the people, thinking I must be going in circles and I'd start to recognize them, but their faces blurred together.

I caught a movement out of the corner of my eye, but when I turned to look, nothing was there. This happened several more times until I started to feel paranoid, like something was following me. Eventually the throng of people thinned, and I was able to breathe a sigh of relief. Finally free from the crowd, I pulled out my cellphone, thinking I would text Tess, but it was dead, which was weird because I had just charged it that afternoon.

I glanced around and got my bearings. The casino area was ahead and to my right. I decided to check there quickly since that was our original destination. If I couldn't find Tess and the others there, I would head to the fountain.

***

The casino was a bust. While not as crowded as the dance floor, I wasn't surprised to find every slot machine busy, their occupants happily feeding in coins and pushing buttons. Every few minutes lights would flash and bells would ring, and a cheer would go up from somewhere in the crowd. It seemed like everyone was winning at Wishes.

I was turning away from the machines when I spotted a familiar face, stopping to stare at her in surprise. It was the woman who had almost died in the ICU the other day. I couldn't believe that she was already out of the hospital and ready to party. And party she was. She held a hamburger in one hand and alternated between whooping and cheering every time she pulled the arm down on the slot machine, and stuffing her face.

"Come on, baby! Mama needs a new pair of shoes!" She took a long swig of beer straight from the bottle and then grabbed a handful of French fries and jammed them in her mouth.

The machine flashed and the bell went off.

"WOOOOOO! WOOOO HOOOO!" She jumped from her seat, arms in the air. "Yes! That's what I'm talking about!" Arms still raised in victory, she threw her head back, her face suddenly slack. A shudder passed over her body, and she moaned, her face contorting into what looked like…well, it looked like she just had an orgasm was what it looked like.

I stared in disbelief. What the hell? As I watched, her body blurred, and a dark shape appeared superimposed over top of hers. It only lasted a second, and when I blinked, it was gone. The woman slumped back in her seat, momentarily disoriented, and then started to plug the machine with coins again.

"Harry!"

Barbie, pulling Tank behind her, her hand firmly in his, came running up to me.

"Omigod, Harry! I can't believe we found you."

"Barbie! Tank! Is Tess with you?" I looked around hopefully.

"No, we haven't seen her. We've been searching everywhere for you."

"Did you go to the fountain?"

Barbie frowned, but it was Tank who answered. "We tried, but it wouldn't let us."

"It?"

"The building, Harry. I don't know magic for shit, but there's something very weird going on here." Tank squinted suspiciously off into the distance, searching the area around us.

"What do you mean the building wouldn't let you?" I gave them a skeptical look.

Barbie shrugged. "We tried, Harry. We really did. We would aim straight at the fountain and start to make our way towards it, but the next thing we knew, it would no longer be where we thought it was. It would be behind us or off to the side. No matter how hard we tried, we couldn't get close to it."

"Yeah, it's fucked up," added Tank. "We need to find Tess and get the hell out of here."

"Okay, yeah. You're right. Something very weird is going on here, but I think you and Barbie should go now." They protested, but I put up a hand, stalling them. "My phone isn't working here. Are yours?" As I suspected, neither of their phones was working either. "I need you to go out and get help. Call Nash. He needs to get his ass down here, and I need Max as well. I can't call out to get them, and I won't leave without Tess, so you need to go."

Remarkably, we were able to find the door we came in easily enough. Although they were reluctant to go, I was eventually able to convince them both to leave. I didn't know what the hell this place was, but I felt better knowing that at least two of my friends were no longer at risk. The idea that I was getting them to send Nash and Max in didn't particularly sit well with me, but I needed Max's magical opinion, and Nash was the biggest badass I knew, and I would feel better having him around.

Once I had Tank and Barbie safely out, I turned back to survey the club. I could see the fountain directly in front of me, but I knew it wouldn't do me much good to make a beeline straight to it. Based on Barbie's story, there was obviously some sort of magic—a redirection spell most likely—preventing people from getting too close. I had a decision to make, but I was torn. On the one hand, I was curious about the fountain. Why was it even there? It was obviously important for some reason—important enough they had built it or brought it in from somewhere because it wasn't there the last time I was at the warehouse. It also had to be important enough they didn't want anyone getting too close to it, or why have the redirection spell? These two facts just made me want to see it up close even more. On the other hand, with the redirection spell in play, it was highly unlikely I would find Tess there, and I really needed to find her. When it came right down to it, the decision was a no-brainer. Tess came first. Besides, I had a plan that not only could lead me to Tess, but also get me closer to the fountain.

A redirection spell reads your intended destination and then, if necessary, redirects you away from what it's supposed to protect. If I could keep my thoughts trained on finding Tess rather than the fountain and used particular landmarks within the club like the dancefloor and casino, I thought I could search for Tess and circumvent the spell.

I made my way back through the club, dodging drunken revellers and wheeled serving staff, my mind fixed on finding Tess while using the dance floor as my destination. I scanned the crowd, searching for her familiar form. When I reached the outer edge of the dance floor, I skimmed its perimeter, intent on making my way back to the casino side of the building. With each pass through the club, I managed to move a bit closer to the fountain at its centre, but there was no sign of Tess. I couldn't stop my growing unease. Something about the place felt very wrong, but I couldn't put my finger on what exactly. After passing by a group of particularly wasted women, who were laughing hysterically and drinking straight from a champagne bottle, it came to me. Why wasn't I feeling drunk or high?

I may be still coming to grips with the whole Salvador-is-my-dad revelation, but there is one thing in which I am definitely my father's daughter. I'm a psychic vampire—well, half vampire, but when it comes to inheriting powers, it's an all-or-nothing thing; you don't inherit half a power. I don't need blood like most vampires, although it provides its own unique high. Instead, I can use the psychic energy released by emotions. When my powers first came online, so to speak, I often found myself overwhelmed in situations like nightclubs and crowds because I couldn't shield myself from the barrage of energy coming from the people around me. I'd end up feeling punch-drunk. While I prided myself to think that my shields had gotten much stronger and I was better at controlling my powers, I should have felt at least some vibes coming from this wild crowd, but I got nothing. Zip. Zilch. Nada.

How was that possible? In a crowd this size, the emotional vibes should have been off the charts. Instead, I was getting less than a trickle. I could get a bigger high at an insurance seminar. Before I could get lost in my thoughts completely, I turned my attention back to my search for

Tess. She had to be my priority. I'd have to try and figure out the rest later.

I was on my second pass around the club when I finally spotted her, and what I saw had me doing a double take to make sure it was really her. She was in the middle of the dance floor doing the bump 'n' grind with two gorgeous men dressed in white. The men were hanging off her—one in front, one behind—their bodies rubbing up against hers, and judging from the expression on her face, Tess was enjoying being the meat in that particular man sandwich. I watched as the man in front leaned down to nuzzle against her neck. Tess threw her head back in pleasure, and the man behind her tipped a bottle of champagne towards her waiting mouth.

"Tess!" I shoved my way through the crowded dance floor. "What the hell, Tess?" I smacked the bottle away from her face and glared back at the man who was giving me a dirty look. "Are you out of your mind? I've been searching everywhere for you."

"Haaarry! Whazzup girl?" Tess's words were slurred, her movements slow. "Look guys, it's my friend Haarrry." She giggled.

The guys didn't appear at all pleased at my arrival. The one who had been in the process of leaving a hickey on Tess's neck scowled at me. "Listen, luv," he said, his accent definitely originating from the other side of the Atlantic, "we're busy here. Why don't you have a drink and wait your turn." He pulled Tess towards him.

"Oh yeah, *mate*?" I replied, grabbing Tess by the elbow and yanking her away. "You had better just push off and find yourself someone else to get busy with."

"Guys, guys," Tess interjected. "Harry, just chill. There's plenty to go around. He's right. Have a drinky-poo. It's da bomb." She laughed as if she had just said the funniest thing ever.

The bottle guy smiled, holding out the champagne. "Come on, doll face, plenty to go around."

I pushed the bottle away and stepped in front of Tess. "Listen, guys. We're done here. Shove off."

Bottle guy scowled and looked at his friend. For a brief second both their forms seemed to twitch like they were holding a glamour that was slipping. What the hell?

Bottle guy took a menacing step towards me while his buddy moved to flank me. He reached out to grab my arm. When his fingers made contact with my bare skin, I felt a tingle, and he yanked his hand back with a jolt.

"Bloody hell!" he cried, holding up his hand. His fingertips were smoking and slightly singed.

"Holy smokes, Harry," Tess said, "you're so hot you set him on fire." She found this to be hysterical and bent over laughing.

I grabbed Tess by the shoulders and dragged her along with me as I backed away from the two men. "We're leaving. Don't try and stop us." I took a couple more backward steps, pulling Tess with me, my eyes never leaving the two men. They scowled at me, but didn't move to follow.

After a couple more steps, the crowd flowed into the space between us, and I turned, taking Tess's arm, dragging her after me. The club's mysteries would have to wait. The only thing I needed to do right now was get both of us out of there.

I hoofed it towards where I thought the entrance should be, half dragging, half carrying Tess. She was completely out of it. I couldn't remember the last time I had ever seen her so drunk—she was a werewolf and could hold her liquor, after all. In fact, I don't think I had *ever* seen her this drunk. What the hell was in that champagne?

As we neared the entrance, I felt the weight of someone's gaze. I scanned the area until my eyes fell on a man wearing a bright, cobalt-blue, three-piece suit complete with a gold watch chain hanging from a pocket in his vest. He was tall and thin, his hair kept long to about his shoulders. Since he wasn't dressed in white nor was he excessively rowdy or drunk, he stood out from the crowd. His face was predatory as his eyes met mine, and it took all my willpower not to squirm under his scrutiny. Without breaking his stare, he tipped back his head and gestured with his finger for someone to approach. Mr. Zed, the man we had met upon our arrival, scurried forward, and the man in the blue suit said something to him.

Mr. Zed nodded and snapped his fingers. As if from nowhere, three large, burly men dressed in white leather appeared and strode across the floor towards us.

I was preparing to drop Tess and take a defensive stance when there was an enormous crash, and the double doors at the entrance burst open.

"Nash!" I shouted in relief as he came striding into the club, bristling with anger. Max, looking equally determined, followed close on his heels. Nash stopped about twenty feet in front of me and said something to Max and then called over his shoulder to shout a few commands. Members of the SRU, dressed in black jumpsuits and bulletproof vests, came jogging in, fanning out across the warehouse. The entire time this was happening, I watched as if from in a bubble. I could see everything, but the sounds were muted, my view slightly distorted. "Nash?" I called his name again, but he just paced back and forth, his face serious as he scanned the room, apparently unable to see or hear me. The SRU team streamed past, also oblivious to my presence.

A sound behind me had me turning back in surprise. I let go of Tess, allowing her to drop to the floor as I reached for my katana, the metal ringing as it cleared its sheath, and moved to stand protectively over her. The man in the blue suit, flanked by Mr. Zed and his goon squad, stood directly behind us.

"Well, well, well, what do we have here? The mystery woman who turned our little scan red." The man in blue, who I had started to think of as Mr. Blue, arched an eyebrow at me, slowly perusing me up and down, his Southern drawl placing him from somewhere in the bayou. "That's a fine-lookin' gator-pokin' stick you've got there, sugar. Are you gonna poke me with it?" His face widened in a toothy grin.

"Maybe," I replied. "That depends on you."

Mr. Blue guffawed loudly, startling me. "Hoo-wee, you got some gumption there, darlin'. I like me a girl with gumption."

"Listen, I don't know who you are, and right now I don't really care. I just want to take my friend and leave." I sidled around Tess, trying to keep my eyes on Mr. Blue and his buddies.

"Now why would you want to go and do that, honey-pie?" Mr. Blue frowned. "We're just startin' to get to know one another. In fact, just to show you what a gentleman I am, I'll even share my name. You may call me Seth. And you are?"

I ignored his question and glanced around nervously. Nash and Max were there behind us and still totally oblivious that we were standing right in front of them. I could see the SRU team leading some of the club patrons out. The people were dazed and confused; many were staring at their surroundings in shock. Others had to be helped or carried out the door.

"You see all those men? They're here for me, for us. Let my friend and me go, and I'll call them off. Otherwise, they'll tear this place apart until they find us."

There was a furtive movement to my right, and one of the burly white-clad bouncers took a step towards me.

"Step back," I warned. "Any closer and I take you off at the knees." I lowered my katana menacingly. Completely ignoring me, another of the bouncers took a step forward. Fuck! I was in deep shit. If they decided to rush me, there was no way I would be able to fight them all off and protect Tess.

For some reason, my thoughts flew to Father Mike and the blessing he had given me earlier. Even with the extra help, I began to seriously doubt I was going to get myself out of this particular mess. As if thinking of Father Mike was a trigger, the mark he had made on my forehead warmed. I winced, squinting at the bright light that burst into being. I blinked in surprise. My katana was glowing! No, scratch that. It was fucking on fire! The fire licked up the sides of the blade from the hilt, flaring to blue wherever the flames touched steel and then flickering to orange and yellow at their tips. I stared at the sword in amazement. Although my hand should have been burning, I felt no heat as I brandished the blade in front of me.

The burly boys jumped back in fear as I waved my fiery sword at them. If I wasn't trapped in some sort of invisible bubble, it would have been totally cool. It was like having my own lightsaber, except without the awesome sound effects.

"Well now, sugar. Aren't you just full of surprises?" Seth eyed me cautiously. I noticed that even he had taken a step back when my sword went all *Star Wars*.

"Harry? Harry, why are you glowing?" Tess roused slightly and managed to sit up.

"It's okay, Tess. Do you think you can stand?"

"So sleepy, Harry." Her words were still slurred, but she moved as if to try and stand.

"Harry? Now what kind of name is that for a pretty girl like you?" Seth grinned, obviously getting over his initial shock at my flaming katana. "Surely it must be a nickname perhaps?"

I was having a serious déjà vu moment. I'd had almost the exact same conversation with Salvador when I first met him. I wasn't in the mood for a repeat.

"Just Harry will do. It's all you need to know." I pulled on Tess's elbow and she struggled to her feet, wrapping her arm around my waist for support. "Now, how about you pop this little bubble you've got going on here and let us out so we can see our friends?"

Seth narrowed his eyes and stared at me, a calculating look on his face. I glared back at him, unwilling to let him see my unease. Suddenly, he broke out in a toothy smile and clapped his hands, rubbing them together. "Alrighty then," he said, sounding pleased. "How about we make ourselves a trade?"

"What sort of trade?" I eyed him suspiciously.

"Now don't get like that, darlin'. It's nothing. A mere trifle."

"Go on," I said impatiently.

"Give me your name, your full name, mind you, and I'll let you—"

"And *all* my friends," I added, interrupting him.

For a moment, something dark passed across Seth's eyes, but then he smiled and tipped his chin in acknowledgement. "I'll let you and *all* your friends leave this place."

"Unharmed. In exchange for my full name, you will let me and all my friends return home unharmed." I bit my lip. Had I covered everything? I figured it was like making a deal with a vampire or a Fae; you had to be careful to make sure you didn't leave any loopholes.

"Deal," Seth drawled. He held out his hand as if to seal the deal, but then pulled it back, grinning slyly. "Normally I would say shake on it." He eyed my flaming sword. "But I do believe we can forego that part of the bargain."

I arched a brow at him and let out a little snort. "Good choice. We have a deal."

The white-clad bouncers stood down, melting into the background. Mr. Zed gave me a less-than-friendly look and then turned and disappeared as well.

"Well now, sugar. It's just us. Alone at last." Seth grinned. "Now give me your name." His eyes turned hard, his friendly demeanor slipping.

I took a deep breath. I suddenly had a very bad feeling about the deal I'd just struck. Why was my name so important to him?

"Come on, darlin'. We had a deal." Seth's smile began to fade. "Don't keep me waiting now."

"Angharad," I said. "My name is Angharad Grainne Russo."

As the last syllable left my lips, there was a loud pop, and cold air wafted up against me. Tess stumbled, going limp, and I wrapped an arm around her, struggling to keep her on her feet. I stared down at my katana. The flames had disappeared, just like Seth.

"Harry!" Nash's voice rang out. I glanced over, and Nash was running towards me, a look of sheer relief on his face. For a moment our eyes met, and it felt like my heart would burst, I was so happy to see him, but then he growled, "For fuck's sake, Harry! Where the hell have you been?"

"Nash," I replied, the warm and squishy moment gone. "Help me. Tess needs help!"

I was so intent on Nash, I didn't even notice Max as he slipped up beside me.

"Good to see you, Harry," he said with a grin. "Need a hand?" Without waiting for an answer, he gathered Tess in his arms, lifting her off her feet. Tess's head lolled back against his shoulder. Good thing she was completely out of it, or she probably would have freaked about being in such close proximity to Max.

"Are you all right?" Nash was suddenly there, in my face. He grabbed my shoulders and held me out to take a good look, his expression darkening when he saw the katana in my hand at my side.

"I'm fine," I replied, stepping back to sheath my sword. "But boy am I ever glad to see you."

Satisfied, Nash pulled me into his arms, enveloping me in a fierce hug. He inhaled slowly, his face in my hair, and some of the anger ebbed out of him.

"Can we get the hell out of here?" I mumbled into Nash's chest, feeling exhausted.

Nash released his grip, and I saw Max, still carrying Tess, striding out the door.

"Fuck yeah. Let's go," was Nash's rough reply.

Chapter Twelve

I was in for a surprise when I walked out of the club and into the daylight.

"What the—?"

I looked around in shock. The sun was low in the hazy, winter sky, but it had to be at least eight or nine in the morning. The street had been blocked off, and police cars and ambulances were everywhere. A small crowd of onlookers had gathered behind the police tape. Isaac and Tomas were long gone in order to avoid the dawn sun, the street empty where their cars had been parked. I turned back to stare at the warehouse. The massive green doors were hanging askew on their hinges, the metal scored and singed. A man in police coveralls was busy putting away a blowtorch, while another threaded a heavy steel chain between the two doors and padlocked them shut.

"Harry!" Tank's voice rang out and I barely had time to brace myself before being caught up in a great big bear hug.

As I struggled to catch my breath in his rib-cracking embrace, there was a loud growl, and I suddenly found myself back on my feet beside Nash. Nash's jacket settled on my shoulders and his arm wrapped around me possessively. Tank took a step back and bowed his head, avoiding eye contact. "Sorry, Harry. I was just so relieved to see you."

I elbowed Nash and gave him what I think of as my stern look. I could do without the jealous-alpha routine, although secretly I was glad to have his jacket. It was cold in the morning air. "It's fine, Tank. Are you okay? Where's Barbie?"

"We're good, both good. It tore Barbie up to leave with you and Tess still missing, but she thought she'd be more help back at the shop with it being morning and all."

I shook my head. I couldn't believe it was morning. "What time is it?"

Nash cleared his throat. "It's almost nine a.m, Harry. You've been gone for almost twelve hours."

"Twelve hours!" I gaped at him. I turned to look for Tess, only to discover she wasn't in sight. "Where did Max go with Tess?" I searched the street and spotted him over by his car. Tess was sitting in the backseat, a blanket thrown around her shoulders. Max was pressing a bottle of juice into her hand and telling her to drink. "Tess!" I pushed off Nash's arm and hurried over. "Tess, are you okay?"

I knelt beside her. She looked like shit, her skin pale and clammy, but she smiled weakly. "I'm fine, Harry. I'm fine. Nothing that a day's worth of sleep won't cure."

I turned to Max, and he raised an eyebrow, shaking his head. "Her aura's in rough shape. What the hell happened in there, Harry?"

I narrowed my eyes and studied Tess with my witchy senses. Max was right. Tess's aura was dangerously thin in places. Something had almost drained her. If I hadn't gotten her away when I did, she could have easily ended up dead.

Just then my stomach growled. I was absolutely ravenous, the last twelve hours suddenly catching up to me and taking their toll.

Nash came up behind me, pulling me up into his arms. "Let's take this conversation back to Harry's. I don't think it's a good idea to stay here."

I glanced back at the warehouse. It looked positively garish in the daylight. I shivered, and not from the cold. I couldn't have agreed with Nash more.

***

"I don't know how it happened," Tess said from her nest of blankets on the couch.

We were back at the firehall—Nash, Max, Tess and me. Tank had left after seeing us safely home and checking on Barbie. Max had insisted on performing a cleansing ritual on Tess to help her aura heal faster, and so while he did that, I had quickly left messages both on Isaac's phone and at Dante's so that the sunrise-challenged would know we were safe once they awoke for the evening. I figured someone at Dante's would listen to the message and let both Salvador and Tomas know what was up.

Tess and I had then gone to our separate bathrooms to shower and change. We had arrived back downstairs, following the smell of bacon, and were treated to the sight of Nash and Max attempting to play nice and cooperate in the kitchen. It was a little surreal.

"One minute there were these idiots shouting, "Chug, chug, chug," and the next I had a bottle pushed into my face and champagne was being poured into my mouth," Tess continued. She shook her head. "Then it gets kind of fuzzy after that."

"It was the champagne. You must have been rufied," I said. "I think that whole place was on drugs. It was nuts."

Over breakfast, I filled Nash and Max in on what we had seen at the club. At first, they both stared at me like I was crazy.

"There were only about thirty people in the warehouse with you, Harry. Not hundreds." Nash frowned at me.

"What?" Tess yelped. "How can that be? The place was packed. We had to wade through the crowd. What about all the waiters on roller skates? The white leather fetish wear? The slot machines?"

Nash and Max glanced at one another.

"I didn't see anyone wearing roller skates," Max replied.

"Or dressed in white leather," Nash added.

"How is that possible? I saw everything with my own two eyes!"

"I'm sure you did, Tess." Max patted her hand, reassuringly. Tess pulled her hand away like it was on fire. Ignoring her reaction, Max continued, "Or at least you thought you did. Perhaps it was some sort of hallucination."

"A mass hallucination? Because Harry, Barbie and Tank saw it all too."

Max shrugged. "Possibly. And I think you're right about the champagne being drugged, Harry. There was probably some sort hallucinogen that also made people more compliant."

"But I didn't have anything to drink, and I still saw what Tess saw," I replied skeptically. "And why did I lose so much time?" I couldn't get over the important detail that what seemed like only a couple of hours had actually been almost twelve.

Max gave a little shrug. "I have some suspicions, but I want to do a bit of research first to confirm my thoughts." He rose from his seat and stretched. "It's been a long night…for all of us." He raised an eyebrow at Tess and then turned back to me. "Let's talk more tonight."

"But…" I stopped, biting my lip in thought. I had some suspicions about what had happened too. I hadn't even had a chance to mention Seth yet.

"Give it a rest, Harry," Nash grumbled. "It can wait until we've all had some sleep."

A soft snore escaped the blankets on the couch, and I looked over at Tess. She was already out like a light.

"Yeah, I could sleep."

Chapter Thirteen

"I thought I was supposed to be sleeping," I mumbled at Nash, half awake.

After getting Tess settled in her own bed and seeing Max (who refused to leave until after Tess was taken care of) out the door, I had crawled into bed and immediately fell asleep before Nash could even finish getting undressed and join me. Sometime later, I found myself naked and spooned up to Nash, his arms wrapped around me, hands exploring various parts of my body.

"You are," he rumbled, and I could hear the smile in his voice. "Don't mind me. I can keep myself occupied."

He buried his face against my neck and inhaled. His lips brushed against his mate mark, and desire zinged through my body. Rolling in his arms, I pulled his face to mine and kissed him. It was a slow, sensual kiss, at least until I thrust my tongue in his mouth which had the same effect as flipping a switch, the kiss going from thirty to a hundred in less than two seconds flat. With a growl, Nash took over, and I found myself flat on my back, my arms pinned above my head while he ravaged me with his lips and tongue.

Just as suddenly, Nash tore his mouth from mine and sighed. "Damn it, Harry," he said, his voice low and rough. "The wolf...I..." He paused, propping himself up on one elbow, and tousled his hair. "I thought I had lost you there for a while."

"I'm here. I'm fine...I'm naked," I replied in a whisper, reaching out to run my fingers through his hair as I pulled him back down on top of me. "Now, what are you going to do about it?" I slid my hand down between us.

With a grunt, Nash captured my mouth with his, and then he spent a very long time showing me just what he *could* do about it.

The next time I awoke, Nash was pulling on clothes.

"Where are you going?" I tried to blink away the sleep, but I was still exhausted.

"Gotta go into work and deal with this shit." He tucked the covers around me and then sat on the edge of the bed. "Try and get some more sleep." He kissed my forehead and ran his hand through my hair.

I sighed sleepily and snuggled down into my pillows. "Nash?" I asked, peeking one eye open. "So it seemed like you and Max worked well together."

Nash shrugged and bent to tug on a boot. "He's okay. I couldn't have got into the warehouse without him." His booted foot fell to the floor with a clomp, and then he picked up the other boot. "He still smells funny though."

"So maybe we could all go on a double date sometime?" I grinned at him, my tone teasing.

Nash snorted. "Go to sleep, Harry."

***

"Wake up, Harry!"

Disoriented, I blinked and looked around. I was in my room, the sun shining wanly through the blinds. I squinted at the clock on the bedside table. It read four twenty.

"Shit!" I said, pushing back the covers. I had slept the whole day away.

"It's about time you got your lazy bones out of bed."

"Gran?" I squeaked in surprise, wrapping the sheet around my naked torso.

"Come on with you. No time for that. As if I haven't seen you in your birthday suit before or wiped your lily-white bottom. Now hurry up, you've got company downstairs." Gran folded her arms across her chest. "*Himself* is here."

There was only one "himself" that Gran would have her panties all in a twist about. "What is Salvador doing here?" I muttered to myself. Gran didn't volunteer an answer, and I wasn't really expecting one.

With an exasperated huff, I grabbed my T-shirt off the floor and pulled it on. After throwing off the covers, I slipped out of bed and padded across the room to the bathroom.

"Where are you going? You can't just leave that vampire downstairs on his own!" Gran floated in front of me, blocking my way.

"Salvador can just bloody well wait. I need a shower."

***

I showered, got dressed and then checked on Tess before heading downstairs. She was fast asleep, although judging from the empty packages of cookies and cans of soda on the floor by her bed, I assumed she had been awake at least once to forage for food.

The smell of roasting chicken had my stomach growling before I was even halfway down the stairs, but the sound of voices raised in argument coming from around the corner in the kitchen made me pause.

"...knew what they were facing and still sent them in unprepared!" Isaac's voice was angry.

"My dear Isaac," Salvador replied, his voice cool and condescending, "I merely suspected. I did not know." There was a pause, and I could imagine Salvador giving Isaac one of his annoying shrugs. "Besides, the girl is more than strong enough—"

"You don't know that!" Isaac interrupted. "You—"

"Harry! Now there are two vampires in your kitchen. Two! It's a damn vampire convention." Gran popped into view right in front of me.

"Shhh! Gran! I'm trying to hear," I hissed, waving her away from my face.

I remained still for a moment, listening, but the voices had fallen silent. Damn vampire hearing. Now they knew I had been eavesdropping. Tossing a dirty look at Gran, who continued to fade in and out of view beside me, I hurried towards the kitchen.

"Ahh, there she is," Salvador said as he rose to his feet, smiling widely, his arms raised in welcome. "My dear Harry, so nice to see that you are none the worse for wear after your adventure last night."

"Not that he really cares," Gran griped, hovering by my ear. "Mark my words, he'll use you up and throw you out like yesterday's trash."

I kept my face impassive, ignoring Gran's interruption.

"Salvador," I said, walking around the far side of the kitchen island, avoiding his arms. I nodded to Isaac and gave him a look that said *what the hell is* he *doing here?* Before turning back to Salvador.

For a brief second, I swear I saw disappointment on Salvador's face, and then it was gone, replaced by his usual sly smile. He lowered his arms, but outstretched his hand to me, waiting.

Rolling my eyes (I don't care what Page Six thinks of my attitude), I huffed out a little sigh and then crossed over to put my hand in his. He clasped it, placing his other hand over mine, and gave me an assessing look.

"Don't put your hand in his, you ninny!" Gran floated in front of my face. It took every ounce of willpower I had to ignore her. "Don't you know what he is?"

"Yes, yes." Salvador patted my hand. "None the worse for wear."

I pulled my hand from his with a frown. "What did Isaac mean that you knew what we were facing?" I turned to walk back to the kitchen, scowling at Gran on the way past. "What *were* we facing? I still don't know, and it almost got Tess killed."

I walked to the fridge and grabbed a couple of beers, cracking one open and taking a long swig. I held the other up to Salvador in silent question. I didn't bother offering one to Isaac. He avoided beer, or at least the cheap, national-brand stuff that Tess and I bought, like the plague, but I figured I should at least offer one to Salvador. I'd drank enough of his liquor over these last few months.

Surprisingly, Salvador smiled and accepted the drink. Yay! A point for me in the good-daughter column.

I took a moment to drink some more of my beer, and Isaac produced a plateful of his homemade hummus and pita bread, setting it down in front of me and giving me a look that said I had better not drink on an empty stomach.

"You're drinking buddies now?" Gran sputtered back into view, hovering between Salvador and me.

Forgetting myself, I turned to Gran and frowned. "That's enough," I scolded.

"It certainly is, Aislin," Salvador said to Gran, using her first name. "You can't shelter her forever, and you only harm yourself with your vitriol."

Gran gasped, shock and outrage warring on her face, and then blinked out of sight. Crap! I didn't even get a chance to ask her about the other night and why she was fading in and out.

I gaped at Salvador in surprise. "You could hear her? See her?" I glanced at Isaac. He shook his head, indicating that he could not. I turned back to Salvador.

Salvador shrugged annoyingly, gesturing with his hands. "But of course. Where do you think your gift came from? I don't believe it runs on your grandmother's side of the family tree."

I stared at him. I hadn't really thought about it. Well, that's not true. Lately, after meeting the piece of work that was my not-so-dead-but-now-definitely-undead mother, I had assumed it was mixed up in a cauldron like the rest of my so-called gifts. My mother had made it very clear that she had used what little magic she had to ensure the fetus she was carrying (me) was powerfully gifted.

Salvador smiled like a Cheshire cat. "Of course my gift is a mere parlour trick next to yours, my dear Harry. I can only see and hear the dead. I do not command them."

Ha! Now that was funny coming from the man who controlled every vampire within a five-state area. But we were getting off topic.

"Listen, let's not change the subject right now. I want to know what happened last night. What is that place? What's going on there?"

Salvador glanced at his watch and rose from his seat. "I must be going. I merely popped in to see for myself that you were unharmed." He paused and smiled at me. "I am genuinely relieved that you are safe, *pequeña*. I am also glad to hear that you have agreed to help *Señor* DeGrasse. He is a valuable ally. You will arrange with Tomas to be present at the time you perform the ritual. He will ensure your safety."

Isaac bristled at Salvador's words. My safety, after all, was sort of his job. I imagine Nash would have a thing or two to say about Tomas ensuring my safety as well. But Salvador, totally unconcerned about Isaac's feelings or what I might want, was already walking towards the door.

"Wait! We're not done here." I started after him. "What about Wishes? What happens next?"

"Good night, Harry," Salvador replied, ignoring my questions and taking his leave.

"Damn it!" I spun on my feet and returned to the kitchen, pulling up a seat at the counter. "That man is so frustrating."

Isaac raised an eyebrow at me and actually snorted. "Try dealing with him for a couple of centuries and then we'll talk."

I looked at him in shock, hummus-covered pita halfway to my mouth. "Isaac! Did you just make a joke?"

"Eat your pita, Harry. It's going to drip on your shirt."

I grinned at him and then stuffed the pita in my mouth. I'd have to tell Tess. We were definitely loosening the old guy up. I got up and hunted for my purse from the night before so I could find my cellphone and left a message for Nash. Then I texted Max and invited him for dinner. I was going to get to the bottom of things, one way or another.

"Is it safe to come out now?" Tess peeked around the corner.

"That depends. Salvador is gone, but Max will be here soon." I gave her a cheeky grin.

Tess paused as if considering going back to bed.

"There is chicken with roasted potatoes and vegetables, Caesar salad, and the sausage cornbread stuffing you like," Isaac added.

"Oh, well....in that case, no problem." Tess smiled and sat beside me.

I reached over and placed an arm across her shoulders. "Are you okay?"

"Ai!" She shook her head. "I feel *chuchaqui*." Tess groaned and put a hand to her forehead.

I couldn't help but laugh. *Chuchaqui* was one of the few Spanish words I knew far too well. It meant hungover. But then I remembered how weak Tess had been the night before and how close we came to losing her, and my mood soured. "You scared the shit out of me last night," I scolded.

"Ha!" Tess gave me a playful punch. "Now you know how I feel around *you* half the time."

***

"So those guys were demons?" Tess stabbed a jellied cherry off her plate and then looked at Max.

We were finishing dinner off with Black Forest cake courtesy of Hilde. Not my favourite, but one of Tess's which was fine, since it was her get-well dinner, not mine.

Max had arrived shortly after Nash, and we had all sat down to eat before moving into the living room to talk about what happened at the club. Nash and I were sitting together on the sofa, while Tess and Max occupied the two comfy chairs. It was like we were having that double date after all, if you didn't count the fifth wheel, Isaac. He was odd man out because Christina wasn't able to join us. She was busy creating her culinary magic over at The Lodge. Isaac had insisted on cleaning up after dinner, so he was listening from the kitchen.

"No, daemons," replied Max, pronouncing the word *day-mon*.

"Po-TAY-to, po-TAH-to." Tess shrugged and scraped her plate clean, licking the last of the whipped cream off her fork before putting her now-empty dish on the coffee table.

Max paused for a moment, watching her lips intently, and then glanced around self-consciously. Interesting. Maybe the crush was mutual?

"It's not just pronunciation," he said after clearing his throat. "There is a difference. Daemons are the lower-level servants of demons. I suspect these particular ones were incubi. They use sex to feed on their prey."

"I didn't have sex with them!" Tess folded her arms around herself defensively.

"No, of course not! I didn't mean..." Max took a long, slow breath. "I mean they use sexual attraction to lure and feed on their victims. You were drugged, more than likely with something that lowered your inhibitions, which allowed them to feed on your aura, draining you of your life energy."

"So they're like the Otherworld version of a vampire?"

"They most certainly are not!" A crash came from the kitchen, and Isaac turned around from the sink to face us.

"Oh, oh, Harry. Now you've done it." Tess waved an accusing finger at me.

I stared wide-eyed at Isaac. I don't think I'd ever seen him lose his cool like that before. "What did I say? I'm just trying to understand." I frowned at him. "Max said that incubi feed on life energy. Well, so do vampires. So do I sometimes!" I gulped. It had taken me a long time to allow myself to admit that. Denial ain't just a river in Egypt, you know. "How is that different?"

"The difference, Harry, is that we have a conscience." Isaac put his hands on the counter and leaned forward to look me directly in the eye. "We have a soul." He glared at me, as if waiting for me to deny it.

"Isaac is right," Max said, quickly filling the awkward silence. "Daemons, demons and other denizens of the Otherworld are purely malevolent creatures, without a soul or conscience. Their purpose is to bring pain and chaos to the world."

"I don't know," Nash deadpanned, "Harry's got the chaos part down."

Tess snorted a laugh, and I threw Nash a playful punch to the arm. He caught my fist and pulled me towards him so that I ended up on his lap.

"Nash! We're trying to have a serious conversation here."

"You can still converse from there," he replied, settling me down to rest in the crook of his arm. I had to admit, it felt kind of cozy—a good feeling to have when talking about demons.

I turned back to Isaac. "I'm sorry," I said. "I didn't mean to offend or insult you."

"Us, Harry. You insult us. Something you are wont to forget. You are a vampire too."

He had a point. I did tend think of myself as a witch first and a vampire only when I had to. But that didn't mean I had to agree with him out loud (there's that denial thing again).

This time it was Tess who saved us from the awkward silence. "So what are these demons and daemons doing here? Why have they taken over the warehouse?"

Isaac went back to cleaning up the kitchen, and Max leaned forward to answer. "I believe that a small portal has opened, and it's allowing a pocket realm to form. The daemons are minions. They're doing the bidding of a stronger, more powerful demon. As he becomes stronger, the pocket will grow bigger, allowing more of his servants to enter this realm."

"So this is DiCastro's fault? He actually opened a portal to hell?" DiCastro had wanted to become the most powerful sorcerer in the world. Obviously that hadn't worked out so well for him, seeing as how he was dead and I was still alive, but there had been a whole lot of chanting and magic going on when things went sideways on him.

"Hell, *Gehenna*, *Duat*, the Netherworld—they're all names for the same thing—what we more commonly think of as the Otherworld. What I think happened was DiCastro managed to start the ritual, but it was never finished or reversed. Instead, a tiny hole in the fabric of our realm was left open. Enough that something, or someone in this case, could slip through."

"But why? Why come here? Why not just stay in their own realm?"

"Why did white man come to the new world?" Max looked around the room at us, reminding me of a teacher waiting for someone to raise their hand.

"To explore," I said.

"To conquer," Nash replied at almost the same time.

Max nodded. "Yes, to both of you."

"But if there's a hole from our realm into theirs, why aren't they just all pouring through it and overrunning us?"

"That's a good question, Tess," Max replied with a nod of appreciation. Tess fussed with her napkin, her face turning a shade darker.

"But what's the answer?" I asked.

"I suspect that the portal is probably too small and too unstable for many of them to cross over at any given time. Also, because they have no souls, the daemons can't fully enter our realm. They're restricted to the small pocket of their realm that now exists in ours."

"So they can't leave the warehouse?" Nash asked. It would make his life easier if the SRU only had to worry about the warehouse and not the entire city being overrun.

"For now. But as we heard from Tomas, the realm is growing outward. I think they're luring people to the warehouse and using the power they steal from them to stabilize and grow the portal. There's also the risk of possession. By possessing a body that already has a soul, they could leave the pocket realm and enter ours."

"So how do we stop them? How do we close the portal?" Nash's body tensed, waiting for the answer.

"Unfortunately," Max said with a frown, "that I don't know." He looked at me. "It might help if we knew which demon has taken up residence."

"What makes you think there's just one?"

"Oh, I know there's just one," he answered confidently. "Demons are territorial and adversarial. In the Otherworld they amass huge armies of daemons in order to display their strength. There's a very strict hierarchy in hell. It has changed very little over time, with the strongest demons having held their positions of power for eons. That's why I suspect this is one of the lesser-known demons making a play for power."

"How do you know all this stuff? I mean, I know you're the Hammer and all, but..." Tess shrugged.

"Well, I do hold doctorates in religious studies and botany, but—"

"You're a summoner!" I slid off Nash's lap so I could sit up.

"A what?" Tess looked puzzled.

"Max can summon demons," I replied. "It's a very rare shamanic gift." It was impressive. It also went a long way in explaining how Max, newly arrived to the Coven, could become the Hammer at such a young age.

"So can't you just summon this demon and tell him to take a hike?" Tess asked, matter-of-factly.

"It doesn't work that way. It takes an extremely powerful practitioner to call forth a demon. Summoning a daemon is more common. Either way, you need to know the creature's name." Max appeared thoughtful for a moment. "I may have a way to find out more about our demon though. I'll have to do some research."

"Well, I doubt if his *real* name is Seth," I said, trying to crack a joke, but not really feeling it.

"What?" Tess looked at me, her face puzzled at first, and then the light began to dawn. "That was real? I thought it was a dream."

All eyes were suddenly on me. I gave them a sheepish smile.

"Harry," Nash growled, his face beginning to resemble a storm cloud. "What haven't you told us?"

"Well, you see there was this guy dressed in a blue suit..."

***

I finished telling my story about meeting the man (or whatever he was) named Seth and how Tess and I finally made our escape, and then looked around the room. Isaac had left the kitchen and pulled up a chair from the dining area to sit and listen. He traded a worried glance with Max.

"What's wrong?" I asked. "Did I do something wrong? Did I miss something when I made my deal?"

"No, no, it's okay, Harry. You did what you had to do."

"But?" Nash's voice was tense.

"But I'm concerned about the demon knowing Harry's true name," Max replied with a sigh. "Names are powerful, especially when it comes to demons."

"What could he do with it?" I asked, biting my lip, dreading the answer.

"I don't know, and that's what worries me. I'll have to do some more—"

"Research," Tess interrupted. "We know, Professor, we know." She grinned, trying to lighten the mood. "I can't believe your sword turned into a lightsaber, Harry. I thought I was dreaming all that. Does it still do it?"

"I don't know!" I jumped up in surprise. "I never thought to check." I hurried over, Tess on my heels, to where my katana was hanging on its rack on the wall, and took it down. Tess crowded in to watch as I pulled the sword clear of its sheath.

"Ahh, nuts," she complained when the flames were a no-show. "I totally missed it. I bet it looked epic."

"It was pretty cool," I agreed with a grin.

Chapter Fourteen

The next day was Sunday, and we were all enjoying a day of rest. The coffee shop was usually pretty quiet on Sundays, so I left it under Tiffy's care. She was a pro at handling customers now, having come out of her shell, and she never took a day off. I had offered one to her once and she had been so angry at me that I'd even suggest something so insulting she didn't speak to me for two whole days.

The SRU had the warehouse cordoned off and were patrolling the perimeter to make sure nothing got in or out. There hadn't been any new HRN incidents, so Nash had the day off as well, at least until the next crisis. He was currently fast asleep in my bed where I had left him after delicious, sleepy morning sex followed by breakfast in bed—okay, so it was a bowl of cereal with banana cut up in it, I still made it, so it counts as cooking.

After everyone cleared off the night before and Tess went back to bed, Nash and I spent the rest of the evening together watching a movie (*Edge of Tomorrow*, which is like a Sci-Fi version of *Groundhog Day*—I needed the laughs and Nash hadn't seen it yet) and eating popcorn before tumbling into bed (two nights of sex in a row! Yippee!).

After breakfast, I was tempted to crawl back into bed with Nash, but I had decided the night before that I needed to go to church. No, I hadn't suddenly found religion. I was quite happy with my current belief systems as they were, but I wanted to talk to Father Mike and thank him. I'm pretty sure his blessing had saved my life, and Tess's too. There was also still the hunch I had after speaking to Tosh at the bingo lady's funeral that I wanted to follow up on, so rather than set the breakfast tray on the floor and snuggle with Nash, I cleaned up our dishes, headed to the shower and then got dressed.

I had checked online, and Mass at St. Anthony's didn't start until ten thirty, and since I was ready in plenty of time, I decided to walk. Half way there, I was beginning to doubt my sanity in making that particular decision. It was frickin' cold. Even bundled up as I was, my face was feeling wind bitten, and the woolly tights I had put on under my corduroy skirt weren't as warm as I thought they would be. I turned my head to the side to deflect the wind from my cheeks, and that's when I noticed I had a tail. It was the furtive movements and the way he stopped to admire a boarded-up window that gave him away. Suspicious, but thinking I could be a bit paranoid after everything that had happened, I quickened my pace and jaywalked across the street. A glance over my shoulder confirmed my fears. I was definitely being followed. And he wasn't being all that circumspect about it.

I was still several blocks from the church, and while I had my katana—not something I would normally wear to church, but I wanted to show it to Father Mike—I didn't want to confront my stalker in the middle of the street in broad daylight. I stuffed my hands in my pockets and hustled along as fast as I could without making it look like I was fleeing something other than the cold.

A couple minutes later, the sound of a car horn startled me, and Max's Lexus pulled up beside me.

"Going my way?" he quipped.

"Max! Am I ever glad to see you. What are you doing here?" I glanced over my shoulder to see that my tail had stopped, ducking into a doorway to wait.

"After our talk last night I decided to stop by and see if I could pick Father Mike's brain on a few things. Hop in, I'll give you a lift."

I gratefully slid into Max's car, revelling in the fact he had heated seats. "Thanks, Max," I said as I leaned over to watch my stalker in the side mirror. "Your timing is perfect."

"Is something wrong?" He looked over at me in concern.

I sat back in the seat and attempted to fasten my seatbelt as Max pulled away from the curb. "I don't know. See that guy back there? He's following me."

Max checked his rearview mirror. "I don't see anyone now."

I shrugged. "It's no big deal. I'm probably overreacting. It was probably just someone who read that stupid Page Six article."

Max grinned. "You're very photogenic. I particularly liked the eye roll."

"Oh hardy-har," I replied, demonstrating my now-famous eye roll for him in person. I wiggled in my seat and finally gave up trying to get comfortable. It's impossible to sit in a car properly with a sword strapped to your back, but it was only a couple of blocks to the church, and I didn't see the point of taking it off and then having to sneak it back on without anyone noticing. The invisibility enchantment only worked when I was wearing it.

Max watched me for a moment and then said, "Sword problems?" His eyebrows arched, and I could tell he was trying not to laugh.

"Just drive, buster."

***

I think I've mentioned before that I like churches, especially St. Anthony's because of its gorgeous stained-glass windows, which are the best in the city. I also like churches because of the peaceful calm you find inside. Today, however, appeared to be an exception; St. Anthony's was anything but calm.

The number of people attending the morning's Mass was so great they were having a crowd-control problem getting everyone into the church. It didn't help that the throng of people, all dressed in their Sunday best, were forced to use the single door that had been unlocked. It was like watching the chaos that ensues when eight lanes of traffic suddenly are compressed down to one.

With a frown I studied the two sets of double doors that remained locked. A young man dressed in cleric robes was doing his best to battle through the crowd to unlock them, but he wasn't making much headway. I shivered at a wind gust, regretting again my decision to wear a skirt. At this rate, we were never going to get into the church before I froze to death. I tossed Max a quick glance, and as if reading my mind, he nodded. I'd take that as permission—not that I needed his permission or anything, but he was the leader of the Coven, and there were certain rules about magic use in front of norms.

Grinning, I refocused my attention on the doors. With a click that I felt more than heard (who could hear anything over that crowd?) I unlocked the doors and gave them a little telekinetic pull. As the doors swung open, the crowd fanned out, streaming through the newly opened portals.

"Nice." Max nodded appreciatively. "I heard you'd acquired that particular talent." He gave me a knowing look.

Ha! I bet he'd heard. I had recently used my telekinesis to physically eject a rude Coven Elder from my store. Of course that particular Elder was no longer in a position to complain about me or anything else for that matter. The Coven doesn't take treason well, and Elder Marshall had sided with the Mariposa in her ill-fated attempt to take over the city from Salvador.

"It comes in handy," I replied. "Now let's get inside before my legs freeze."

If the crowd outside had been my first indication that today was going to be different, the next came the minute I walked in the door and passed over the threshold. As I stepped into the narthex, I was hit by a wave of psychic energy. It was so strong all the little hairs on my arms stood up as the energy popped and fizzed like an electrical current over my skin. I stumbled, and Max grabbed my elbow.

"Harry! Are you okay?"

I stood for a moment, dazed, and took a deep breath, trying to centre myself. "Yeah, I'm okay, it's just...can't you feel that?"

Max paused then shook his head. "No. What do you feel?"

"Spirits. A lot of them." I took another deep breath and steeled myself against it. "I'm okay. Let's go."

As was expected after seeing the crowd outside, the church itself was packed, and most of the pews were already full. It didn't matter. I didn't want to sit with the congregation anyway. Instead I led Max down a side aisle that ran the length of the nave to a small chapel just off the sanctuary at the front of the church. It was the spot where I usually liked to hang out unseen during services to avoid having to partake in all the religious mumbo-jumbo. I'm a witch after all, and we don't particularly have the best history with the church, especially the Catholic Church.

I was so intent on getting across the length of the nave and hidden away in the chapel that I didn't pay attention to what was going on around me. When I finally reached my desired destination, I turned and looked out over the sanctuary.

"Holy...!" I gaped in shock, covering my mouth with my hand to keep from blurting out something totally inappropriate for the venue.

"What's wrong?" Max scanned the church, following my gaze.

I didn't answer him at first. I was too transfixed by the sight before me.

The church was packed with congregants, but that's not what grabbed my attention. High above the faithful, in the soaring rafters of the church, a less-corporeal congregation had amassed. The air above swirled with the filmy horde of ghosts. I had never seen anything like it.

With a gasp, I ducked back into the chapel as quickly as I could. The last thing I wanted was for all those ghosts to discover I was in their midst. Although I might not have a choice as I was pretty much a spirit magnet, and ghosts tended to be drawn to me.

"What's going on, Harry? Is there a ghost here?"

"Yeah, you could say that." I gave him a halfhearted smile. "It's like ghost central out there. I thought I could just talk to a couple, but..."

"You might get more than you bargained for? How many are we talking about?"

"There must be dozens—too many to count."

Max looked impressed and with a nod, pulled something out of his pocket.

"What's that?" I asked, eyeing the small bottle. The liquid inside had the consistency of oil with bits of leafy matter floating in it.

"Just a little something I threw together this morning—some fennel, dandelion, yarrow, lemongrass and peppermint." He dabbed the oil on his forehead and underneath his eyes using his finger, his lips moving as he chanted silently. Next he wiped some on his ears.

All the plants he mentioned had known properties for aiding in spiritual sight. I looked at him skeptically. "I thought all you shaman types liked to smoke your herbs."

Max grunted in reply and continued chanting. A few moments later, he stopped and glanced around sheepishly. "You can't always smoke 'em," he said with a grin.

"So did it work?"

"I'll let you know in a minute." He strode to the entrance of the chapel and peered out into the much-larger church. A moment later he let out a low whistle. "Whoa," was all he said, but it spoke volumes. "Is it always like that?"

"No," I answered in surprise. Would that stuff would work on anyone? Tess would probably pay a fortune to see a ghost.

I told Max as much, but he shook his head. "Unfortunately, it only works on those who have a gift. It enhances what is already there." He paused briefly and then attempted to appear nonchalant as he asked, "What else does Tess like?"

I smiled slyly and was about to reply when an uninvited guest arrived.

"Hey, Harry! Pull my finger!"

"Mofo? What are you doing here?"

Max jumped back, startled, his eyes wide as he took in all that was Mofo from his candy-cane-striped shirt to his green polka-dotted pants. He turned to stare at me and mouthed, *Mofo?*

Long story, I mouthed back and then turned to Mofo. "Why aren't you at the hospital?"

"It's not safe, Harry." Mofo clutched at his bow tie nervously. "Not safe at all."

"Not safe? For a ghost? What could possibly scare a ghost?"

Before he could answer, a commotion filtered into the chapel as the congregation rose and began to sing. Father Mike and his fellow clerics entered the sanctuary.

"I've got to go tell the others," Mofo mumbled, distracted. "Wait until they hear my friend, the famous Harry Russo, is here." He started to fade.

"What? No! Mofo, wait!" I whispered loudly at him to come back, throwing a little will behind my words. Mofo popped back into view, looking antsy. "Don't take off yet.

Tell me what has you so afraid. Why are you here instead of the hospital?"

"I need protection, Harry. I can't risk getting caught by the Collector."

"The who? What are you talking about?"

"It's bad, Harry. Spooks are going missing all over town. They disappear and never come back."

"Maybe they're just finally passing over," I said, thinking it was obvious.

Mofo shook his head vigorously. "No, Harry. They aren't passing over. They've been snatched." His spectral body visibly shuddered. "Father Mike will protect us. That's why we're all here."

"Do you know who this Collector is? What does he look like?"

"He's bad, Harry. Eee-vil. A soul-stealer." He wrung his hands again. "I ain't ever seen him, and I don't ever intend to change that."

"Do you know anyone who has? Can you send them my way?"

Mofo nodded. "I'll get Junie for you, Harry. I think she's seen him."

He faded again, and I quickly added, "Listen, Mofo, you should head back to the hospital. Father Mike's prayers are potent enough to speed you on your way, so unless you want to cross over, you'd better make yourself scarce. Hang out in the hospital chapel if you need to feel safe." I added that last bit, thinking of Tosh and her idea that any hallowed ground would do.

"Okay, thanks, Harry." Mofo tipped his hat and disappeared.

"That was phenomenal," Max whispered. "Can you have conversations like that all the time?"

I shrugged. "Sort of, depending on the ghost. They aren't all as...interactive as that."

The service was in full swing by the time Junie arrived. Aptly named (she was a ringer for a younger version of June Cleaver), she was the epitome of a fifties teenage girl. Dressed in a bright-pink poodle skirt with a wide black belt and a white button-down shirt with butterfly sleeves, she could have been a stand-in on the set of a Gidget remake, except for the whole being-dead part.

"Far out! It really is the famous Harry Russo. Isn't that the ginchiest? And here I thought Mofo was lighting up the tilt sign." Junie looked at me and simpered.

I shook my head, trying to decipher the lingo. "Hi. You must be Junie?"

"In the flesh..." she paused, a mischievous smile hovering on her lips. "...so to speak. What can I do you for? Mofo said you needed some information."

"I do. What can you tell me about the Collector?"

Junie faded out momentarily and then popped back into view, a scared look on her face. "Now why do you want to know about *him*? He's the reason this joint is antsville."

Antsville? Ha! That was a good way of describing all the ghosts floating around I guess. "That's why I need to know. Why are all of you afraid of him?"

"I'm not sure I want to be talking about him, even here." She glanced around nervously.

"Tell me what you can. Please? It's important."

Junie crossed her ghostly arms over her chest. "Well, I've never seen the Collector. You see him, it's already too late. What you have to worry about are his henchmen. You never know where or when they're going to jump out and get you. Suck you right up and you're gone." She snapped her fingers. "Just like that."

"Can you describe these henchmen?"

"They could be anyone!" Junie floated around the room, agitated. "Just the other day I saw it happen."

"What exactly did you see?" Junie was ready to bolt, but I pressed on. "What happened?"

"I was out and about at my usual spot down by the old radio hall and the Earl of Sandwich was there, also as usual."

I nodded to let her know I was following her. The old radio hall was a dance studio from the fifties that had been converted into trendy condos. The Earl of Sandwich was a repeater ghost who spent all his time reenacting eating a hoagie in the courtyard just outside the hall. "And then what happened?" I coaxed.

"Well, the Earl was just minding his own business, eating his sandwich as he does, when this fella comes walking along all jittery. The next thing I know this, this *thing* jumps up out of nowhere and grabs the Earl and sucks him up like a Hoover. Just like that, no more Earl. Well, I burned rubber getting out there, let me tell you."

"What did this henchman look like?"

Junie shivered. "Like nothing I've ever seen. I don't know where to begin to describe him."

"Was he short and round with wrinkled, grey skin and spindly arms and legs?" Max asked, speaking for the first time since Junie's appearance.

Junie smiled at him. "Why yes, Daddy-O, that's him to a T. How did you know?" She narrowed her eyes in thought. "Hey, wait a minute. You can see me too? There's two of you?"

"It's just temporary," Max replied, but it was too late. Junie was gone.

"Crap! I bet she's gone to blab to all the others. We should try and get out of here." I stuck my head out to see what part of the service they were at. "Perfect timing! They're at the crackers and wine part. Let's duck out and wait for Father Mike at the back of the church."

We slipped out of the chapel and made our way through the few stragglers still getting out of their seats to go and get in the Communion line that had formed down the centre aisle of the church. As we went, the air around us filled with ghosts, swooping down from the rafters.

"Hey! It really is her!"

"Junie said he can see us too."

"Harry! Harry, I have to ask—"

"Hey, new guy—"

The ghosts hovered around us, vying for our—mostly my—attention. I fought through them, my skin tingling the whole way.

"Harry!"

"Harry!"

"Harry!"

"Argh!" I whisper-shouted the moment we were out of the nave and into the narthex. "Will you all just can it!"

"But, Harry!"

"I want—"

"Could you just—"

"Harry, I—"

They circled around us, closing in. It was like being at the centre of a snowstorm. I was surrounded by a swirling mass of white that blocked my view of anything else. My skin felt like pins and needles from the electric buzz they were creating around me. I glanced at Max beside me. His eyes were wide in wonder, but it didn't look like he was feeling the same effects I was.

"Harry, can't you—"

"I need you to—"

"*No!*" I yelled, and then checked myself. Several people in the pews closest to the back of the church turned to frown at us. "No," I said again more quietly. "Be gone! Your time on this plane is over. Leave, I compel you." I pushed the ghosts away with my power. I didn't want them near me any longer.

Father Mike's voice echoed through the church. "Go in peace. Amen," he said, just as a blinding flash of light burst out of the narthex, rippling across the church to the sanctuary. The lights hanging above swung slightly back and forth as if a great wind had rushed by. As quickly as it appeared, the light was gone, the swirling host of ghosts with it.

The silence in the foyer was deafening, and then everyone in the church started to speak at once. I looked at Max across the newly cleared void. His eyebrows arched, and he gave me a wide-eyed stare.

"Be gone?" He quirked a smile.

I shrugged. "I sort of got caught up in the moment." Not to mention I'd seen *The Exorcist* one too many times.

***

Despite the cold, I needed to get some fresh air after my unintentional banishment of the ghosts taking refuge in the church, so Max and I headed out to the parking lot to wait for Father Mike. As you can imagine, the congregation was all abuzz over the explosive finale they thought the priest had provided.

"It will be standing-room-only next service," Max joked.

"Yeah, I guess. They'll be disappointed though," I replied, shaking my head. "I don't plan on a repeat performance."

Father Mike seemed to be taking it all in stride, oblivious to his new rock star status. He stood by the doors, clasping hands and patting backs, bidding everyone goodbye.

Suddenly, a chorus of shouts rang out across the parking lot.

"Now what?" I muttered, turning to see what was causing the commotion.

A group of men were escorting (more like dragging) a man towards Father Mike. The man was thrashing and yelling, refusing to enter the church, but there were enough burly men in the group to force their reluctant captive along.

Father Mike stepped towards the man who started to wail, the sound changing to a terrified shriek when the padre reached into his cassock and pulled out a familiar little bottle (the guy must carry that stuff around everywhere). When the holy water touched the man's forehead he gasped, his body going rigid.

I gasped too, not because of the man, but because of what I saw crawling out of him.

"What the—?" I blinked, not believing my eyes, but it was still there. I turned to Max. "Do you see that?"

"See what?" He squinted towards the mob and the man who had started to convulse. "I don't see anything, other than the obvious."

I frowned at him and turned back to the scene before me. The group had lowered the man to the ground, unsure what to do during their captive's seizure. They were completely oblivious to the small, grey creature clawing its way out of the man's body. I don't mean like in the movie *Alien* when the monster exploded out of the guy's chest, it was more subtle than that, of a metaphysical nature, like the creature had been wearing the man like a suit and was now trying to wiggle out of him like a pair of wet jeans.

"Harry?" Max's voice sounded alarmed. "Harry, you're glowing."

"What?" I looked over my shoulder and started in surprise. My katana was glowing, the light escaping out the top of the sheath. Shocked, I turned back to watch as the little grey man, it must be a daemon of some kind, finally worked himself clear and hopped a few steps away from the crowd that had surrounded the fallen man's body.

"Harry?" Max asked again, concern in his voice. "What's going on?"

The creature, as if hearing Max, turned and looked at me. He cackled gleefully, and then spun around, running away across the parking lot.

I shook my head, rousing from my shock. "C'mon! We have to try and catch him." Not waiting for Max, I dashed down the steps after the daemon, but I was too late. He had disappeared.

***

It took some explaining, but we brought Father Mike up to speed. He was pretty open-minded for a norm. I guess if you spend your life preaching the word of a god that claims to have created the earth in seven days it helps to be open-minded. Funny, though, many of the people I meet who are religious seem to lack that quality. Lucky for us, Father Mike had it in spades.

"The little grey man was an imp," Max was saying. "They're considered minor creatures in the hierarchy and generally are slaves to the more powerful daemons and demons.

Father Mike nodded, and sipped his tea, taking a moment to process everything we had told him. We were sitting in his office. As you can imagine, after the grand finale I inadvertently provided for Mass, it took quite a bit of time to get the congregation to disperse, so Father Mike had offered us some refreshment in his study while we talked.

"Demons only exist to create chaos and harm," the priest said. He rose from his seat and walked across the room to a bookshelf. He perused the titles for a minute or two then pulled out an old book with a tattered cover. "What did you say the demon told you his name was, Harry?" He thumbed through the pages of the book carefully.

"Seth," I replied.

"Oh yes, Seth." His finger scanned up and down the pages until he found what he was looking for. "Yes, here it is. It's in Latin, so I'll translate." He skimmed the page, silently reading, his lips moving as he translated the text for himself. "Yes, yes, I remember now. Seth, or Set as he is often known, was the Egyptian storm god. He was said to be the son of Nut and Geb, and the brother of Osiris."

"Osiris!" Well, that couldn't be a coincidence.

I gave Father Mike an apologetic look and then waved at him to continue.

"Yes, where was I? Oh, here we go. Set was jealous of his brother Osiris and had him killed. When Isis, Osiris's wife, found out, she searched until his body was found. Afraid that Isis would raise Osiris from the dead, Set stole the body and had it cut into pieces and spread across Egypt."

"Wow, sounds like a really nice guy. How did he end up a demon of hell though?"

Father Mike continued to read from the book. "It says here that Set was defeated by Horus, the son of Isis and Osiris, and condemned by the other gods. He serves in hell as a lieutenant of Asmodeus and also goes by the name Zaebos." He flipped the pages back towards the front of the book and started translating again. "Asmodeus is one of the seven princes of hell under its king, Lucifer. According to this, Asmodeus has seventy-two legions of demons that serve him."

"I guess old Seth is making a power play to move up in the ranks."

Max held out a hand to Father Mike. "May I?" he asked, indicating the book.

"Do you read Latin, Mr. Hart?"

"*Sed ego modicum patiuntur*."

Ha! The show off. I rolled my eyes at him.

I hadn't a clue what Max said, but Father Mike understood and, chuckling, handed over the book. "You may borrow that for a while, if you'd like."

"Thanks, I'll take good care of it." Max smiled and held the book reverently against his chest. I rolled my eyes again. He was as big of a book nerd as Tess. I'd have to make sure to tell her that.

"All right then," said Father Mike, clapping his hands together. "Let me see that sword of yours."

Chapter Fifteen

"Thanks for the ride, Max. You sure you don't want to come in for something to eat?" I hopped out of Max's Lexus in front of the coffee shop and reached in to grab my katana. I hadn't bothered to put it back on after Father Mike examined it. It hadn't glowed again, but the Father didn't seem all that surprised about it—it was a sign that I was doing "God's work," according to him. He even carried my sword back out to the font in the sanctuary of the church and blessed it with holy water.

"Take a rain check? I've got somewhere I need to be."

"Sure, no problem." I waggled my eyebrows at him. "Gotta hot date or something?"

"What? No! I..." Max blushed and he looked a little flustered. "No, I'm just going to the gym. I have my first sparring session with Tess."

Well, well, well. Wasn't that interesting? The signs were all there that Max was crushing on Tess as much as she was crushing on him. I smiled at him, but then my thoughts turned to Tess's close call from the other night and I began to worry. "Do you think she's up for that after what happened at the nightclub?"

"Don't worry. I'll keep an eye on her and make sure she doesn't over do it." His face warmed again.

Oh yeah, he'd keep an eye on her all right.

***

"I've got my eye on you, old wolf," I said, narrowing my eyes at Nash. "That's my butter tart. You already ate yours."

We were snuggled up in front of the TV for another movie (*Kingdom of Heaven*, Nash's pick, but one I could definitely support). Our bellies were full of Christina's homemade chili and cornbread that she had dropped off earlier and a tray full of baking I had commandeered from the coffee shop.

"How do you get that? I counted four tarts on the plate to start."

"Yeah, one for you and three for me," I replied, giving him a look that said it made perfect sense to me.

His eyebrows arched and he opened his mouth to speak just as his phone rang. "Damn," he growled, grabbing the offending device and thumbing it on. "Yeah, Nash here."

As Nash sat up to listen to his call, I scrambled to my feet and stole the tart from the plate, skipping to the other side of the coffee table. I held my prize up and smirked at him as I brought it to my lips to take a little nibble. "Mmmmm," I moaned.

Nash glowered, still listening to his phone. It appeared to be a rather one-sided conversation, or else Nash wasn't able to get a word in edgewise. He narrowed his eyes when he saw the tart in my hand, and pointed his finger at me.

I shook my head, the smirk turning into a full-blown smile. I licked my lips, and then took a big bite out of the tart, moaning again in satisfaction as I savoured the sweet, ooey goodness. Sure, I was playing it up a bit to tease Nash, but Isaac really does make butter tarts that are to-die-for. Trust me on this.

"Yes, sir. Of course. I'll see you in an hour, sir." Nash ended his call and tossed his phone on the sofa beside him. "Minx, you are in so much trouble," he growled, springing to his feet and stepping around the table towards me.

Yikes! I scrambled backwards, shoving another bite of tart into my mouth, trying to eat without laughing as I put myself on the far side of the kitchen table, keeping it between me and the now-grinning Nash. He pursed his lips and mock-glared at me, trying to keep the smile off his face, and then began to stalk me, looking positively predatory.

I feinted left and right, holding the last piece of tart, the syrupy middle dripping down my fingers. "You want it? Come and get it," I challenged.

I expected Nash to round the table and come at me, but I should have known better than to challenge an alpha. His eyes flashed, and with a leap he was over the table and on me before I could even blink. His momentum took us both to the floor, Nash's arm cradling my head to protect me. With a grunt of satisfaction, he straddled my hips and captured my hand, eating the last of the butter tart (that I had somehow miraculously managed to hold on to), licking my fingers clean in the process.

"Mmmm," he purred, sucking my finger back into his mouth, "that tastes good."

I swallowed as the fire was stoked somewhere south of my belly button, and squirmed underneath him. "Maybe you better take another sample," I said, pointing to the corner of my mouth. "I think I have some here too."

Nash grinned and released my hand, folding himself over my body, his chest pressing against mine. He pinned my arms above my head and then transferred their captivity to one hand so he could use the other to grasp my chin. He made a show of examining my mouth and then tilted my head to the side, bringing his face close to mine. "Yes, I think you might be right," he whispered, his voice low and rough.

When his tongue rasped across the corner of my mouth, sending a shiver down my spine, I moaned. His eyes widened for a split second before his mouth descended, his tongue plunging in to ravish mine.

I felt him hard against me, and I slipped my hand from his to reach down between our bodies, tugging at the button on his jeans.

With a groan, Nash tore his mouth from mine. "I have to go in to work," he said, his voice flat.

"Not even time for a quickie?" I slid my hand past his waistband. Mmmm, he was going commando today. Nice.

"Only if I take you right here, right now," he grumbled and my nether region quickly agreed.

There was a quiet sound at the door and then a muffled voice said, "I'm coming in! Your private bits better all be covered."

The door swung open, and Tess stomped in, shaking off a few flakes of snow. She kicked off her boots and hung up her jacket without even looking at us and then headed across the room to the stairs.

"Hi, Tess!" I shouted after her, trying not to giggle.

"And you wonder why I need my own place," she griped without slowing her pace.

***

Tess's arrival kiboshed whatever sort of quickie Nash and I were going to have, and since she had thumped off to her room in a mood and Nash had gone into the office, I suddenly found myself all alone with nothing to do.

Reluctantly, I pulled out several of the ancient books Isaac had found on necromancy. I still had to figure out what all I needed to do to raise William Koenig's zombie. With everything going on, I hadn't been able to spend much time doing research.

I was ready to call it quits for the night when Bryce's computer screen blinked on.

"Hey, Harry," Bryce's computerized voice called out through the speakers. *"I've got something for you."*

I sat down at the desk in front of the computer and gave a little wave to the camera perched on top. "Hey, Bryce. What's up?"

"I've been playing around with the recording from the GhostCam 3000, trying to clean it up a bit, and there's something you've got to hear."

The robot animation Bryce often put up on the screen popped into view, holding a sign that said *One Moment Please*. After about ten seconds, he dropped the sign and picked up another one. This time it said *Don't Get Your Panties in a Twist*. I couldn't help but chuckle.

Suddenly the screen went black, and then a window popped opened. A video of the inside of Susan Cooper's house started to play.

"I'm going to fast forward to the end," Bryce said.

The video sped forward, stopping just as the whirling vortex of books and cups came to a halt. Up until this point, the volume had been muted, but as the amorphous, red-and-yellow blob that was Darryl Leroy Sutcliffe appeared again and the vortex came to a sudden stop, Bryce turned up the volume so I could hear.

On the recording, Tess yelped in surprise just as Darryl's tremulous voice asked, "*What's happening*?"

"You need to leave now, Darryl. You don't belong here."

"I-I…yes, I need to go."

There was another pause in the sound on the recording, and then I heard a small shuffling, followed by Tess's, "*What the fuck's happening, Harry*?"

At this point in the recording, I remembered that I had felt something weird, a sudden chill in the room before there was a draw of energy on my aura. I still didn't know what happened, and truthfully, I had sort of forgotten all about it until Bryce started playing the video, so what I heard next chilled me to the bone.

"*Well, well, well. What do we have here*?" The voice was neither mine nor Darryl's, the Southern drawl becoming more pronounced as the speaker continued. "*Don't you look like a right tasty, little morsel*?"

"Omigod!" I stared at the computer screen in shock. "Play that part over again!"

Bryce complied, and as I watched, or rather, listened, the tiny hairs on the back of my neck stood up. My stomach clenched, and for a moment I thought I was going to lose my dinner.

"I know that voice," I said, shaking my head in denial.

"There's a bit more," Bryce said. *"Do you want to hear it?"*

"Play it," I replied, feeling numb.

The recording started to play again, and Seth's distinctive voice purred, *"So nice of y'all to open this handy little window for me here. It's like, what is it called? Oh yes, drive-thru."*

"No!" Darryl cried out on the recording *"Who are you? Wait! Stop!"*

"Stop it, Bryce. Stop the recording." I couldn't listen anymore. I knew the rest. And now I had an explanation for why Darryl sounded so terrified when it came time for him to cross over. Because he didn't. Instead, his soul was taken by the creature that I now knew as Seth, a.k.a. the Collector.

Chapter Sixteen

The air was filled with laughter and music, lights flashed and bells rang.

I was surrounded, the press of people crowding in on me.

After a moment's disorientation, I realized where I was—back at Wishes—but thankfully it was only a dream. It had to be. How else could I be there? Nash's team had the club shut down. No one could enter or leave, and yet it seemed to be in full swing.

I looked around to orient myself and discovered I was very close to the fountain that had eluded my inspection last time. Elbowing through the crowd, I made my way towards it. Unlike my previous visit, there no longer seemed to be any sort of enchantment preventing me from drawing close. Although perhaps there still was for everyone else because as I shoved my way through the dancing, writhing bodies, the crowd thinned, and I stumbled forward when I encountered no further resistance. I caught myself before I fell flat on my face and came to a stop in a space in front of the fountain, devoid of anyone but me. Curiosity won over caution, and I turned my attention to the watery monument, ignoring the rest of my surroundings.

As I had surmised from my last visit, the fountain looked like something more at home in Rome than a warehouse full of horny, dancing norms. Carved from marble, there was a large central figure rising up from the middle. Definitely male—it was kind of hard to miss his massive semi-erect penis and set of *cojones* that would do a horse proud—the statue had a body to match his manly bits, muscular to the point of being beefy. He had a full and flowing head of wavy hair and a long, bushy beard that would make even the most enthusiastic lumbersexual proud. The oddest thing about him (*cojones* not withstanding) was the small brazier he held in one hand. The flame burned brightly, dancing in its marble bowl to the tune of the splashing water. I had never seen the two elements, fire and water, juxtaposed like that before.

Still, it wasn't until I looked closer at the rest of the fountain and the remaining statues that I began to feel uneasy. From a distance, the central figure appeared to watch over the other scantily clad statues as they danced and cavorted in front of him. On closer inspection, however, it was much more disturbing. The figures were men and women of all shapes and sizes. They were naked and the men were much more modestly endowed. Their faces were contorted in grimaces of pain and terror because what I had mistaken for wisps of clothing were actually flames licking up the sides of their bodies. The smaller statues were writhing in pain as they were burned alive at the feet of the much bigger central statue who wore an unmistakeable look of pleasure. The entire thing was disturbing.

Unable to look at it any longer, I leaned on the side of the basin and gazed down at the water below, only to gasp in surprise. The pool was an eerie glowing blue colour. The water itself appeared to be just water (at least the stuff spraying out of the various jets around the fountain appeared to be nothing out of the ordinary), but the pool below was teeming with something that appeared almost eel-like, if eels were long, glowing blue, amorphous blobs.

"Why, Harry, sugar, so glad you have finally arrived."

Startled by Seth's voice behind me, I spun, reaching for my katana, but it wasn't there. I looked down at myself. I was dressed Nash's old RPD Academy T-shirt and nothing else. It was what I had worn to bed. Even my feet were bare.

I glanced furtively around me, keeping my eye on Seth. There was no sign of any of his cronies; I was alone with him standing in front of the fountain. He grinned and winked at me. "I thought you were never going to fall asleep and join us."

Say what? Seth's words sent a shiver down my spine. I *was* dreaming. I know I was. So why did it feel so real, and how could I dream such a vivid description for something I had never seen up close?

I peered at the bare skin of my arm and pinched it.

"Ow!"

"Now, sugar, don't go abusing your pretty self."

"I felt that! How could I have felt that? I'm dreaming. I'm not really here."

Seth smiled slyly and shrugged. "Well, you are dreaming, but you are here just the same—at least the important bits."

"That's impossible," I said with more confidence than I felt.

Seth arched his eyebrows at me. "Is it *really* now, Angharad Grainne Russo?"

My name! Of course. Max was worried about what Seth could do with my full name, and now I guess I had found out. I glanced around the packed club. Maybe not as busy as it had been before but still crowded. "Are all these people dreaming like me?"

"All your dreams come true at Wishes," Seth replied with a toothy grin.

So that's why Nash and the SRU only found about thirty people in the club the night they raided it. The rest of the people weren't physically there. They were astral projections—their souls had left their physical bodies at home and had come out to play. When Nash and Max had broken in, they only entered the warehouse in our realm. The pocket realm had remained hidden from them.

"What do you want from me?" I asked suspiciously.

Seth made a clicking sound with his tongue, shaking his head. "Harry, may I call you Harry?" He continued without waiting for an answer. "Harry, let's not be hasty here. We can be friends. I just know it. Join me for a little libation." He gestured with his hand like he was Vanna White, and a small round wicker table and chairs appeared (in white, of course).

"No, thanks." I crossed my arms and stared at him, unwilling to move.

Seth's eyes locked with mine in a game of who would blink first. After a minute, his blue eyes narrowed, and then they changed. It was like he blinked, but didn't. Instead of his eyelids closing over his eyes like they would for a normal blink, a clear membrane slid across the surface of his eyes from the corner of his nose outwards, and his pupils elongated until they were tiny upright slits of black in an iris of yellow.

"Please, I do insist." He smiled at me with his lizard eyes and then blinked and it was if it had never happened.

He stepped towards me, reaching out, and I jumped back. "Don't touch me."

"Come now, sugar. You already know I don't need to touch you to get a taste."

As if to demonstrate, the air around me cooled as something pulled on my aura, siphoning energy from me. I sucked in a surprised breath, and my knees buckled.

"Sit," Seth said, his voice hard.

The wicker chair appeared behind me, and I sank into it, more because if I didn't, I would fall on my ass than because he told me to.

Seth sat in the chair across the small table from me, looking pleased as punch. "There now, isn't this nice?" He picked up the pitcher of lemonade that wasn't there a moment ago and poured two glasses. "Have a drink. You have my word as a gentleman that it is only lemonade."

With a shaky hand, I reached out to the glass to take it. "I'll hold you to your word Set Zaeb—"

"*SILENCE!*" Seth roared at me, casting away the pitcher so it landed on the floor with a crash. "Where did you learn that name?" he asked, his voice dripping with menace.

I set the glass back down with deliberation and looked at him squarely. "I have my resources," I replied, trying to play it cooler than I felt. My heart was pounding in my chest. I struggled to slow it down and restore some calm, hoping to buy time while I strengthened my shields. I didn't feel like being a Harry-flavoured milkshake again. "What I don't understand is why you're here and not your brother."

"Asar!" Seth all but spit out the name. "My brother was nothing more than a mewling, puny king. He thought he was a god, and yet now he is nothing but dust, and I shall be an Emperor in Duat."

Whoa, talk about your career aspirations.

"Does your boss know about your plans to usurp him? Somebody better tell Asmodeus not to go to any dinner parties with you."

For a split second, the skin around Seth's eyes tightened and I could have sworn I saw fear. Wow, Asomdeus must be a real badass if this badass was afraid of him. Suddenly Seth smiled, his pearly white teeth glowing under the lights. "You know, darlin', you are awfully bold for someone in your situation. I like it."

"And what situation would that be? The one where you plan on sucking me dry like you nearly did my friend, Tess? Like you're doing to all these people?" I waved a hand out over the nearby crowd. They were dancing and partying, oblivious to the danger they were in.

"Ahhh, the dear Therese Fuentes. She is a tasty morsel and oh so easy to read." Seth leaned back in his chair as if reminiscing. "So many of these pathetic souls come here seeking fame and fortune, full of lust and greed. They want it all. But not your dear Miss Tess. All she wants is to be loved. She dreams of finding a mate like your Cian Nash."

I frowned at Seth's use of Nash's name. What else had he found out from Tess? Poor Tess. I knew she was having a hard time with the idea that I was mated to Nash. Not that she was jealous of me or anything. I know she's happy for me. But I also know it is her deepest, darkest desire to be mated and have a family of her own. I scowled at Seth. How dare he use her like that?

"So that's what you do? Suck people dry while feeding them illusions of their dreams coming true? Like you did to Tess?"

Seth appeared unaffected by my accusations and merely shrugged. "Your friend was never in danger. The dual-natured cannot be bought, but they do make for a tasty snack. And they recuperate so quickly." With a flash of his teeth Seth tipped his chin at the crowd beyond, and I followed his gaze.

"Tess?" I rose to my feet, pushing back the chair. "Tess!"

Tess, dressed in an extremely short, tight red dress, was dancing in the centre of a mob of men, booty bumping and grinding, running her hands all over herself and them. Most of the men were dressed in variations of the white leather fetish wear that seemed to be the uniform for Team Daemon.

"What is she doing here?" I glared at Seth. "What are you doing? Send her back."

"She's here of her own free will, just like all the others." He waved a hand out over the club. I looked around at all the people—men and women, many acting out similar scenes to Tess's. A woman who appeared to be in her fifties was being double-teamed by a couple of daemons disguised as buff young men, an expression of pure pleasure on her face. The daemons were kissing her arms and neck, sucking her life force. Suddenly, the woman gasped in shock and keeled over. The daemons backed away, letting her fall, apparently indifferent to her distress. Before her body hit the floor she disappeared. A second later, an imp popped into view beside me, and I jumped back in surprise. The imp ignored me, running around my chair to the fountain. He leaned over the edge of the basin and proceeded to regurgitate a glowing blue mass into the water below, before popping out of sight. WTF?

"Ahhh," Seth purred. "Another for my collection. How nice."

I gaped at him. That's what the glowing blue things were? Souls? I quickly found Tess in the crowd again. "Tess!" I shouted, trying to get her attention. "Wake up!" I moved to go to her only to find my way blocked. The beefy goons from my previous visit were standing in front of me like a wall of muscle between me and Tess.

"We are not finished with our conversation yet, sugar. Do sit down."

"No. I have nothing to say to you." I made a move to dash around the goons, and the closest one stepped forward, holding a black police baton. He gave it a flick, allowing the baton to expand to its full length, and smiled at me menacingly. I hesitated. I was dreaming, so could he really hurt me? The realization that I had felt it when I pinched myself seemed answer enough for me.

"Don't be tiresome, sugar." Seth sounded bored. "Sit yourself down." At his words, the goon squad advanced, all brandishing batons. Where was my flaming sword when I needed it?

With a scowl at Seth, I flopped back down in my chair and crossed my arms. "I have nothing to say to you until Tess is back home safe."

Seth rolled his eyes with much exaggeration. "Fine. She's gone. She's of no use to me anyway." He waved his hand, and the wall of goons parted. Tess blinked out of sight and I breathed a sigh of relief.

"And you promise not to lure her back here or let her come back here ever again." I leaned forward so only he could hear me. "Swear on your name, Set Zaebos."

Seth's eyes became deadly, the reptilian pupils snapping back into place as his body seemed to swell, the muscles in his arms and neck bulging, until he towered over me from his seat. "You will not use that name," he roared. He reached out a bloated hand, the veins bulging under his skin, as if to grab me by my nonexistent collar, and I steeled myself against the draw on my aura. I waited, holding my breath, but nothing happened. A surprised look came over Seth's face and I blinked, realizing my shields had held. He wasn't able to steal my life force. Seth's eyes widened and then quickly narrowed as he scowled at me. "I swear, on my name, Set Zaebos, your friend Therese Fuentes will be safe. I will not lure her here again."

Trying not to push my luck, I did my best not to appear gloating and simply nodded as I slumped back in my chair. "I'll take that lemonade now," I said calmly.

Seth straightened his clothes, his body returning to normal. A new pitcher of lemonade appeared on the table. Now I just had to kill time until Tess woke me up. I was sure she would figure things out and know I was in trouble. If not, Nash was bound to be home soon. He'd wake me for sure.

We sat in silence for a few minutes, drinking lemonade, like we were sitting on the porch on a sunny, summer day. It was weird to say the least.

"Now isn't this nice?" Seth said, laying his Southern accent on thick, drawing out the word *nice*. "You've got gumption, sugar. I'll give you that. That's why you and I will make a mighty fine team."

I coughed, trying not to choke on the lemonade I had just sipped. What the hell was he talking about? Team up with him? Me? Time for more stall tactics.

"Why do you talk with a Southern accent?" I replied, ignoring his comments. "I know the devil went down to Georgia and all, but it's not like you're actually from the south."

Seth looked at me in surprise and then smiled. "Well now, sugar, I'm a perfect Southern gentleman, don't you know? It puts people at ease, it does. 'Specially the ladies." He winked at me.

"And the white fetish wear and roller skates?" I asked, continuing to stall. I arched an eyebrow at him. "Did you last visit this plane in the seventies or something?"

Seth's congenial expression faltered, and his eyes narrowed. "What are you up to, sugar?"

"*Come on, Harry! Wake up!*" I silently willed myself. "*Wake up, wake up, wake up.*" It wasn't working...or was it? I felt a flutter in my belly, the kind I feel when Nash is nearby. As inconspicuously as I could, I looked around, but there was no sign of Nash, which was sort of a relief because I wasn't sure what good he would do me if he showed up dreaming like Tess.

"Enough with the nonsense questions," Seth said impatiently. "Let us get down to the nitty-gritty." He leaned forward, and I self-consciously drew back in my seat. He smiled at me, and his teeth appeared pointy, like an alligator's. He blinked, and his eyes instantly matched his teeth.

I gaped at the transformation. He looked truly like something from out of this world. "What nitty-gritty?" I asked, my voice unfortunately sounding a bit shaky. "What do you want from me?"

"Why, to make you an offer you simply can't refuse, of course," Seth replied, the Southern gentleman making a reappearance. He winked a baby-blue eye at me. "I want you to come work for me."

"Doing what?" I was equally horrified and intrigued.

"To do what you do best of course, darlin'. Open me a portal."

Before I could reply, a shiver ran down my spine. A completely inappropriate shiver. It wasn't disgust like the situation warranted, but rather sexual arousal. I let out a long, slow breath as another wave followed the first.

"*Harry*! *Harry, wake up*!"

Shocked, I looked around. I was sure I heard Nash's voice. I stole a glance at Seth. He was studying me through narrowed eyes. I bit my lip, pretending to be thinking about his proposal as another tremor pulsed over me. Oh boy, this was weird.

"Are you all right there, honey pie?" Seth's eyebrows drew together as he examined me. He took a deep breath. "You seem a little peaked"

"*Harry, goddammit, wake up*!"

I jumped, turning towards where I thought I heard Nash's voice again. My body felt flushed and needy. I shifted uncomfortably in my seat.

"What's going on here?" Seth rose from his chair, his expression turning angry. "I am not yet done with you. Don't you go anywhere now, sugar."

He grabbed my bare arm in a fierce grip, just as an overwhelming sense of vertigo took me. I cried out in pain as his hand burned my skin and suddenly everything went black.

***

"Fuck!" I sat up, flailing my arms, gasping for air.

"Harry!" It was Tess.

"It's okay, minx. I've got you. I've got you." Nash's voice was right in my ear.

I slowly opened my eyes and looked around. I was in my room and it was still dark outside. I was lying on my bed with Nash's arms around me, the sheets twisted around my bare legs. Tess, Max and Isaac were all staring down at me with concern.

"Omigod, Harry! I was so scared. We couldn't wake you up. It's been hours!" Tess rushed towards me to give me a hug, stopping short as Nash's arms tightened around me, a low growl rumbling from his throat. She dipped her head and backed up a step, avoiding eye contact with Nash.

Normally I would be pissed at Nash's alpha bullshit, but the sexual arousal racing through my body hadn't lessened now that I was awake. Instead it felt amplified, like I was going to spontaneously combust at any minute. Worse, I could hear and smell the blood coursing through Nash's veins, and I was overwhelmed by an aching hunger to taste it.

"Out!" I said, my voice cracking. "Everyone who isn't Nash, get out."

"Harry?" Tess gaped at me in confusion.

"Tess, I'm sorry. We'll talk later, but you need to get out of this room right now."

Isaac gave me a thoughtful look, and his nostrils flared. He could smell my sexual arousal, and for once I didn't care that he was sniffing me, as long as it meant everyone got the hell out of the room. "Come, Tess. Let us give Harry and Nash some time alone." He placed a hand on her arm, pulling her towards the door.

"But..." Tess backed up a step and yanked her arm from Isaac's grasp.

Max chuckled. He had figured out what was happening too. "Let's go, Tess. I have a few more questions for you."

"But we haven't heard what happened to Harry," Tess replied.

"There will be time for that later. I think Harry has...um, more important things on her mind right now."

"What could be more important than...?" Tess's voice trailed off, and she took a deep breath. "Seriously? You're going to do that now?" She rolled her eyes and then spun on her heel, stomping out the door while muttering under her breath. Max trailed close behind her.

"We will see you tonight, Harry," Isaac said as he followed them out the door, pulling it closed behind him.

"I thought they would never leave," Nash said as the door clicked shut.

I turned in his arms, taking him by surprise as I pushed him to the bed. "Shut up and get your clothes off." I grabbed at his shirt, yanking it off over his head.

Nash laughed. "Okay, okay." He pushed my hands away from his pants where I had been trying unsuccessfully to undo them. "Here, let me get that." He deftly unbuckled his belt and opened the fly of his khakis. "I guess using the mate mark to wake you had an unexpected side effect."

"Omigod, Nash. I am so horny. If I don't fuck you right now, I swear I'm going to explode."

With a growl, Nash reached for me, pulling me down on top of him, his mouth on mine. My hands went to the bottom of my T-shirt and I ripped it off, relishing in the feel of skin against skin as my mouth found his again, my breasts pressed against him.

After a few minutes, I slid off him and grabbed the bottom of his pants, stripping them off his legs. I jumped back on the bed, straddling his thighs and wrapped a hand around his hard length and stroked.

Nash sat up and reached for me. "Slow down, minx. Let me—"

"No," I growled, shoving him back on the bed. "We're doing it my way right now." I gave him a couple more strokes then slid up his hips, rising on my knees. I lined up our bodies and then pushed down to impale myself on him.

"Ahhhh, fuuuuckk," Nash groaned.

"Yessss," I moaned at the same time.

The ache between my legs became a fire as I began to piston my hips, our bodies grinding together. Nash put his hand on my hips, guiding my movements as he bucked his body in rhythm with mine.

I grabbed his arm and ripped the leather bracer from it, holding his wrist to my face. I could smell the tangy copper of the blood pulsing beneath his skin. My fangs fell into place so smoothly I didn't even notice until they were suddenly there. I inhaled deeply against Nash's wrist and looked down at him. Nash's face was filled with a hunger to match my own, his eyes wide as he watched me lick his wrist. The veins were like bulging blue ropes under his skin, and with each stroke of my tongue I took a small taste of his life essence. Nash groaned, enjoying each tiny, pleasurable pull.

"Fuck, Harry. I'm so close. Just do it already." He shoved his free hand between our bodies, sliding his fingers between my legs.

I gasped at the extra stimulation and brought his wrist back to my mouth. My fangs slid through his skin like a hot knife through butter and as the first drop of blood touched my tongue, my orgasm exploded across my body. With each pulse of blood, I poured my ecstasy out and into Nash, sharing what I was experiencing. Nash's body jerked as his own orgasm followed, and he wrapped an arm around my waist, holding me firmly as he pumped his hips against me.

Finally spent, Nash fell back against the bed. I licked the two dainty little marks on his wrist, sealing them, and then fell down beside him, breathless. Nash pulled me up against him, and I wrapped my leg over his, my head on his chest. His heart was pounding to match mine. He tugged at the sheets and settled them over me.

After a few minutes, Nash sighed, his arm tightening around me. "Fuck, minx. You had me worried. When Tess called me and told me what had happened and that she couldn't wake you up..." Nash ran a hand through his hair and let out a deep breath. "What the hell happened to you?"

I quietly told Nash everything I could remember. I knew I would have to tell it all again for Tess and the others, but Nash deserved to hear it first. As I finished my story, getting to the part where I woke up in Nash's arms, Nash reached for the arm I had draped across him, pulling it closer to have a look.

"Shit, Harry. Doesn't this hurt?" He sat up in bed, bringing me with him.

I looked down in surprise at my wrist. There was a bright-red handprint like a sunburn across my skin where Seth had grabbed me.

I shook my head. "No, it doesn't hurt at all." Which was a relief. The burn was such an angry red colour it should probably hurt like, if you will pardon the pun, hell. At least I didn't end up...

"Omigod!"

I scrambled out of bed and gaped at Nash. "I completely forgot! There was a woman. I think she was killed in her sleep. You need to find out for me."

"What?"

"I'll explain in the shower. Get your ass out of bed, old wolf." I glanced over my shoulder and winked at him. "I'll make it worth your while."

Chapter Seventeen

A woman had indeed died in her sleep that night. It took some cajoling on my part to get Nash to let me see police records, but when I reminded him I could just get Bryce to poke around for me, it didn't take long for him to cave. The woman I had seen the night before was Betty Appleton—fifty-five, lived alone—whose body was found when the super of her building had let himself in to fix the dripping faucet she had complained about the day before. The coroner had called it a death due to natural circumstances, listing a heart attack as the cause, despite Betty having no history of heart problems.

More startling was the fact that when we did a bit of snooping, there had been over a dozen deaths of people (all norms) in their sleep attributed to natural causes over the past few weeks. Did they all have a connection back to Seth's club? I set Bryce digging to see what he could find on the potential victims.

"See if you can find a link between all the HRNs too," I said to Bryce after setting him up with his task.

"HRNs?" Nash looked at me in confusion.

"Oh, that's short for Homicidally Rampaging Norm. It's what I've been calling all the weird cases you've been assigned to lately."

Nash snorted. "HRN. I'll have to try that one on Dev. He'll get a kick out of it." He slipped on his worn leather jacket, taking care not to get it hooked on his gun. He crossed the room to where I was sitting behind the desk and pulled me to my feet. "Try and stay out of trouble, will you minx?" he said with a grin.

"Hey! It's not my—"

The rest of my protest was swallowed by Nash's kiss, which had me throwing my arms around his neck and rising up on my toes to meet him. I ran a hand through his hair and grabbed a fistful, giving it a playful tug. "...fault I was dream-napped," I finished breathlessly.

Nash grunted, obviously having his own opinion on my proclaimed innocence but choosing not to elaborate. "Just remember not to go to sleep before Max brings over his protection spell."

Max had called to say he had prepared something for Tess and me to keep us safe in our dreams. I had put a few talismans together myself—using anise, fennel and holly—and they were already tucked safely under our pillows, but I was more than willing to take any extra help I could get to prevent a repeat dreamtime visit with Seth.

After Nash left, I headed down to the coffee shop for my shift. Despite my harrowing night, I was feeling great—fully rested and energized. I wondered how Tess was fairing. She hadn't gotten much sleep the night before but had gone into work anyway. Better to keep busy than risk falling asleep before we had ensured there would be no return visits to Wishes.

The afternoon was uneventful. Well, uneventful except for one strange incident. It was the midafternoon lull, and I was restocking the shelves with clean coffee mugs and espresso shot cups when I noticed my katana glowing. Ever since we had the run-in with Juan Carlo (now a vampire pin cushion), I had gotten into the habit of bringing my sword with me and tucking it under the counter. I had been caught unarmed once, I wasn't going to let it happen again.

It seemed like my caution was paying off when I spotted the thin blue line of light coming from my sword.

Luckily, it was under the counter and nobody but me and Tiffy noticed.

"What does it mean, Harry?" Tiffy reached out to the sword tentatively, pulling her hand back before she touched it.

"Nothing good, I imagine." I slowly straightened from my crouch behind the counter, leaving the sword where it was, and scanned the shop. Three of the people were regulars I recognized, plus my two werewolf guards, Jon and Eric, were on duty. The "Harry-sitters" had arrived, presumably on Nash's orders, shortly after he'd left for work. They had given me a nod and then headed for their usual booth in the corner from where they could watch the whole shop.

There was only one other customer, a woman, who sat with her back to me. There was nothing unusual about her until I noticed she had been pouring sugar from the dispenser into her cup for about a minute or more. The sugar was creating a mountain in the middle of her coffee mug.

Grabbing the carafe I used for refills for some of the regulars, I walked out to her table. "Would you like me to warm up your coffee?" I asked, holding up the carafe.

The woman looked up at me, and I started in surprise. She was so familiar, but I couldn't place her. She also appeared a little, well, a lot weird. Her lipstick had been applied thickly as if she had used it over and over again, not bothering to colour in the lines. Her cheeks were smudged bright red, and her eyelids had been brushed with blue eyeshadow.

The weirdness didn't stop at her face. Her clothes were mismatched and dishevelled, her button-down shirt buttoned incorrectly.

The woman cackled nervously and set the sugar down with a bang. "Nooooo," she said. "I'm fine." Her face tightened in a grimace as she spoke as if the words were painful to say, and that's when I remembered where I knew her from. She was the blonde from the hospital, the one I saw have a near-death experience. I examined her closely. Was she possessed by one of those creepy, little imps? She looked so different from the last time I saw her, playing the slot machines at Wishes. Her head twitched to the right like she had a nervous tic.

"Are you sure you don't need anything?"

Ignoring me, the woman picked up her spoon and stirred the sugary sludge in her cup.

Suddenly she yelled, "No! Leave me alone!" The spoon clattered to the floor. She paused, clearing her throat. "I mean, no thank you, dear." Her voice sounded robotic, and her head ticked to the right several more times. Without warning, she pushed away from the table, sending her coffee cup skittering towards the edge, and headed for the door. I was about to reach out with my telekinesis to keep the cup from smashing, but Jon, one of the Harry-sitters, was already there beside the table, palming the cup.

"What was that about?" he asked, sliding the cup back on the table.

"I'm not sure."

I watched the woman leave. As she exited the shop she turned left towards the city centre, but then she abruptly made an about-face and stalked off to the right. I hurried back over to the counter where Tiffy was giving me a funny look. I pulled out my sword, but the light was gone.

"Weird," Tiffy said.

"You can say that again."

"Weird?" Tiffy replied, her face full of confusion. I guess we still needed to work on teaching her some common expressions.

***

"Thanks, Max," I said, reaching out for the elaborate dreamcatcher. He had made one each for me and Tess. They were about six inches in diameter and had been wrapped using red thread. Max had tied them with several recognizable herbs, including holly and marigold. As my fingers made contact, the magic imbued in the circle zinged across my skin.

"No problem, Harry. Let's get them hung up. I brought some sage to purify your rooms as well." Max patted his black leather satchel.

Tess, who had been pretending to be engrossed in an old episode of *Castle* so that she could avoid talking to Max, suddenly jumped up. "You want to go in my room?"

Max looked uncertain. "Yeah, if that's okay."

"Uh, sure. Just start with Harry's first," she replied as she dashed across the room.

"Do you want a beer or something?" I asked Max. "She's going to need extra time to plow a path for you." I couldn't help but laugh. Tess is the biggest slob I know. Even Mrs. P's brownie magic couldn't tackle her room. Gran had blamed Tess's messy nature on her denning instinct. Now that I think about it, Nash tends to throw all his clothes on the floor too. Maybe it's a werewolf thing.

Max and I sat for a while and enjoyed a beer and some of Hilde's soft German pretzels. Just as we were heading upstairs to cleanse the bedrooms and hang his dreamcatchers, there was a loud *whomp* on the roof above us.

"What was that?" Max turned to me in alarm.

"Don't worry. It's just Isaac announcing his arrival."

"On the roof?"

"Yeah."

"But doesn't he live across the street now?"

"Yep." I nodded, enjoying Max's confusion.

Max's forehead screwed up in thought. "You mean he can fly?"

"It's more of a long leap," Isaac replied drolly as he came down the spiral staircase that led to the roof. He arched an eyebrow at me. "I planned to make lasagna. It will serve a crowd, if necessary."

I smiled at Isaac and then glanced at Max. "You staying for dinner?"

Max blinked, having trouble switching topics because he was still hung up on the whole flying-vs.-leaping thing. He shook his head as if to clear his thoughts. "Yes. That would be nice. Thanks."

I shrugged. "No problem. The least we can do for these babies." I held up the dreamcatchers. They felt all warm and tingly in my hand. I turned back to Isaac. "I guess there's a crowd. Thanks, Isaac."

***

We were enjoying a plate of antipasto and a bottle of Chianti (I can never say that without seeing Anthony Hopkins) after cleansing and protecting both bedrooms. Tess had managed to clean hers up in the extra time we gave her so that the floor was actually visible. She had even made the bed. I was sorely tempted to sidle over to her closet and throw open the doors, but I suspected it would end up looking like something out of a cartoon with an avalanche of clothes crashing down on me. Besides, every time I took a step towards it, Tess would glare at me, muttering something under her breath about shaving my head while I slept. I decided not to chance it.

Nash had called and said he would be by for dinner, so when I heard footsteps on the landing, I hurried over and opened the door.

"Oh. It's you." I frowned at Tomas.

He raised a single dark eyebrow and smiled wryly. "Are you always this polite to your guests, Russo?"

"Only the uninvited ones. The zombie thing is tomorrow. Come back then." I turned, shutting the door in his face. I didn't want to deal with any of Salvador's drama today, and I couldn't think of any other reason for Tomas to be at my door.

"Very funny, Russo." Tomas's voice was muffled through the thick wood.

"Go away, Tomas. I don't want to deal with any vampire stuff today."

"Russo, just open the door."

I stood in front of the door, hoping to hear his footsteps heading back down the stairs. Instead I heard a faint clicking sound, and my phone began to ring. It wasn't a surprise when the ringtone announced it was Salvador calling.

"Hello, Salvador."

"Good evening, Harry," Salvador purred. "You will quit being childish and let Tomas in. That is no way to treat your brother."

"My *what*? Excuse me? My *brother?*" I turned to look at Isaac, who merely shrugged in the same annoying way Salvador often did. "What do you mean he's my brother?"

"But of course, I wasn't aware you did not know this. Just as Diego was a child of Catalina,"—that was the Mariposa's real name—"Tomas is mine. That makes you brother and sister of a sort." I could almost hear the Cheshire-cat-like smile in his voice. "We are one big, happy family now, so let your brother in like a good girl."

I rolled my eyes, even though Salvador wouldn't be able to see them, and opened the door to Tomas's smug grin. With his vampire hearing he hadn't missed a single word.

"Hey, sis."

"Don't call me that."

I stalked away, leaving the door open for him to come in. He paused on the doorstep, scowling, and I started to smile. Now that he was a true vampire, he couldn't come in without my invitation. That meant even though Salvador seemed to be able to come and go as he pleased because he considered the building his, Tomas could not.

"Harry." Salvador admonished as if he knew exactly what was happening.

"Don't stand there all night, fangboy. Come in." I turned away again and spoke into the phone to Salvador. "Why is he here? I really don't have time for any vampire politics right now, Salvador. I'm tired, and I have to get ready for tomorrow."

"Tomas is simply there as my representative. I believe you will be speaking with our dear friend Elder Hart regarding your encounter with the demon last night. I would prefer to be apprised of the situation." There was a chiding tone to his voice. I guess I should have called him and told him what happened.

"Okay, fine. And I'm sorry I didn't call you."

"Apology accepted, *pequeña*."

As usual, the call cut off abruptly. I looked at Tomas, who was standing just inside the doorway. "Well, come in and take your coat off. Leave your boots on the mat so you're not tromping snow around everywhere." I walked back towards the kitchen. "I guess there's one more for dinner, Isaac."

I turned back to Tomas and stared in surprise. He was wearing jeans and a charcoal grey Velvet Underground T-shirt. I had never seen him in anything other than a designer suit.

"Quit undressing me with your eyes, Russo." Tomas grinned.

"It's not...oh, put a sock in it. I didn't recognize you without your suit. Besides, that flirty shit was creepy before, and now it's just plain wrong."

"I never would have taken you for an alt-rock fan," Tess chirped, adding her two cents. "You strike me more of a Lawrence Welk sort of guy."

"What would you know about me, fluff ball?" Tomas turned a sneer to Tess.

"Children, children," Isaac intoned, stemming the protest it appeared Max was about to make, "could you all just put a sock in it?" He gave us a chilly look. "Tess, the salad needs tossing. Harry, we'll need another place set at the table. Max, pour Tomas some wine."

There was a beat while everyone stood stunned at Isaac's parental-like hijacking of the evening, and then we all scurried to do his bidding like the children he accused us of being.

Nash arrived with Dev in tow just as we were about to sit down to eat, and so we rearranged the table to add one more plate and then all chowed down. Just as well Isaac had cooked for a crowd.

Between bites of Isaac's out-of-this-world lasagna (he could give Mama Minetti a run for her money) and bread oozing with butter and chunks of garlic, I rehashed my impromptu and unwanted visit to Wishes the night before.

"The dual-natured cannot be bought…he said those words exactly?" Max sat forward in his chair with interest.

"Yeah, I'm pretty sure that's what he said, that werewolves weren't in any danger from him, but they made tasty snacks."

Max nodded slowly, deep in thought.

"Why?" I asked him impatiently. "Have you figured something out?"

"I believe so. I think I know why there's a barrier keeping vampires out."

"Well, don't keep us in suspense, Professor," Tess replied.

Max quirked a grin and sat back in his chair. I could almost see the professor's robe settling on his shoulders as he began to speak.

"As we have discovered, a small, unstable portal to the Otherworld was opened several months ago. This has allowed a pocket of the other realm to leak into ours. The demon known as Set Zaebos has taken advantage of this opportunity and has been very slowly increasing his hold on the pocket and expanding the realm's boundaries. He's been doing this by stealing life essence from both norms and werewolves."

"We knew that already," Tess complained.

"Right. Well then..." Max grimaced as if trying to think of a way to break a piece of news delicately. "As you may know, the currency of the Otherworld is the soul."

I shifted uncomfortably in my seat. I hadn't known that. I looked across the table at Tess. She seemed just as shocked as I was.

"This, of course, is why norms are so valuable. They have a soul to lose," Max continued.

I saw Isaac straighten in his seat, but Tomas spoke first. "Are you implying, Elder Hart, that vampires have no soul?" Geez, it seemed to be a touchy subject among the fanged set.

"No, of course not," Max replied hurriedly. "What I am getting at is that vampires don't have a soul to barter because their souls are already spoken for...by Hecate." He pronounced the ancient goddess's name as EK-a-tee (the ancient Greek language from which the name is derived has no sound for the letter H) rather than the incorrectly anglicized HEH-kate.

Whoa. This really was a night full of surprises. Hecate, as many norms know even if they do pronounce her name wrong, is the goddess of witchcraft, among other things. Many of the incantations I use, like the more intense protection spells, call upon Hecate's blessing. If vampires were also connected to Hecate, did that mean that witches and vampires were more closely related than I thought? And what the heck did he mean their souls were already spoken for?

"Because their souls are already owned by a goddess with access to hell, vampires can come and go to the Otherworld with no consequence, and since they also feed on the life essence contained in the soul, they're a threat to the demon way of life."

"So that's why Seth has created the barrier to keep vampires out?"

Max shook his head. "I don't think Seth is responsible for the barrier at all. I think it's an organic result of the Otherworld realm being pulled into ours. The barrier keeps vampires out of hell."

"So there's no enchantment to break. The vampires just can't cross over?"

"Yes, but no. There's no enchantment that I can work a counterspell on, but bringing down the barrier should be possible. We just need to close the portal to the Otherworld."

"Oh, is that all?" Tess rolled her eyes, her voice dripping with sarcasm. "Should be a piece of cake."

"Wait. Can we back up a minute?" I put out a hand to stall any arguing about to break out. "What do you mean that vampire souls are already spoken for? You mean my soul belongs to Hecate just because I'm part vampire? I don't get a choice?"

"Well, you can choose not to undergo the ritual after your first death and not become a full vampire, but I doubt if Salvador would honour that request."

I thought of Diego, the Mariposa's son, and how she had forced the change on him after he had lost his mortal life in the Spanish Civil War. Yeah, Salvador wouldn't hesitate to do the same to me.

"You get a choice," Tomas said quietly, his eyes distant as if he was remembering something.

I frowned at him, thinking of all the questions I had about his recent transformation. "I think you and I should talk," I said quietly.

"I don't owe you anything, Russo."

"No, but if you answer my questions, I'll owe you."

"Harry!" Nash growled at me. "Don't indebt yourself to him."

I ignored Nash, keeping my eyes on Tomas. His eyebrows arched, and he tipped his chin up. "Deal," he replied with a grin. "When this demon stuff is done, we'll talk."

The dinner party pretty much broke up after that. Nash continued to glare at me, and Tess kept throwing shy glances at Max. No one was able to come up with an idea of how to close the portal.

"Don't we have to send all the daemons and Seth back to hell first before we close the portal?" Tess asked Max.

"No. They can return to their realm, even without the portal, but they won't be able to reenter ours. If we can just close the portal, they'll probably return on their own once they start to get hungry again."

"So, like a siege? We close the portal, surround the warehouse to keep anyone from getting in and find a way to keep anyone from visiting via their dreams, and then starve the bastards out." It was my turn to sound sarcastic. "Just like Tess said, should be a piece of cake."

Chapter Eighteen

"When we get back to the coffee shop, I want a double-shot, no, a triple-shot, extra hot, extra foam with cream and a squirt of caramel," Tess grumbled. "And cake. I want cake."

"Oh, quit your griping. I'm almost done. Besides, I told you that you could wait in the car." I looked over to where Tess stood stomping her feet against the cold. "*And* I told you to wear your warmer boots." It had turned bitterly cold, and a light dusting of snow had fallen earlier in the day, which was why I was at the cemetery ahead of schedule, sweeping snow from around William Koenig's grave. My original plan had been to use salt to set my protective circle, but with the snow I was worried about melting and the salt getting diluted or washed away. Instead, I was going to set my circle with fire. "You're a werewolf, for Pete's sake," I added, throwing another glance at Tess over my shoulder. "You shouldn't even notice the cold."

Tess brought her bare hands to her mouth and blew on them. "Tell that to my frozen fingers."

I finished clearing the last of the snow and paused to admire my work. I had cleared a circle approximately ten metres in diameter with William Koenig's grave and its impressive angel statue at the centre. Despite believing I would be able to control the zombie once I called it, I decided to err on the side of caution and set a protection circle to prevent the zombie from straying too far. It would also keep the Koenig children and their lawyers from getting too close.

I stepped over to the black duffle bag I had packed with everything I needed for the night's ritual. Pulling out a tall, cylindrical, cardboard dispenser of smokeless rifle powder and starting one foot in from the edge, I painstakingly poured a thick line to create a slightly smaller inner circle of the black gunpowder. Contrary to what you might have watched on an episode of *Looney Tunes*, the line of gunpowder would burn relatively slowly (kind of like a sparkler), although it would throw up enough flame to put on a bit of a show.

As a secondary precaution, I planned to use a timing candle in my spell. Four inches tall and a half inch thick, the candle was hand-dipped by a witch I knew from back home in Aldergrove. Each candle was guaranteed to burn for exactly two hours and had been spelled so it wouldn't blow out by accident. If you wanted to extinguish the candle before the two hours were up, you had to use the magic words "*mali ex fine*" which was the Latin equivalent of "mischief managed"—the candlemaker was a big *Harry Potter* fan and had a whimsical sense of humour. When I raised William Koenig from the grave, I would invoke the spell using the candle. This meant his family would have two hours to talk about whatever they felt they needed to discuss—more than enough time, I hoped—and then William would return to the grave whether I put him there or not.

I turned at the sound of a vehicle pulling up. Isaac and Tomas, who had been patrolling the cemetery, both materialized from out of the dark and took up defensive positions. Isaac relaxed before Tomas did, recognizing Nash's truck.

"There are two limos coming up behind me," Nash said as he stepped out of the truck.

"Good. They're right on time." I leaned into the quick one-armed hug and peck on the cheek that he gave me and turned to Isaac and Tomas. "Remember, once I have the circle set, no one will be able to cross over."

Isaac frowned but kept his misgivings to himself. We had already hashed the issue out and he wouldn't bring it up again. He didn't like that he wouldn't be able to enter the circle and come to my aid if needed. From the look on Nash's face, he was just catching onto that fact himself.

"Tess will be in the circle with me. We can handle whatever happens," I said quickly, before Nash could start an argument by going all alpha male. "I need you three to make sure we don't get any unexpected guests and keep the Koenigs from trying to cross the circle."

Not that it mattered. They could try, but they wouldn't be able to pass. Anyone who touched the circle would end up with a pretty decent electric shock, so I'd rather they just didn't try. Although now that I knew more about the son, William Jr.—Bryce had done some background research for me—it wouldn't upset me one iota if the jerk got a zap.

I really hoped this worked and DeGrasse got whatever it was he needed to legally make sure that Elise Koenig took over the business and not her brother. My opinion of the late, great Koenig Sr. was tarnished after hearing what Bryce had discovered. It seems our dearly departed, well-known philanthropist was a sexist. He overlooked his much smarter and talented oldest child, Elise, in favour of the one with testicles, even though William Jr. had been nothing but a screwup his entire life. Flunking out of two different schools, getting into trouble with the law, the usual things the young, rich and entitled get arrested for—drunk and disorderly, public nudity, destruction of property, driving under the influence. Elise, on the other hand, had been a model student and faithful daughter. First in her class at law school, serving on the boards of two charities, employed by the company but insisting on starting at the ground floor and working her own way up. She had never so much as even had a parking ticket.

The first limo arrived pulling me from my thoughts, followed closely by the second. "Alright! It's show time!" I sounded more eager than I felt. I had butterflies in my stomach like before-performance jitters. Why did I ever agree to do this?

***

"If I ever agree to do this again, just shoot me," I said, leaning close to Tess so only she could hear me. We had been waiting twenty minutes while DeGrasse and William Jr.'s lawyer refereed a sibling squabble. The two had practically launched themselves at each other the moment their cars came to a stop. I had long since tuned out what they were saying, but the gist of it was that Jr. had already started to help himself to the family heirlooms, even though their father's will had yet to be read.

"Enough!" DeGrasse's voice cut through the bickering. "We've held up Ms. Russo long enough. There's been a full accounting of the items in question, and I have taken it upon myself as executor of the estate to have the locks changed on the family manor. We will settle this after the reading of the will."

DeGrasse turned to look at me. "I'm dreadfully sorry for this, Ms. Russo. Do accept my apologies for keeping you waiting."

I nodded, accepting DeGrasse's apology, and then drew closer to the little group as DeGrasse continued.

"If you will allow me to introduce my client, Elise Koenig. And this is her brother, William Koenig Jr., and his attorney, Matt Hayes."

We traded handshakes all around. Elise seemed genuinely friendly and eager while Jr. all but sneered at me, his impatience and skepticism evident.

"I'm sure your lawyers have reviewed everything with you, but I'd like to remind you that what goes on here is confidential. Tonight I'll be attempting to call forth your late father's spirit *in corpus*, better known as a zombie." At this, Jr. didn't even try and cover his derisive laugh. I ignored him. "I just want to go over with you what I will be doing so that you know what to expect."

I looked at DeGrasse, and he nodded to continue. "Okay, first, I'll ask you to wait here until I indicate that you can draw closer. As you can see, I've cleared a large circle around your father's resting place. Please do not attempt to cross into the circle or you could be injured. To begin, I'll cleanse the area by burning some sage. The sage will smoke, but it won't harm you in any way. Immediately after I've completed the cleansing ritual, I'll set a protective circle around the grave. I'll be using a black powder to ignite a small ring of fire. It will spark, but there's nothing to be alarmed about. Once the circle has been set, nothing can get in or out until I break it. This includes the zombie, so you're perfectly safe. Next I'll call forth Mr. Koenig's spirit and reanimate his remains. If you're squeamish at the sight of blood, you might want to look away for a minute during this step. When the zombie has risen and I'm satisfied with the result, I'll signal for you to come closer, but remember not to touch or cross the circle." I paused to let them process everything then waved a hand, indicating Tess. "This is Tess, and she'll be assisting me tonight. Detective Nash from the RPD is also present this evening, and you may notice two of my associates patrolling the cemetery to ensure we don't have any uninvited guests. Do you have any questions?"

"Yeah," Jr. replied, his voice dripping with contempt. "Do you seriously expect us to believe all this mumbo-jumbo?"

"Mr. Koenig," DeGrasse warned. "You've already agreed to this attempt. Mr. Hayes, please suggest to your client that he refrain from speaking if he has nothing informative to contribute."

Hayes pulled Jr. closer and whispered something in his ear. Jr. scowled and tore his arm from Hayes's grasp. "Bloody waste of time and money," he muttered.

"Will my father be able to recognize me? Can I talk to him?" Elise looked at me hopefully.

"Yes, he should have no problem recognizing you and holding a conversation with you." Jr. snorted at this, but as before I chose to ignore him. "Mr. DeGrasse, Mr. Hayes, did you prepare a question for me to ask Mr. Koenig Sr. in order to establish credibility?" I had suggested earlier in the day to DeGrasse that he and Jr.'s lawyer might want to provide me with a question or two that I could ask the zombie. Something only William Koenig would know the answer to in order to prove I was in no way directing his responses.

"Yes, we have." DeGrasse reached into his pocket and pulled out two folded slips of paper. He handed them to me, and I shoved them into my jacket for later.

"Great. Let's get started then."

***

I held the white sage smudge stick above my head and waved my free hand with a flicking motion, pushing the pungent smoke outwards over the circle. I was on my third trip around the perimeter and was preparing to set the protective ring. I glanced over at my audience. DeGrasse and Elise looked on with fascination while Jr. and his lawyer both appeared to be bored. Obviously neither of them had truly bought into the whole idea.

"And now for the show," I said to Tess, nodding at the line of black powder.

I finished my last cleansing pass then brought the compact smoking bundle closer to my mouth. I puffed out several short breaths until the end of the smudge stick glowed orange and a tiny flame licked the edges. Bending down, I touched the burning bundle to the line of black powder. For a moment, nothing happened, and then sparks began to fly and a small flame burst forth. The flame split, slowly crawling around the circle in both directions, burning the black powder as it went. When at last the entire circle had been scored by the fire, I walked to the centre and chanted, letting my magic flow outwards:

"Hecate, Goddess of the Crossroads,
Queen of the Night,
By the dark moon I call you,
By fire I invoke you,
By magic I entreat you,
Cast out your mantle of protection
over all those present,
Keep us from harm until we return to the light."

As I spoke the last word, a sense of calm washed over me like a soft caress of acceptance and my magic melded with the natural energy surrounding us like two waves coming together in sync. I didn't need to feel the tingle of energy at the periphery of the circle to know my invocation had succeeded.

I turned to Tess. "It's set. I'm going to call Koenig now, so you might want to wait behind the headstone until I need you." I thought it was best if we limited the amount of stimulation the zombie had when it first materialized, so I had also positioned the waiting Koenigs out of sight, behind the grave.

Tess nodded and moved behind the statue marking Koenig's resting place while I dug around in my black duffle bag, pulling out the candle and my athame. The hilt instantly warmed to my touch as if the dagger was eager to participate in the upcoming ritual. The six-inch blade was etched with Celtic runes of protection, and the hilt had been carved from ebony, years of use polishing it to a smooth, glossy finish. The knife had been given to me by Gran, and it had belonged to her mother before me.

Tucking the athame into my pants at the small of my back, I came to stand in front of William Koenig's grave, the butterflies that had disappeared with my cleansing ritual returning in full force. I looked self-consciously across the circle where the Koenigs and their lawyers watched with varying degrees of interest. A movement to their left drew my eye, and I saw Tomas leaning against a nearby monument. His arms were crossed and his pose casual, but his eyes were fixed on me intently.

Holding up the candle in front of me, I murmured the quick charm used to light it. As the flame came to life, I heard a soft "Ah" of appreciation from Elise, followed by a cynical snort from Jr. After letting some wax drip from the candle onto the corner of Koenig's headstone, I set the taper down, the quickly cooling wax securing it in place. The flame flickered in the light breeze, and I paused to take several deep breaths, calming my heart rate as I watched the fire dance.

Pulling the athame from its sheath, I held it above my head and began to chant.

"Spirits of the dead,
Attend my words."

I pushed my power outwards as I spoke, feeling it ripple out and over the cemetery. In my peripheral vision I saw Tomas suddenly stand straight, his body tense. Isaac appeared at the edge of the circle.

"Harry, you may want to turn it down a notch. Unless it was your plan to call to every vampire in the city?" His voice held a hint of mirth although his face remained serious.

"What? No, of course not." I bit my lip. "I'll tone it down," I mumbled, my cheeks flaming with embarrassment.

Isaac turned to go just as his cell phone vibrated in his pocket. He stopped and pulled it out, glancing at the screen, the smile he had been suppressing escaping from his lips. He answered the call and spoke a couple of quiet words before slipping the phone back into his pocket. He looked at me, humour evident in his eyes and said, "Hilde and Willow also say hello."

Great. Isaac obviously hadn't been exaggerating when he said I was calling every vampire in town if Hilde and Willow could feel it back at the firehall on the opposite side of the city.

Isaac melted back into the darkness and I glanced at Tomas. He stood at attention, his fists clenched at his sides. This was the first time he had ever experienced the touch of my powers as a full vampire. Obviously he was less than thrilled.

Taking another slow breath, I grounded myself again and started over.

"Spirits of the dead,
Attend my words."

This time I kept my power to a low trickle, letting it simply flow out rather than pushing it.

"William Henry Koenig, heed my call.
As flame burns bright, in dark of night,
Avail yourself from death's thrall.
Meld body to soul.
This I do command."

As I spoke the last words, I held out my left arm and drew my athame across my palm, slicing it open, ignoring the sharp pain. Dark red blood welled from the cut, and I cupped my hand, letting it pool for a moment before closing my fist over it. I repeated my chant several more times as the blood dripped from my hand to the ground below. After a moment there was a stirring beneath my feet, and the blood that had splattered on the ground disappeared, absorbed into the earth, my gift accepted.

I held my fist clenched and Tess hurried around to my side. Taking my hand, she quickly wrapped it with gauze she had prepared earlier and tied it off to stem the flow of blood. I gave her a nod of thanks and sent her back to her spot to wait.

The ground continued to stir until I felt a draw on my power. Suddenly it cracked, and William Koenig's spectral body appeared, crawling up from his grave, his hands breaking through the surface followed by his head as he pulled himself out. At this point he was simply spirit, his incorporeal body flowing from the ground like fog. The fog continued to flow, rising up in a column that grew thicker and taller, filling in until it was the shape of a man.

"William Henry Koenig, do you accept my gift?"

"Y-y-y-e-e-sssss," a hoarse voice replied.

"Will you heed my command?"

There was a longer pause and then, "Yessss."

I let out a small sigh of relief and gave one last push of my power, directing it at the column of fog before me. The grey mist swirled and slowly dissipated to reveal a very solid William Koenig. He looked pretty damn good for a dead guy, if I do say so myself. Only the sickly grey pallor and dead, sunken eyes gave him away. His suit was a little worse for wear as well, but that couldn't be helped. The guy had been dead and decomposing for a few weeks after all.

"William Koenig, do you know where you are?"

"I-I..." Koenig blinked and looked around. "I'm in a cemetery."

"Do you know why you're here?"

Koenig frowned.

"Daddy?" Elise called from behind Koenig.

He turned towards his daughter's voice, but I put out a hand.

"Stop," I commanded.

Koenig froze.

"Do not turn away. Keep your eyes on me."

Koenig's body relaxed, his eyes returning to mine.

"I'm going to ask you a couple of questions, and then I'll explain why you're here. Do you understand?"

"Yes."

"Do you remember your friend and solicitor, Reginald DeGrasse?"

"Yes."

I glanced at the piece of paper with DeGrasse's question. "Do you remember what you said to him when you first met?"

"Yes."

I waited a moment and then shook my head. Of course he wasn't going to elaborate; he had already answered the question. Apparently zombies take things literally.

"Tell me what you said to him when you first met."

"I told him that I had never met a lawyer worth knowing, but I hoped he proved me wrong."

I glanced over Koenig's shoulder to look at DeGrasse. He was smiling. I guess we passed his test.

I looked at the second question on the sheet. It was from Jr.'s lawyer.

"Do you remember your son William Jr.'s tenth birthday?"

"Yes."

"Do you remember what type of car he wished for when he blew out his candles?" I frowned. How would Koenig know that? Jr. must be trying to sabotage us by asking a question the zombie wouldn't be able to answer. I glanced over at DeGrasse. He was frowning as well.

William Koenig—the zombie, not Jr.—began to shake. Startled, I stared at him in concern. What was happening? Did something go wrong?

A moment later, a hoarse laugh burst from him. "You're trying to trick me. My son didn't want a car when he was ten."

Surprised, I glanced at Jr. He appeared shocked that the zombie knew the answer.

"What did he want?" I asked the zombie.

"He wanted a pony, but I told him ponies were for girls, and he would have to wait until he was sixteen to get some real horsepower."

"Th-that's right!" Jr. was shaking his head and backing away. "How the fuck could you know that?" He directed the question to me.

"I didn't. Your father knows."

"I believe I'm satisfied with the demonstration," DeGrasse said, turning to look at his counterpart. "Do you agree, Mr. Hayes?"

Hayes, looking pale and jumpy, nodded slowly. "Y-yes. I concur."

DeGrasse turned back to me and nodded. I studied the zombie in front of me, biting my lip. I hadn't given this part as much thought.

"William, your family is here, and they'd like to speak with you."

"Elise is here?"

"Yes, and your son."

Koenig Sr. frowned. "I don't understand... He's not supposed..."

"Daddy, it's me, Elise." Elise stepped closer to the circle, and suddenly Isaac was there beside her. He grasped her arm and said something quietly to her.

"Elise?" The zombie smiled.

"Would you like to see your daughter?" I asked, but the answer was evident on his face.

"Yes," he answered. "Yes."

"Turn around and you'll see your family. Don't try and cross the circle."

The zombie turned, and I led him closer to the edge of the circle, stopping about four feet from the boundary. Elise clasped her hands to her face, tears on her cheeks.

"Oh, Daddy, I miss you so much."

William looked confused. "Have I been away?"

"Yes, Daddy..." Elise glanced at me, unsure what to say.

"You were very sick, William. Do you remember?"

"Yes. Damn cancer just wouldn't quit." The zombie frowned and then looked at DeGrasse. "Reggie, why are you here? Why did you bring Elise to this place? This is no place for a lady at night."

DeGrasse cleared his throat, obviously uncomfortable. "We need your help, William."

"William, you're dead," I said. "You only have a short time to talk, and we have a few questions for you. Do you remember being at home, dying? Do you remember Mr. DeGrasse visiting you there, in your bedroom?"

William frowned in concentration. "Yes, I remember."

"What do you remember?"

"I remember the pain." The zombie grimaced.

"Yes, there was pain, but you're beyond that now. You can't feel the pain any longer. Tell me what else you remember?"

"I remember Elise sitting in a chair reading to me. Dickens."

"Yes, Daddy, we were reading *A Tale of Two Cities* right before you..." Elise paused, her eyes teary. "I read to you every night after work," she said finally, after composing herself.

"I remember, I remember." The zombie became agitated, rubbing his arms and rocking back and forth. "*It was the best of times, it was the worst of times...*" He frowned. "But now I'm dead, what of the business? What has happened to the company?" He stopped rocking and shook his head slowly, as if remembering. "There was a will." Suddenly he looked up and turned to face Jr., noticing him for the first time. "You!" he said vehemently.

Jr. started to back away, holding his hands out in a keep away gesture. "No....no...this isn't real. This is a trick."

"I remember everything," the zombie growled. He reached out, his hands like claws, as if he wanted to throttle Jr., and rushed towards the edge of the circle.

"Stop!" I shouted, throwing out a wave of power. Koenig froze.

Jr. continued to scuttle away until Tomas appeared behind him, his face grim. Trapped, Jr. stopped and defiantly crossed his arms.

"Tell me what you've remembered," I said to the zombie.

"I remember changing the will so Elise could take over the company. I couldn't let Billy destroy all my hard work. I remember signing the new documents and asking Reggie to leave them with me so I could discuss them with Elise that evening."

"Yes, you did sign the new will, William. But we can't find it. Do you know what happened to it?" DeGrasse took a step towards the circle and then stopped when he realized he'd almost crossed the edge.

William's agitation grew, and he clenched his fists at his sides. "It's gone. Destroyed in the fireplace by my own son right before he murdered me."

Whoa. Totally didn't see that one coming.

There was a collective gasp as William's words sank in. Elise let out a little mew of despair, her hand at her mouth, as we all turned to stare at Jr.

"This is bullshit! There's no way you can prove any of this. The old man died from natural causes. I wasn't even there." He faced Hayes. "Let's get out of here. I don't have to stand here and listen to these accusations."

"Billy, you didn't." Elise reached out to her brother. "How could you?"

"You stupid bitch. I didn't do anything. This is another one of your stall tactics to try and steal the company out from under me. Well, I won't stand for this…this…freak show." He turned as if to leave, but stopped as Nash joined Tomas, blocking his way.

"You can prove it," Koenig replied. "There is proof."

"What sort of proof? Where can we find it?" I looked skeptically at the zombie.

"He said there was a camera in the bedroom. It was how he kept tabs on what was going on. He said it recorded to a file, and he planned on watching me die over and over."

"I think I've heard enough," Nash said, grabbing Jr. by the arm.

"Wait just a minute," Hayes complained. "You can't arrest my client on the word of…of a…" he frowned at a loss for words, "…of a dead person. You'll never get it to court."

"He won't need to take it to court if he gets a confession." Tomas stepped in front of Hayes. "You will be silent." He snapped his fingers in front of Hayes's face, and the lawyer fell still.

Huh. Neat trick. I guess Tomas picked up a few upgrades along with his transformation.

Tomas glanced at Isaac and some sort of unspoken communication took place. Isaac raised an eyebrow and shrugged.

"Detective," Isaac said, "if you would like some assistance, we can arrange for a full confession."

"What do you mean?" Nash appeared skeptical.

"Only a little coercion to ensure that Mr. Koenig Jr. has a rapid onset of a guilty conscience and turns himself into the police, along with any evidence."

"Works for me," Nash replied.

I left them to work out the details, and while Tomas worked his mojo on Hayes and Jr., I drew Elise to the side, bringing her father along.

"If you have anything you'd like to say to one another, now would be the time to do it. Just remember to stay on your own side of the circle."

I backed away, giving them some privacy. Tess came up beside me.

"That was cool. It was like watching an episode of *Murder She Wrote* but with zombies."

"Omigod, are you comparing me to Angela Lansbury?" I gave her a playful punch to the shoulder.

Tomas had finished with Jr. and his lawyer, and Nash was leading Jr. away in handcuffs to wait for a squad car to pick him up and take him to the station. Hayes followed behind as if in a trance. I glanced at Elise and her father. They were saying good bye.

"Looks like I'm up again," I said to Tess with a grin. It had gone much better than I expected.

I turned to the zombie. "William Koenig, it's time." Koenig turned and walked towards me.

Tomas stepped up to Elise and snapped his fingers. "You will remember everything that has occurred here this evening, but you will be unable to discuss these events with anyone at any time. You will keep these events in your subconscious, and you can visit them as memories only. When news of your brother's confession breaks tomorrow, you will be genuinely surprised."

"Yes," Elise replied.

"Well, there goes my chance at ten million bucks," I deadpanned. "Come on, William. It's past your bedtime."

***

Putting Koenig back to bed should have been as easy as blowing out a candle. As I led him back to his grave though, I found myself at a loss as to what to say. I mean, what do you say to someone you basically ripped out of the afterlife and stuck back into their decomposing body?

"Uh, well, thanks for your help," I said.

"No, thank you. I can rest in peace knowing my company is safe and there will be justice."

"Sure. No problem." Cue the awkward silence.

I traded a look with Tess where she leaned against the base of Koenig's gravestone and she smirked at me. Fat lot of help she was.

"Okay then. Off you go," I said to Koenig, giving him a push with my power. I had a whole chant prepared, but it didn't seem necessary. The words were just for show anyway, and Gran would say they were a crutch.

I felt the release of energy as William's spirit left his body, and watched as his physical shell crumbled to dust, returning to the ground from which it came. I let out a deep breath, glad to be finished.

"Well now, what do we have here?" The voice cut through my calm like a knife.

"Tess!" I yelled a warning as Seth's head appeared at the base of Koenig's grave. It was like some sort of cartoonish scene with just his head sticking out of the ground, his lizard-like eyes glowing. His arm snapped out, grabbing Tess's ankle as she tried to get away. She fell backwards, landing on her ass, crying out as smoke rose from his burning grip. "Tess!"

Ignoring Nash's swearing as he arrived back at a run, trying fruitlessly to pass the protective barrier of the circle, I hurried towards the grave.

"Let her go!"

I pulled out my athame and struck out, catching Seth across the wrist. He roared something in a language I neither recognized nor understood, and Tess took the opportunity to kick out at his face with her free foot. She scored a hit, and Seth fell back, letting go of her ankle. The demon disappeared, and I grabbed Tess by the armpits, dragging her away from the grave.

"Shit, Harry. Where did he come from?" She scrambled to her feet, pulling out her own blade.

"I—"

I didn't get a chance to answer because suddenly a grey, wrinkled body flew at us, hands like claws, teeth bared. Unlike Seth, the imps were having no problem fitting through the small portal over Koenig's grave, and the little grey man was quickly joined by a second and then a third as they scrambled out of the ground and tried to flank around us. I swiped out with my athame at the closest of the little buggers, but he was too fast.

More of the little grey creatures continued to spill out of the grave, forcing Tess and me back to back as they circled around us. They seemed content to keep us penned in, only occasionally risking my or Tess's blade. Each time we struck, they dashed out of harm's way. I glanced across the circle to where Nash paced, practically pulling his hair out. I had to get to the edge and bring it down, otherwise we were on our own.

"Harry! Look out!"

At Tess's shout I turned just in time to see an imp leap at me. I swung out with my athame, and the blade hit home, plunging into his chest. With a squeal and a pop, he disappeared, black ichor-like blood splattering everywhere. Well, at least now we knew we could harm them.

"Tess, I have to try and take down the circle."

Tess nodded and pulled at the zipper on her coat. "Give me a second," she replied. She slipped off her jacket, tossing it at the imps, tangling a couple of them in the heavy fabric. I gaped at her. She was naked under her coat.

"Where the hell is your shirt?"

Tess grinned as she unbuttoned her fly and dropped her pants to the ground. There was a second where she stood in nothing but her birthday suit, and then she shimmered, and in her place stood a large, grey wolf. She turned her wolfy face to mine and bared her teeth in what could only be a grin and then threw back her head and howled.

As if it was their cue, the imps rushed at Tess, and she growled and snapped, tearing through them, wrinkled bodies flying. I turned, using the distraction to move towards the edge of the circle, intent on getting to Nash and Isaac.

"Not so fast now, sugar." Seth rose from the grave and I felt a tug on my aura. "I'm not done with you." He continued to feast on my life force, drawing it from my aura like soda through a straw, and I fell to my knees, lightheaded. "But seeing as how you opened this lovely little doorway for me, I am inclined to forgive you. Provided you be a good girl now and come with me." He gestured for me to come to him. Ha! Like that was going to happen.

I struggled to my feet and braced for his attack, athame held at the ready, but he remained where he was, his reptilian eyes burning into me.

"I'm losing patience with you, sugar," he hissed. "Come to me."

"Never!" I snapped at him. A wave of vertigo hit me and I stumbled backwards a step, feeling drained and weak. I watched him warily; waiting for him to strike, but he didn't move from the portal. He was tied to it somehow and couldn't come after me.

"Wrong answer, witch." Seth flashed a mouthful of sharp, pointy teeth and then uttered something in another language. Several of the imps peeled away from the melee with Tess to rush at me. They swarmed me, knocking me back to the ground, pinning my arms. One of them tore at the bandage on my hand, reopening the cut I had made earlier, his tongue lapping at the seeping blood. Disgusted, I flailed out, managing to get my blade hand free only to have it grabbed again. A sharp pain stung my wrist, and I cried out as my athame fell from my hand. One of the little buggers had bitten me! I thrashed my arms and legs, attempting to knock them off, but more piled on. Suddenly, a hand wrapped around my ankle and began to drag me towards Seth.

Frantic, I increased my efforts to get away. I couldn't let Seth get a hold of me. How could he even be here? What was it he said? I'd opened a door for him?

That was it! I had to close the door I had opened to the Otherworld when I called Koenig.

"Tess! Tess, I need the candle." I wasn't sure if she even heard me as I struggled against my attackers. Finally getting one foot free, I kicked out at the imp dragging me by the ankle, catching him square in the face. His grip loosened, and I tried to scramble free. A growl erupted behind me, and a huge grey bundle of fur landed beside me, what was left of the candle clenched in her teeth. It was still burning and would continue to do so until I put it out. Tess dropped the candle into my hand and then sprang on the nearest little grey man, tearing him off me.

"What are you doing, sugar?" Seth said, his voice harsh and angry. "Do not do this. Come to me now, or there will be consequences."

"No, never," I replied, struggling to my feet again. Tess had ripped through the last of the imps, and she came to stand beside me, her muzzle black with ichor. I placed a hand on her furry shoulder, and it comforted me, lending me strength.

Seth assessed the situation through narrowed eyes and then scowled, pointing a finger at me. "You will pay for this, Angharad Grainne Russo. Just you wait and see. You *will* submit to me, my little twitchy witch." With a snarl, he spun away, disappearing through the portal.

I had to get the door I had opened to the Otherworld shut before anything or anyone else came through. I held up the candle and chanted the words of the extinguishing spell, adding a quick prayer to Hecate as I willed the portal shut.

"Mali ex fine!
Hecate, Queen of the Night
Aid me in my task
Close that which was opened
And set the world to right."

The candle snuffed out with a small puff of smoke, and I felt a shift as the portal closed. Exhausted, I collapsed where I stood. My aura was scraped raw after Seth's attack and the energy I had expended earlier raising the zombie. My knees simply went out from underneath me.

"Harry! Harry, you have to bring down the circle." Isaac's voice rang out into the silence. "Harry, we can't get to you to help if you don't break the circle."

I was vaguely aware of Nash's and Isaac's voices calling to me, but I was so weak I could barely keep my eyes open.

"GRRR-UH!" A sticky, wet nose poked itself into my ear, the wolfy equivalent of a wet willy. Tess nudged me again.

I struggled to my knees, and Tess dipped her head under my arm until my hand rested on her shoulders. She yipped encouragement as I pushed myself to my feet, using her to keep my balance. It took every ounce of what little strength I had left to make the trek to the edge of the circle.

"Goddammit, Harry. Open this damn circle." Nash stood on the perimeter, looking tense.

I took one last faltering step, shuffling my foot across the sooty black line that formed the perimeter and the protective ring dissipated as I fell into Nash's arms.

"Harry!" Nash's voice was full of concern.

"Nash! I know how to close the portal at Wishes," I rasped and then promptly passed out.

Chapter Nineteen

The next twenty-four hours were mostly a blur. I have vague recollections of being in the shower with Nash and getting the sticky black ichor washed off. Later, I can remember waking up in bed sandwiched between two furry bodies—Nash must have shifted and Tess was still in her wolf form. It was amazing that she had been able to shift so far from the full moon—previous to this, she had never been powerful enough to do it—so it was understandable that she would remain in her wolf form for a few hours.

The next time I woke up, Tess was gone and so was Nash's wolf. Instead, I was wrapped in a pair of very human, very possessive arms, holding me tightly against Nash's chest.

"Nash," I murmured, wiggling against him. "Nash, you're crushing me."

The arms loosened but didn't move from around me. "Go back to sleep, Harry," Nash grumbled in my hair.

I guess I must have listened because I can remember waking up yet again, only this time I was alone. I could hear voices though, just outside the door.

"She's still asleep," Nash was saying, "but her colour looks better."

Isaac replied something, but my stomach chose that moment to grumble loudly. I was starving.

"I'm awake," I called out. "Tell me someone will feed me."

Isaac chuckled as he and Nash stepped into the room. "Your food radar is impeccable as always, Harry. Max has just arrived with food from Minetti's."

"If you tell me there are meatball subs, I'll kiss you."

Nash leaned over the side of the bed, "There are, and if you hurry, Tess might just save you one. Now give me my kiss."

"I wasn't talking to you," I teased.

Nash growled and raked a hand through my hair. He pulled my face to his and then paused to look at Isaac. "We'll be down in ten minutes."

"Ten minutes? Who needs ten minutes when there are Minetti's subs waiting?" I gave him a push and started to toss the covers back only to grasp them tight again with a little "Eep!" when I realized I was buck naked underneath.

Isaac shook his head with a grin, averting his eyes, and turned and left the bedroom.

"We'll be right down," I called after him.

***

I washed my face, brushed my teeth, ran my fingers through my hair to fix the bed head and spent a precious few minutes necking with Nash to reassure him and his wolf that I was fine, and still made it downstairs in less than ten minutes.

Max had arrived with a veritable feast from Minetti's—their famous meatball subs, two extra-large deep-dish pies with pepperoni and Italian sausage, and a double order of spaghetti carbonara. He was my new favourite person. Of course Mama Minetti had included all the fixin's too—buttery garlic bread, Italian salad with slices of salami, and extra red sauce for the subs.

Tess was already tucked in to what appeared to be her second meatball sub, judging by the wrappers. She smiled at me, marinara on her cheek, and pushed a sub towards me.

"Better hurry, Harry, and get one while you can. I can't believe how hungry I am."

"Your first few moonless changes will do that to you. You did well." Nash reached over and squeezed her shoulder.

Tess's face flushed, and she dipped her head in acknowledgment of her alpha's praise. I glanced at Max. His eyes were intent on Nash's hand on Tess's shoulder. I grinned into my sub. Things were going to get interesting soon. Not that they weren't way too interesting already.

"I can't believe you were naked as a jaybird under your jacket," I said to Tess, setting down my sandwich and helping myself to some carbonara. "Whatever possessed you to do that?"

"It was Max's idea."

She smirked as Max almost choked on the big swallow of beer he had just taken. "I certainly don't remember saying that," he replied.

"No, but you did tell me that if I were to encounter any more demons, I should shift if I could because the wolf would be immune to them, and since I figured if anything was going to go wrong last night it was going to be demon-related, I wanted to be prepared for a quick change."

"Well, it's a good thing you did. I couldn't have done it without you. You really saved my ass." I frowned. "I should never have agreed to the whole zombie thing."

"Don't be too hard on yourself, Harry," Max said. "No one could have predicted what happened last night."

I sighed, not sure if I agreed with Max. "At least I know what we need to do to close the portal at the warehouse."

***

"I don't know, Harry, it's kind of a stretch," Max said, shaking his head. I had finished a quick recap of what had happened at the zombie raising and shared my suspicions about why I thought the portal had remained open.

"It has to be the fire. Why else would it be there as part of the fountain?" It all made sense (at least to me). When I summoned Koenig, I had used the candle to set the spell. As I had found out the hard way, this meant that when I sent him back to his grave, the door to the Otherworld remained open because I had tethered it to the fire. I had to put the candle out before the portal would close completely. When DiCastro and his cronies kidnapped me and made me part of their sick ritual to raise Osiris, they had also started their spell with fire—a large cauldron-like brazier. Somehow, that flame must have been kept lit, allowing the rift to the Otherworld to remain open. If Seth had discovered the portal around the same time Isaac and his crew of vampires cleaned up the aftermath, it would certainly have been possible for the demon to hide the brazier and the existence of the rift.

"Does it matter?" Tess asked with a frown. "Let's say Harry's right. How are we supposed to snuff out a demon-controlled flame? Not to mention, how do we even get close enough to try? It's not like Seth will just let us waltz back in there."

I bit my lip and glanced at Nash. Seth might not let just anyone waltz back in, but we already knew someone he really wanted on his dance card.

As if reading my thoughts, Nash looked at me and growled. "Abso-fucking-lutely not. There has to be another way."

***

The next few days were frustrating for everyone. Nash and Dev were still on the hook with their norm police department bosses to figure out the HRN crisis, and they really had no leads, or at least anything they could tell the norms, so it didn't look very good for either of them. On the plus side, bringing in William Koenig, Jr. for murdering his own father was a big, fat checkmark, maybe even a gold star since Koenig, Sr. had been such a highly respected man in the community.

I was frustrated because I was the one with the "in" back into Wishes, yet I had been completely kept out of the loop in regards to any plans they were making to get rid of Seth and his minions. Even Salvador, who was usually pushing me towards danger as some sort of messed-up test, had told me in no uncertain terms that the problem was no longer my concern.

To add to my frustration, it quickly became apparent that Seth wasn't going to give up on me easily. Unable to reach me through my dreams anymore, he had taken to sending imps to harass me. Riding poor possessed norms, the imps would follow me every time I left the coffee shop. A few had become brazen enough to enter the shop to speak to me, but the glow from my katana was always a dead giveaway that they were nearby. The first couple we had managed to capture and hold until Father Mike could come and work his mojo, separating confused and frightened norm from imp. Unfortunately the imps had quickly learned that getting caught wasn't a good idea, so they became more evasive, dashing in to shout Seth's threats at me, often to the bewilderment of my customers, and then streaking out again before we could give chase.

It was Tess who came up with the brilliant solution for handling the little buggers. She arrived at the shop on what I was beginning to think of as day three of my captivity with a cheeky grin and a five-gallon bottle of water.

"What's with the water jug?" I asked as I followed her into the kitchen.

Tess set the bottle on the counter and connected a manual pump to the top of the jug, and then flashed me a mischievous smile. "You'll see. Have you had any of your little visitors today?"

"No, it's been pretty quiet on the demon-minion front. Why?"

Tess shrugged. "No reason. I just thought we could try out the genius idea I had to get rid of them." She shrugged off her backpack and bent over it to rummage around. With a little "Aha!" she straightened, a small water gun of the super-soaker variety in her hand.

"What do you plan to do with that?"

Ignoring me, she proceeded to fill the gun from the jug. "An experiment," she finally replied, giving the gun a squirt into the nearby sink to test it out. "Let's go out front and wait."

We didn't have to wait all that long. Less than half a cup of coffee and an everything bagel later, Tiffy hissed at us from across the room and pointed under the counter where my katana was stored. Just then, the bell above the door announced the arrival of a customer. He was a middle-aged man dressed casually, although not warmly enough for the cold winter wind howling outside, in a short-sleeved T-shirt and jeans, and if his lack of winter wear didn't give him away, his jumpy, furtive behaviour certainly did. Luckily the shop was almost empty, and what few customers we had were all werewolves, so I didn't have to worry about whatever Tess was going to do. The man's eyes scanned the room nervously, as if looking for something, until they came to a stop on me.

"My masterrrr orderrrrsss your pressssence," he hissed, his head beginning to twitch towards his right shoulder. He pointed at me, taking a step towards our table. Tess leapt from her seat, super-soaker in hand.

"Oh yeah? Well, take that, you evil little hitchhiker."

She gave the man a blast with the water gun, aiming right at the bare skin at the base of his neck. His hands flew to his throat, and he made a choking sound as a small puff of white smoke rose from between his fingers. He stumbled backwards, and I shifted my sight to watch as the imp wriggled out of the man, scowling. The little grey beast hopped away from the man's now-collapsing body.

"My master's patience wanes," he warned and then ran out the door.

We hurried over to the no-longer-possessed man who sat bewildered on the floor, looking around in confusion.

"Wh-wh-what happened?"

"I don't know, sir." I bent over to help him to his feet. "You were waiting in line for coffee and then passed out or something. Do you suffer from low blood sugar?" I directed him towards a chair. "Here, take a seat. Can I get you a drink?"

Tiffy hurried over with a glass of water, and the man took it, still appearing dazed.

I pulled Tess to the side and fixed her with an incredulous look. "What the hell was in that water?"

"It's holy water. I asked Father Mike to put a whammy on it." She shrugged. "It worked so well for your katana, I figured it wouldn't hurt to try it."

"Genius," I replied. "Absolutely genius."

***

Finding a solution to the imp problem wasn't Tess's only brilliant move that week. She was on a roll.

"I know what's happening with the HRNs!" Tess shouted as she came in the door, breathless, a waft of winter air following her.

"What?"

"I know what's going on with the HRNs," she said again. She peeled off her boots and coat and dumped them on the bench by the door.

I looked up from the onion I was chopping. I was in the middle of getting a cooking lesson from Isaac. We were making steak and mushroom pot pies with some puff pastry Hilde had made.

Tess went to the fridge and cracked a beer open before hopping up on a stool at the kitchen island where I was working.

"They all died," she said, looking smug.

"Uh, duh...yeah, most of them killed themselves after going whacko. We already know that."

"No, I mean before. They all died before they went whacko." Tess grinned with pride. "Each one suffered a near-death experience where they appeared to die for a few minutes before coming back to life in the weeks leading up to their murderous rampage."

"Seriously?" I stared at her incredulously, still chopping onions. "How in the world did you figure that out?"

"Harry, I asked for diced, not annihilated." Isaac examined the onions that had gone well past minced at this point.

"Oops, sorry." I set down the knife, giving Isaac a look of chagrin. "Should I start again?"

"No, they'll be fine." He took the cutting board over to the counter by the stove-top. "We'll continue your lesson another time so that Tess can fill you in on her discovery."

"Okay. Thanks, Isaac." I turned back to Tess as Isaac finished getting dinner ready. "So? How did you figure it out?"

"I got the idea when I was talking to Father Mike the other day. I remembered you mentioned that man from the church who had been possessed. I asked Father Mike how he was doing, and in the course of our conversation he mentioned that the man had previously had a near-death experience. That made me think of the woman you told me about from the hospital. She had a near-death experience and then you saw her at Wishes. It just seemed like too much to be a coincidence, so I went to talk to the bingo lady's family and...same thing!"

"Wow! Great detective work, Veronica Mars." I grabbed myself a beer and sat down beside her. "But why did you do all the sleuthing?"

Tess's cheeks coloured, and she put her head down, staring at the beer bottle in her hands. "That meeting with Salvador got me thinking." She fidgeted at the label on her bottle. "I mean, I never thought I'd work at Uncle Rigo's forever, so I've been thinking about what I want to do, and what I really want to do is be a detective."

"You want to join the police force?" I gaped at her. She had never mentioned a desire to serve and protect in all the years I had known her.

"No! Not that kind of detective. A private investigator."

"You *do* want to be Veronica Mars!" I exclaimed with a smile.

"Why not? Think about it. We have access to the world's only talking supercomputer. With Bryce on our side, we have a leg up on the competition."

"We?"

Tess grinned. "Of course. Why break up the band? If having a supercomputer is a plus, imagine having the ghost whisperer on our team as well."

Ha! She was joking, but some days I really felt that Melinda Gordon was the only one who could truly understand me.

"One problem," I replied. "Ghosts don't pay very well."

"I never said they were the clients. They'd be our confidential informants."

"But—"

"Don't answer now," Tess said hurriedly. "Just say you'll think about it."

"Okay, I'll think about it."

***

By day six of my self-imposed house arrest, I was growing stir-crazy, so I decided to go grocery shopping.

"I don't think that's a good idea, Harry," Jon said, hands on his hips as he watched me pump water from the jug and then fill the brightly coloured plastic gun.

"I'm just going a couple of blocks to the grocery store. How much trouble could I possibly get into? Besides, I'll have you and Eric at my back." I thrust the loaded water pistol at him, slapping it against his chest. "Take this, and we'll be set."

Jon eyed the dripping gun. "What the hell am I supposed to do with this?"

"Trust me. It could come in handy. Just squirt it at anyone acting shifty." Ignoring any further protests, I strode from the kitchen and across the shop, Jon and Eric hustling after me. "Tiffy, I'm going to the store. I'll be back in half an hour or so."

Not waiting for a response, I zipped my jacket up against the cold and set off. The day was one of those bright winter days where the air feels exceedingly crisp, but you're so glad to see the sunshine after weeks of grey clouds you don't care if it's cold. I kept my pace brisk and my attention focussed, but the only tails I picked up were Jon and Eric, the Harry-sitters, who strode purposefully behind me.

The local supermarket was two blocks over and, as it was a Tuesday afternoon, the store was relatively quiet. I passed through the double set of sliding doors, pausing to stomp the slush off my boots and tuck my mittens in my coat pocket.

Jon came up beside me and put a hand on my arm. "I don't like this. Nash told us you should stay at the firehall until they figure out the demon problem."

I scowled at him. "Despite what Nash may think, he's not the boss of me. I can't stay locked up in the coffee shop forever."

"Easy for you to say, Harry, you don't have to answer to him."

I chewed on my bottom lip, feeling a bit guilty, and gave him a little shrug. I hadn't thought of that. "Fine. Here," I said, taking out my list and tearing it in two. I shoved one half at Eric. "Take this and get everything on it, and Jon and I will do the other half. That way we'll be twice as quick and be back at the jailhouse, I mean firehouse, before you know it." I gave Jon a look. "Satisfied?"

Jon nodded. "Thanks, Harry."

My half of the list was mostly fruits and vegetables, so Jon and I headed over to the produce section on the far side of the store to start. At first, everything seemed to be going fine, although there were a few loud crashes, like someone had knocked over a display, that set Jon on edge.

I was squeezing the melons (not a euphemism) when Eric came trotting up, his face full of concern.

"Hey! Where's your half of the groceries?" I asked, looking down at his empty hands.

"Not now, Harry. We have to go." He gave Jon a look that obviously spoke volumes to Jon, but said nothing to me.

Jon grabbed my arm. "Let's go, Harry."

"Wait!" I pushed his hand off my arm. "What's going on?"

"There's a woman going berserk in the cereal aisle. She's ranting and knocking everything off the—"

"YOU!"

The shout surprised us, but not as much as the egg missile that whipped past my head and took Eric right in the chest. He didn't even flinch at the impact, although he scowled down at the yolk staining his shirt and dripping to the floor.

We turned as one to regard the crazy woman with the egg carton, momentarily shocked into inaction. Jon roused first, grabbing my arm and dragging me around a display shelf stacked with apples as eggs continued to fly and the woman continued to rant.

"Harry Russo! Come out, come out wherever you are. You're a naughty girl. Yes you are, yes you are."

Jon raised an eyebrow and looked at me. "Do you know her?"

I shrugged. I didn't really get a good look at her before we dove behind the apples. There was a crash, and a display of salad dressing toppled over. I risked a peek and started with surprise. It was the woman from the hospital, again! She was in even worse shape than when I saw her at the coffee shop the week before. Her hair was a bird's nest of tangles and her clothes, the same ones she was wearing last time, were filthy.

"Harry, oh, Harry," she crooned, her voice sounding raw. "Get out here, you bitch. My master is not happy with you."

"Now see here, just you wait a minute!" A man, probably the store manager, strode into view. "I'm going to have to ask you to leave. I've called the police."

"Go away, you puny meatsack," the woman screamed. She threw the carton of eggs at him and then pulled a sharp kitchen knife from her purse.

"Oh shit." I looked at Jon and Eric. "We've got a problem, guys."

"You think?" Eric gaped at me incredulously.

"Come on, let's get out of here while she's distracted," Jon said.

"We can't just leave. What if she hurts him?"

"It's not your job—"

"Yeah, but it's my fault." I sighed heavily. "Look, we just have to distract her until the cops get here. Move around and try to get behind her and then hit her with a blast from your squirt guns." Not waiting for a reply, I quickly stood up, waving my arms. "Woo-hoo! Over here."

The woman, who had been brandishing the knife at the manager, swiveled her head to stare at me.

"Yeah, that's right. It's me, Harry. I'm the one you want. Let him go." I waved my hand at the manager, and he scuttled backwards a few steps away from the woman. Thankfully, I could hear sirens in the distance. The police would be here soon.

Faster than I would have thought possible, the woman leapt forward, slashing out with the knife, catching the manager across his exposed neck as he turned away to flee.

"No!"

I watched helpless as blood spurted from the gash at his throat. He slapped a hand to his wound, shocked, as the blood continued to spray from between his fingers.

"There'll be more where that came from the longer you ignore my master's wishes," the woman hissed. She lifted the blade to her mouth, her tongue darting out to lick the blood coating its surface. She looked at me from over the blade, her face frozen in a rictus of pleasure.

I rushed forward, pushing Jon and Eric, who had stepped in front of me, out of the way, and pulled the squirt gun from where I had tucked it at the small of my back.

"Go back to hell, you little bastard," I yelled as I opened fire with the squirt gun, dousing her with holy water.

The woman screamed, dropping the knife to swipe at her face. Jon and Eric stepped up beside me and opened fire as well, and the woman fell to her knees, writhing and screaming. I crouched on the floor, clamping my hands on the manager's neck, trying to stem the blood that continued to spray.

I glanced around me at the crowd that had gathered. "Call an ambulance!" I yelled, as a man ran forward, pulling his scarf from around his neck.

"Here," he said, dropping to his knees beside me. I shuffled over, giving him room beside me, while keeping my hands on the manager's wound. When the scarf suddenly looped around my neck, and I was pulled tight against the man I thought was a would-be rescuer, I was, to say the least, surprised.

"My master wants you baaaack," he whispered in my ear, his voice low and gravelly. He tugged me backwards, dragging me to my feet. I scrabbled at the scarf, my hands covered in the manager's blood, as I struggled to loosen his hold on me. The scarf was so tight I couldn't breathe, and my pulse began to pound in my head as a wave of dizziness came over me. Letting my knees buckle, I threw all my weight to the floor. Surprised, the man let go of the scarf.

"Jon," I rasped. "Water!"

Jon turned from watching the woman who continued to writhe on the floor in pain, his eyes wide with surprise.

"Water!" I croaked again.

Jon aimed his water pistol and blasted the man, who screamed, his hands flying to his face. I crawled back to the manager to check his pulse, but I knew I was too late. I looked up at his spirit as it gazed down in disbelief at its own body.

"I'm sorry," I said. "You should go to the light. Don't linger, there's evil about."

"My family," the ghost moaned. "I-I…"

"I'll tell them you were thinking of them at the end."

"Thank you." He glanced away, his sad visage turning to one of amazement. "Is that…?"

"Yeah, go to the light.

"Harry, are you okay?" Jon knelt beside me, pulling the scarf from my neck. He winced at the bruises that must have already been starting to form.

I looked over at the man who'd tried to strangle me. He had stopped screaming and was sitting almost comatose, his back against the shelves. A sudden movement to my left drew my eyes. A wrinked, little grey man was scampering away. The imp paused as if sensing my attention and turned back to glare at me before thumbing his nose and blowing a raspberry at me.

"Harry," Jon said again. "Are you all right?"

"Yeah, yeah. I'm fine."

I looked back to the woman who had started the attack. She was frothing at the mouth and tearing at her clothes as if burned by acid. The imp must still be in possession. Why didn't the little bugger let her go?

"Everybody freeze. Don't move."

Two police officers dashed into view, guns drawn. Jon and Eric quickly dropped their squirt guns to the floor and put their hands up.

"Harry? Is that you?" One of the cops glanced over at me in surprise as the other crouched beside the manager to check his pulse.

"Georgia, hey. Yeah, it's me." Georgia was a local beat cop who often stopped by the coffee shop.

"What the hell happened here?"

"I won't do it anymore!" Pushing to her knees, the woman from the hospital grabbed the knife and sprang to her feet. "I won't do it anymore!" She waved the weapon in front of her and charged towards the cop kneeling by the manager.

"Look out!" I shouted, as the crowd erupted into chaos.

BANG!

BANG!

Georgia fired her gun, hitting the woman centre mass. She lurched backwards, her body stiffening and then falling to the floor.

She was dead instantly. Her spirit stood beside her body and looked at me pleadingly. "This isn't what I wanted. I just wanted to live again. Not this. Never this."

An imp peeled itself from her fallen body. It ran towards the ghost, and as I sat stunned, it sucked in a deep breath, swallowing down the woman's spirit. It turned to face me, smiling with sharp crooked teeth, and then disappeared from view with an audible *pop*.

"All I wanted was a few groceries," I said to no one in particular, but I couldn't fail to hear Jon's derisive snort.

Chapter Twenty

"He has to be stopped. We can't just sit back and let him kill more norms," I said as I paced the length of the room. I was still wound up from the events of the afternoon. "And making deals with them, bringing them back from the dead only to drive them crazy so they kill themselves? It has to end!"

"I absolutely agree with you, *pequeña*."

"We have an obligation, *you* have a... Wait a minute." I came to an abrupt halt and stared at Salvador in surprise. "Did you just say that I was right?"

Salvador arched an eyebrow and looked at me from over his fingers, which he held steepled at his chin. As usual, he had arrived uninvited to the firehall with Tomas in tow while I was in the shower. I had only been home a short time after I'd finally been allowed to leave the grocery store. As expected, when the police and dead bodies were involved, the remainder of the afternoon had entailed a lot of sitting around and waiting, as well as numerous repetitions of our story. And, since dead bodies were involved, it also meant I had to suffer all the dirty looks Nash threw my way once he arrived on scene. Luckily for me, Nash seemed to prefer to bawl me out the old-fashioned way, so he kept our telepathic communication—a side effect of the mate mark and blood sharing—to a brief, "*Are you okay*?" followed by an "*Are you fucking out of your mind*?" Jon and Eric hadn't been quite so lucky. They had left the store shortly before me, their metaphoric, if not actual, tails between their legs after a thorough reaming out by Nash.

"I was never merely sitting back and letting anyone do anything, my dear Harry. I have my own irons in the fire, as they say." Salvador's tone had lost some of its amused edge.

I narrowed my eyes at him. I didn't like the sound of that. He was up to something and knowing him it was more for his benefit than the norm population's.

"Now, tell me about these," Salvador continued. He gestured at the water guns I had dumped on the coffee table during my recounting of the afternoon's events. "I'm most curious to know if they would work directly on the daemons themselves or only on those possessed?"

I shrugged. "I don't know. It was Tess's idea."

Tess glared at me and then turned to Salvador. "I really don't know, Magister. I would imagine so. Although maybe only the imps?" She gave a little shrug, her cheeks colouring. "I mean from what Harry said, the one imp seemed to be more resistant than the other. I wonder if that's because that particular imp was stronger? And, by that logic, the more powerful daemons might also be immune."

Salvador nodded. "Yes, yes. I see your point." He made a show of checking his watch. "You seem to have it all under control, *pequeña*. I will leave you to your plans. Tomas will remain as my liaison." He rose gracefully and stalked towards the door.

"Under control? Wait a minute. That's it?" I chased after Salvador, heading him off at the door. "You told me to butt out a few days ago, but now you're just going to leave it to me to figure out?"

Salvador paused, giving me an appraising look. "Why, yes," he said, followed by one of his trademark shrugs. "That's exactly what I am doing."

I opened my mouth to tell Salvador what I thought of that idea, but a ruckus across the room interrupted me.

"What the hell?" Tomas jumped from his seat, the chair falling backwards with a crash. He glared down at Tess from across the table and pulled a handkerchief from his pocket to mop his face. "Did you just shoot me with a squirt gun?"

Tess smirked. "I thought we'd better test it out. Wouldn't want any vamps going up in smoke if we decide to use these on the daemons."

Stifling a laugh—Tomas didn't need to know that Isaac had already safely tested the water—I turned back to Salvador, but he was gone.

"So what's the plan, Harry?" Tess looked at me, the smirk still on her face. "It's not like you can just walk right up to Seth and say, 'Excuse me, I'm here to close the portal.'" She held her fingers up and made air quotes as she spoke. "And I doubt if he'll believe in a voluntary change of heart."

Heaving a sigh, I flopped down on the couch. I sat for a minute, my mind going a mile-a-minute, and then I smiled at Tess. "No, but who said it had to be voluntary?"

Chapter Twenty-one

"I got it... I got it..."

Pop!

I watched in disgust as my protective dome imploded on itself. I had been trying for several hours under Max's guidance to learn to set a circle without having to prep the area first. "I don't got it," I groaned, unable to keep the dejection from my voice.

"*Pew, pew.*" Tess grinned evilly as she pelted me with pennies.

"Ouch! Tess! Will you knock it off already?" I ducked as another copper projectile flew past.

"It wouldn't hurt if you had your shield up," Tess replied with a smirk.

"Gee, thanks for pointing out the obvious. Whatever would I do without you?"

"No problem. Glad to help."

Max breathed a tired sigh. "I have to agree with Harry, Tess. I don't think you're helping at this point. Harry needs to concentrate."

I beamed at Max for coming to my defense. When Salvador had made his exit, leaving me in charge of coming up with a plan to defeat Seth, I had called the mage, hoping to elicit some assistance. Max had offered to teach me to create a snap circle, an instant protective circle. It was meant as a personal defense and piggybacked on a witch's or mage's existing shields, requiring no prior preparation. Just set the spell, and *Bam!* You were protected from harm under your own personal magical dome. So far I hadn't been able to do much, except temporarily protect myself to the height of my knees for about three seconds before the bubble burst.

"Try it again, Harry." Max moved to stand between Tess and me, blocking me from Tess's abuse.

I rolled my eyes and sighed, finally turning my back to them to try and centre myself to make another attempt. If I could just get this safety precaution mastered, I would have a better chance of getting Nash to go along with the plan we had hatched.

***

"Absolutely not. I forbid it." Nash crossed his arms and pinned me with a fierce glare.

"Excuse me?" I gave him my best WTF face. "I don't remember asking your permission, nor do I need it."

"Oh, boy." Tess looked around the room, gathering Max and Tomas up with her glance. "Maybe we should give them some privacy."

"Just when it's starting to get interesting?" Tomas smirked and leaned back in his seat as if preparing to watch the entertainment.

"Put a sock in it, fangboy. There's not going to be any show." I turned to look at Nash but addressed the group. "If Nash would just dial back on the alpha male crap, he'd realize that I'm our only option. I'm the only one who can close the portal."

Nash's nostrils flared as he took a deep breath, and then another. "How long until she's able to put up the protection without fail, every time?" Nash directed his question to Max, ignoring me.

Max shrugged. "I don't know. It's a fairly advanced skill. I've had students require months to master it." He gave me a pensive look. "Harry has a strong foundation for her shields and is a quick study. I imagine she'll get it sooner than later."

"The full moon is in ten days. We should strike when our force is at its strongest. You have until then."

Great, no pressure.

***

"I'm sorry."

Nash grunted in response and nuzzled his face against my neck. We were in bed and despite doing our best to wear each other out, I couldn't sleep. The afternoon's incident at the grocery store kept replaying in my head.

"Go to sleep, Harry." Nash tightened his arm around me where I lay spooned up against him. "What's done is done. No point worrying about the past."

"Easy for you to say. It's my fault the manager is dead." I rolled to my back and stared up at the ceiling.

Nash stirred, rising up on his elbow to look down on me. "No, it's not. You aren't responsible for that man's death, the demon is."

"But—"

Nash put a finger to my lips. "No. Quit torturing yourself and get some sleep. You need your strength so you're ready for when we face Seth."

I lifted my head and gave him a kiss. "Thank you."

Nash arched an eyebrow at me. "For what?"

"For understanding that I can't just sit on the sidelines."

Nash grimaced and took a deep breath. "Just promise me you'll stay in the safety of your circle and not take any unnecessary risks."

"I promise."

***

"I'm just running upstairs. I won't be long." I gave Barbie a quick wave and then ducked down the hall to leave through the back door.

"Harry, wait!" Jon hustled after me. "You're supposed to let me go first."

I sighed in exasperation and stopped in front of the door, allowing him to pass by. "Fine. After you," I huffed.

My temper was a bit frayed. Three days had passed since what I would forever think of as the Piggly Wiggly Incident, and I continued to be on lockdown, my movements restricted to working at the coffee shop or hanging out upstairs. Cabin fever was beginning to set in, even though I had plenty of company. The apartment had become a war room with Tomas representing the vampires and Nash speaking for the pack. Max was also a frequent visitor as the resident demonologist.

Our plans had been laid, but I had only successfully raised a snap circle twice, so I was feeling the pressure. It was still a week until the full moon and the waiting was killing me, making me feel antsy. I hated just sitting around while norms continued to die. Seth had carried out on his threat, and the HRN incidents had increased with Nash and Dev called out every day to at least one new gruesome death. It meant I had hardly seen Nash since the fiasco at the grocery store.

I followed Jon out the door into the parking lot behind my building and stopped in my tracks.

"What the...?"

Jon lay on the ground, a feathered tranquilizer dart sticking out of his neck. I crouched beside him and checked his pulse. It was steady.

"Harry! Get back in—"

Phhht!

Eric, who had come up behind me, slapped his hand to his neck and then toppled to the ground.

I blinked in surprise, coming to my senses, and I jumped to my feet, turning back towards the shop. A man stepped out of the shadows from behind the recycling bin and raised his hand.

Zzzttttzzzttt!

The sizzling tick of a stun gun was the last sound I heard as the probes of the Taser took me square in the chest and my body began to convulse uncontrollably.

Chapter Twenty-two

I was having another nightmare, or at least a serious case of déjà vu. I was back at the warehouse, my arms bound above me, suspended between two columns. The air was filled with chanting and the screams of DiCastro's victims. I shook my head, feeling groggy and tested the chains holding me. They held tight. There was a movement to my right, and I turned a blurry gaze to see a man approach. It was DiCastro, dressed in his Egyptian finery.

"You're awake at last," he said.

I shook my head slowly in denial. This felt too real to be a dream, but how else could DiCastro be here?

"No. You're dead. Go away," I said, tugging at my chains again. This couldn't be happening. I had to be dreaming.

DiCastro leaned towards me, leering at me. "You're mine now."

"No!"

I smashed my forehead into his face, gasping at the very real pain it caused. DiCastro reared back, holding his nose. Good. I hoped it was broken.

"Now, sugar, that's no way to greet a friend."

What the fuck? Confused, I watched as DiCastro's face slowly melted and his body swelled, his clothes morphing into a distinctive, cobalt-blue suit, until finally Seth grinned back at me. The chanting and screams fell away, replaced by the sound of dance tunes and slot machines.

"I was just messin' with you, darlin'. All in good fun, don't you know?" He turned away, snapping his fingers and the chains holding me disappeared.

My arms fell to my sides, stinging with pins and needles. How long had I been hanging there? I rubbed them, trying to get the blood flowing again, and looked around. I was back at Wishes, standing beside the fountain, but the usual crowd was nowhere to be seen. Hopefully that meant it was still early and I hadn't been unconscious all that long. The sting of being electrocuted came back to me as I remembered what had happened, and I rubbed the spot on my chest where the prongs of the Taser had bit in.

"You have a strange definition of fun." I scowled at Seth.

He snapped his fingers again, and a table, the white wicker one, appeared. "Ah now, sugar, don't be angry. You brought it on yourself, after all, with your willful misbehaviour." He waved a hand at the empty chair. "Have a seat, and we'll kiss and make up."

I glared at him, unwilling to move. "I think I would prefer to—"

"SIT!"

Unused to his commands being ignored, Seth's composure snapped, his eyes flashing and his teeth elongating as his human visage slipped. He pointed at me, and I found myself scooped up by an invisible force and deposited roughly in the chair. He cleared his throat and smoothed his hands down his suit, tugging at the bottom of his vest.

"There now, was that so difficult?" He arched an eyebrow over his once-again blue eyes and glared down at me. I inclined my chin but refused to answer, watching him warily. Unbuttoning his jacket, Seth sat down across from me and reached for the pitcher of lemonade. "Now we can sit like two civilized people and discuss our partnership."

I watched as he poured us each a drink, my mind reeling. What was I supposed to do now? This wasn't what we'd planned. I wasn't supposed to get kidnapped until *next* week. Oh, well. I'd just have to wing it and hope for the best.

Seth held his lemonade up. "C'mon now, sugar. Down the hatch." He smiled toothily and took a long sip.

Leaning forward, I started to reach for my glass, and then pushed up from my chair, springing backwards away from the table.

"*Circulum*!" I shouted, coming to a crouch low to the floor.

There was a crack and a green flash of light, and then I found myself surrounded by the steady hum of a protective circle. I did it! The hours of practicing with Max had paid off. The protective dome was only big enough for me to sit on the floor, but it was intact. What can I say? Beggars can't be choosers, and mastering the skill was still a work in progress.

"What is this?" Seth roared, pushing the table away. It flipped, the lemonade crashing to the floor. He strode towards me, becoming less human-looking with each step, and I flinched involuntarily, barely remembering in time to hold my ground and not break the circle. He stopped at the edge, which was discernible only as a thin, film-like sphere, similar to a soap bubble. "What have you done, you little twitchy witch?"

Seth reached out a gnarled finger to touch the edge of the dome and it sizzled—so close to my head it made me duck—and a spark of light raced across its surface to zap his finger. It reminded me of one of those lamps I wanted as a kid, the kind that looked like a glass ball with coloured lightning inside.

"What is this?" Seth roared again. He paced the edge, ranting.

Sitting cross-legged and stooped over in my circle—I really needed to practice making them bigger—I held my hands out in front of me and began to chant quietly.

"What do you think you're doing?" Seth slapped his hands against the barrier, the resulting electric crack causing me to jump. "Stop it! Stop what you're doing!"

I ignored him and kept chanting. In my mind's eye I could see my magic flowing out from my centre, drawing my power and shaping my will as I spoke the words:

"Hecate, Queen of the Night,
Goddess of the Crossroads,
Hear my plight.
Lend me strength to close
that which should not be open,
To put this wrong to right."

I continued to chant, my magic taking on an amorphous green form, circling above me—the bounds of my ring of protection had no effect on it—and then it arced away to encapsulate the flame in the fountain's small brazier. For a second, nothing happened, and I found myself holding my breath. I pushed again with my power, willing the portal to close, but it had been open so long, it wouldn't budge.

"*Please, Hecate, aid me in my task,*" I prayed silently.

There was a sudden rush of wings as a waft of air passed over me, and then, as easily as blowing out a candle, the flame extinguished.

"No!" Seth bellowed, his fingers elongating into claws as he raked at the barrier, attempting to get through to me. Luckily, the circle held.

For a brief moment it felt like time stood still. The water in the fountain ceased flowing, the music stopped playing and the slot machines fell silent. Into the deafening silence, another sound rose as the room shook, the metal roof of the warehouse above us rattling as if a hurricane passed overhead. There was a mighty crash, and I turned to see the statues beginning to crumble and fall into the water below.

"This cannot be! This cannot be!" Seth gazed around in denial.

The rattling and the crashing became a roar, and the fountain trembled, pieces of rock splashing into the water until it imploded, disappearing as if sucked inwards through an invisible hole. At last it was gone, and the room fell silent.

"I. Will. End you!"

Seth towered over me, all vestiges of humanity gone, his reptilian eyes and long, pointed teeth more suited to his green, scaly skin. His suit was in tatters, now that he had hulked out to more than twice the size he was as a man.

"I will crack your bones and suck the marrow. I will dine on your liver and drink your blood. You will pay for this, you filthy mortal."

"Stick and stones, Seth." I smiled at him and shook my finger, feeling cocky and safe behind my shimmering bubble. "Face it. Your time here is done."

"Harry?"

"Isaac! I'm all right. Hurry!"

The relief flowed over me when I heard Isaac's voice in my head. It was a good thing I had already let him take some of my blood before I was kidnapped. Even Nash had agreed it was a necessary precaution, since we couldn't rely on our telepathic communication if he was in his four-legged form.

Already I could hear the sounds of fighting as Nash and the rest of the cavalry came to my rescue. They would have known the moment the portal closed because the vampires would have been able to cross the boundary.

There was a crash as the inner doors to the warehouse were blown off their hinges and a stream of werewolves, all in wolf form, surged in. The imps and other daemons that had been left standing around in confusion when the portal closed, rushed to meet them.

"You may be safe, but what about your fellow mortals?" Seth growled at me, pulling my attention back to him. He stood in front of me, his hand wrapped around the neck of a middle-aged man. The terrified man struggled in Seth's grip, his feet dangling above the floor as Seth slowly choked the life out of him.

"Stop it! This will get you nothing. Your time here is over. Leave him and return to hell." I shifted uneasily, my circle suddenly feeling small and constrictive. I was helpless, unable to do anything but sit and watch.

With a look of disdain, Seth tightened his fist around the man's throat. There was a sickening crack, and the man's head fell backwards at an impossible angle, his body going limp. For a brief second I saw the man's spirit flickering beside his body, but then Seth inhaled, and it was sucked up as he tossed the now-lifeless shell away.

"You can't win this fight, Seth. Look around you." I swallowed back the bile, revolted by what Seth had done.

I glanced out over the warehouse. The werewolves, immune to the glamour of the daemons, were chewing through the ranks of imps. A familiar black wolf grabbed an imp and shook it between his teeth until the imp popped out of existence. The wolf, black ichor on his jowls, raised his head and howled. He was answered by a resounding chorus.

The vampires were proving just as lethal against the daemons, using their claws and fangs and superhuman strength to tear through the enemy.

"You may not care about a mere human, but what about your precious Therese?"

I turned back to stare at Seth in shock. He had his hand wrapped around Tess's throat.

"I'm sorry, Harry," she croaked. "He caught me by surprise."

"Tess!" I started to jump to my feet, remembering in time not to break the circle. "Let her go!" I growled at Seth.

"A trade. You for her. Whose life do you value more?" Seth regarded me and grinned, his forked tongue flickering out between his teeth. He gave Tess a little shake, and she cried out.

"Stop!" I threw out my hands. "Okay, okay."

"Harry, no—"

"Let her go, and you can have me," I said, cutting Isaac off from my thoughts. I couldn't sacrifice Tess, even if it meant my own life. I waved my hand through the circle, and it fell away as quickly as it had formed, allowing me to leap to my feet, my hand reaching for my katana that rested invisible on my back.

Seth smiled in triumph and tossed Tess at me. I braced to catch her one-handed, but her body never fell. I gaped. It had all been an illusion. He never had Tess!

While I stood momentarily stunned, Seth lunged at me, knocking my sword away. He grabbed me by the throat and pulled me off my feet, giving me a gleeful shake. I dangled helplessly from his clenched fist, his claws gouging into my throat. He raked his free hand across my chest, ripping through my clothes and tearing through my skin. It stung like a bitch, bleeding profusely, but it was only a minor wound.

"You're mine," he rasped, his tongue flickering between his teeth as he sank his fist into my abdomen, his claws slicing into me like knives. The pain was almost unbearable, the copper smell of my blood filling the air. I hissed, my fangs suddenly appearing, as I tore at his hands, trying to loosen his grip on my throat.

"Stop!" The voice rang out across the room, its power shaking the rafters above. The warehouse fell silent as the fighting came to a standstill.

Seth's deadly grip loosened slightly, and I sucked in a ragged, painful breath, turning my head to see Salvador striding towards us across the warehouse. Mr. Zed, the daemon I had met on my first visit to Wishes, followed in his wake. He clapped his hands twice, and the imps and daemons bowed down to Salvador as he passed.

"Your daddy can't save you now. Your soul is mine." Seth's tongue flicked out, licking my cheek.

"I think Hecate might have a thing or two to say about that," I rasped, lashing out with the small blade I had managed to pull from my pocket. It was irregularly shaped, wrapped carefully on one edge with duct tape, but its exposed edge was extremely sharp. I had taken to carrying it, hidden in the lining of my pocket, after the attack at the grocery store. I brought my arm up between Seth's outstretched arms, scoring the blade across his face.

Seth shrieked, tossing me away as his hands flew to his face. Despite being the size of a razor blade, my makeshift weapon had opened a wide furrow across his cheek up to his eye, his green skin oozing black ichor.

"What have you done to me? What have you done?"

"You've been marked by your brother's blade, the Dagger of Asar." I winced, pressing my hands against my side, trying in vain to stop the bleeding.

"No!" Seth's voice held a note of terror as smoke rose from the rapidly spreading wound and his skin turned a sickly grey. He lowered his hands and looked at me. His eye was melting in its socket even as his flesh decayed and fell from his skull. "You haven't heard the last of me. You will never be safe from me. I will haunt your dreams and revel in your nightmares, and when you die, I will eat your soul." With one last hiss, he flicked his tongue at me and then disappeared with a pop, returning to hell where I hoped he died from his wounds.

I fell back on the floor in relief, my hands pressed to my side. A large black wolf landed beside me, giving me a butt with his head.

"Nash!"

He butted me again with his nose, sniffing at my wounds before plopping down on his haunches to look at me and growl.

"I know, I know," I replied weakly, reaching up to run my fingers through his sticky, ichor-covered fur. "I broke my promise. I'm sorry." I let out a shaky breath. Nash whined and licked my face.

"Harry!"

Isaac strode towards me. He knelt beside Nash, his hands pulling mine away to examine my wounds.

"I'm sorry I didn't listen when you tried to tell me—"

"Don't worry about it now, Harry. Let's get you fixed up first."

"It's not that bad." I shifted, trying to sit up. "I can barely feel—Oh! Ow!" I fell back to the floor as pain lanced through me. Nash's wolf barked in alarm.

"Try not to move. The wounds are deeper than you think."

I nodded, trying to suck in a breath, but the air bubbled in my chest, my lungs refusing to fill. I rasped for air, panicked. Nash leapt to his feet, growling and snapping as my vision started to fade. It felt like I was going to pass out.

"The demon must have nicked her lung; she's not getting any oxygen." Isaac's voice, despite my panic, sounded calm and clinical.

There was a commotion and then Salvador and a huge black cat—a panther—appeared beside me. Nash growled, his wolf moving to stand protectively over me.

"Be at ease, my wolfy friend," Salvador said. "He can help."

The panther hissed and yowled at Nash, sitting back on its haunches. There was a flash of light, and then Max crouched in his place.

"Hi, Harry," he said. "Let's get you fixed up."

Salvador laughed heartily. "Well, that certainly lets the cat out of the bag."

Epilogue

"And then they argued about whether or not it would be better to give you vampire blood to heal you or just let Max do it, but you croaked out Max's name, so they let him heal you," Tess said, shaking her head. "I can't believe that Max is a cat. A cat!" She made a funny face. I couldn't put my finger on it, but she looked more than just surprised.

We were both still shocked by the revelation that Max was a skinwalker, able to take the shape of his totem animal—the black panther, in Max's case. Nice to know I wasn't the only special snowflake around. A shaman with both the ability to summon demons and shapeshift? That was about as rare as a half-vampire witch with the gift of necromancy.

"No wonder Nash thought he smelled funny," I replied, stuffing another donut in my mouth. It was a BMG—bacon maple glazed—from Dorfman's. They seemed to be our new tradition for the morning after I almost get killed and end up in the hospital. Although this time, because Max worked his magic, I was at home recuperating instead of in a hospital bed.

"So, speaking of Nash, is he still mad at you?"

"Yeah, he's barely said two words to me. He spent the entire night as a wolf rather than speak to me, I think." I set my half-eaten donut down, my appetite suddenly gone.

"I'm sorry, Harry. I feel like it's my fault."

"No way! It is *not* your fault." I frowned at her. "I don't care what I promised Nash, I couldn't let Seth hurt you, even if it did turn out to be an illusion."

Tess crawled up beside me in bed and gave me a hug. She put her head on my shoulder and snuggled up against me. "Well, up until that part, it all went according to plan, if a little ahead of schedule."

"Yeah, although I could have done with skipping the Taser part. I don't remember that being part of the plan." I took a long, slow breath. Despite being healed, I was still a little sore. I rubbed my chest where the Taser had left a burn. The mark was gone, but I could remember how it felt to have twelve hundred volts coursing through me.

"So what's with Salvador and Mr. Zed?" Tess asked. "I didn't see that coming."

"Neither did I, but no surprise really. Salvador never misses an opportunity to turn a situation to his advantage, and he did say he had an 'iron in the fire.'" I fingered quoted.

And, while it was certainly fortuitous that Salvador and Mr. Zed had made some kind of deal giving Mr. Zed and his loyal minions the chance to remain here and serve Salvador in return for turning traitor on Seth, I wasn't sure how I felt about Wishes being allowed to reopen, even in a modified, less deadly form.

"Can we go back to the 'Max is a cat' part?" I asked Tess, giving her a pointed look. "What's going on with you and him?"

Tess squirmed beside me, grabbing a pillow and covering her head with it. "Heeb by bait," she said, her voice muffled to the point of being incomprehensible.

"What?" I laughed, pulling the pillow from her face. "Say that again."

"Crap, Harry. Isn't it obvious?" Tess let out a loud sigh. "I think he's my mate."

The End

Thank you for reading *Hell to Pay*. I love writing about Harry's adventures and I hope you have fun reading them too. As an independent author, I rely on word of mouth to help sell books. If you are so inclined, please consider leaving a review online at your favourite bookseller's website.

My gratitude also goes out to my editor, Sasha Knight. Without you there would be so many homeless commas. Please note that I take full responsibility for any mistakes that remain.

A final shout-out to Isabella, my go-to girl when I had some questions about Catholic Mass. Thanks, Izzy!

Want to know if there is more in store for Harry? Don't miss a thing! Keep up with all the news and receive exclusive offers and content by joining my mailing list. Visit my website at www.lisaemme.com and sign up today!

Cheers!
Lisa

Other novels by Lisa Emme

The Harry Russo Diaries
Don't miss Harry's first adventures! Find out how it all began.

Dead and Kicking - The Harry Russo Diaries, volume 1

What's a girl to do when her date is D.O.A?

Angharad 'Harry' Russo is just your ordinary twenty-something, with one exception - she's a witch with an out of the ordinary gift. When her blind date goes sideways and she ends up face to face with a dead body, her life starts to go sideways too.

Harry soon finds herself right in the middle of the mayhem, dealing with Cian Nash, a homicide detective that is as aggravating as he is sexy; the biggest, baddest vampire in town; and a parcel of pesky zombies that keep popping up everywhere. It's all connected to her date's unfortunate demise, or is there more to it than meets the eye?

Tooth and Claw - The Harry Russo Diaries, volume 2

Q: When is a witch, not a witch?
A: When she's a necromancer.

Angharad 'Harry' Russo has had to adjust to some major changes in her life. Her computer is haunted, she accidentally acquired a vampire servant and she's attracted to the most aggravating alpha male on the planet. Her friend betrayed her, a lunatic tried to sacrifice her to raise a god and she accidentally 'outed' herself to the Magister, the most powerful vampire in town. What else could go wrong? Oh yeah, she's just discovered that her father is a vampire and her dhamphiric powers are emerging prematurely. Poor Harry doesn't know what weird ability could pop up next.

When werewolves start to go missing, and two young men die suspiciously, not to mention horrifically, Harry believes it's all connected. It could be just a hunch, or it could be the big, grey wolf that stepped out of her dreams to haunt her waking moments; either way, Harry knows that she needs to help solve the mystery. Now if she could just convince the sexy police detective, Cian Nash, to take her seriously.

Deadlocked - The Harry Russo Diaries, volume 3

When life gives you brownies, make coffee.

Angharad 'Harry' Russo has had a busy week. She's fended off a swarm of pixies, battled blood-thirsty redcaps and put an end to a maniacal Fae prince hell-bent on eradicating the entire werewolf population. She's also decided to open a coffee shop. Is it too much to ask for things to settle down so her life can go back to normal?

Apparently it is. As if being metaphysically bound to Cian Nash, the most aggravating yet desirable man she's ever met, isn't enough, Harry's just found out that the Magister, the scariest, most powerful vampire around, is her father. Talk about your daddy issues!

Harry just wants to concentrate on getting the coffee shop open, but between the freaky ghosts that keep haunting her and rogue vampires terrorizing the city, it looks like normal is a thing of the past.

LISA EMME ALSO WRITES ROMANCE!

Home Again

They say you can't go home again. Allie Daniels hopes they are wrong, whoever they are. After a series of misfortunes, she and her small son have come home to the town she thought she had left behind. She's just looking for a safe place to raise her son. The last thing she wants is any more complications.

Mike Finn didn't roll into town on his Harley looking for love; he just wants to find a place to call home. Hoping to escape the fast-paced, anonymous life in the city, he's bought a partnership in the local veterinarian practice. The small town has a lot to offer – especially after a chance encounter with Allie.

When Mike first sets eyes on Allie, sparks fly. He knows there's something there, but the reluctant, single mom is going to take some convincing. Good thing Mike is a persistent man. When strange things start to happen around town, his protective instinct is sent into high gear. It's just as well, because when Allie starts playing detective, she may find herself in over her head.

Coming soon to print for the first time!

The Yacht Club

Welcome to the Yacht Club - Vancouver's exclusive BDSM club and best-kept secret - where few are asked to play, fewer still invited to stay. Each sexy story brings a bit of ink, a lot of kink, topped with a hint of magic.

Daisy

Daisy Andrews has been burned by love before. Now she prefers to play it safe and keep things casual. So how then, does a woman that prefers her sex with a little kink, satisfy her need to be owned?

Kimi

With a vicious killer loose Kimi Jones is on the hunt, and she'll stop at nothing to get her man. But when she meets a sexy stranger on the beach and a one-night stand turns into more than she bargained for, will Kimi be able to keep her own secrets?

Pax

Pax Lightfoot struggles to make it day-to-day without losing her mind, until a chance encounter brings her the peace she's been yearning for. It doesn't hurt that it comes in a ruggedly handsome package. But can Pax win the heart of a man that craves more than just vanilla?

About the Author

Lisa Emme is a Canadian who proudly ends her ABC's with 'zed'. A self-professed book-a-holic, she has spent the last few years trying to stem her book hoarding tendencies by writing her own stories and by avoiding the bargain table at the bookstore like the plague.

A bit of a thrill seeker, Lisa has tried such death defying activities as bungy jumping off a bridge and rappelling down the side of a 17 storey building. She's also single-handedly raising a teenager.

Lisa has worked as a veterinary assistant, playground instructor, bank teller, store clerk, waitress, telephone solicitor, research writer for an environmental think tank, computer programmer, and systems analyst. Her passion however, is writing. What else is she going to do during the long, cold prairie winter?

Lisa would love to hear from you. Drop her a line at lisa.emme@mymts.net or you can find her online:

Website: www.lisaemme.com
Facebook: www.facebook.com/LisaEmmeBooks
E-mail: lisa.emme@mymts.net
Twitter: @LisaEmmeBooks
Pinterest: www.pinterest.com/LisaEmmeBooks/
Instagram: www.instagram.com/lisa.emme.books/

67715425R00143

Made in the USA
Charleston, SC
20 February 2017